PHOENIX
CHOSEN

An Heirs of Huaxia novel

Ekaterine Xia

Phoenix Chosen

by Ekaterine Xia

This is a work of fiction. Names, characters, businesses, events, places and incidents are either a product of the author's imagination or used in a fictitious manner. Any resemblance to actual persons, living or dead, or actual events is purely coincidental.

Cover design: Digital Dragon Designery

Cover Illustration: Phoenixlu

Editing: L.B Briggs

Publisher: Innamorata Press

ISBN: 978-9781634650007

For everyone who's kept me breathing: I love you and I
love how you love me.

When a spell saves her life by sending her to her mother's homeland, Estyria finds herself in a world she'd believed to exist solely in bedtime stories – a realm where gods walk the earth, magic is real, and political intrigue strikes close and hard.

As Scion to a noble House and caught in a competition for the throne, she has mere weeks to learn to navigate the murky waters of court and tangled loyalties.

More than a crown and the well-being of a country is at stake. Two men are bound to her by destiny and their fates depend upon her choices.

Sethalor, who holds secrets and memories lost to her, vows to defy the very gods to keep her safe.

Aedrian, who agreed to protect her out of love for his prince, but comes to see in her a ruler he would give his soul to protect.

Through assassinations, poison, and shifting alliances, can Estyria keep the realm, her heart and the people she loves safe?

TABLE OF CONTENTS

PROLOGUE

I strolled across the street, hands in my pockets, head bowed against the rain. The plastic bag holding my lunch dangled from my wrist and banged against my knee with every step.

The wind drove pinprick rain against my skin, colder than expected for fall, but I didn't hurry my pace. I had nowhere to be and no one waiting for me at home. Not anymore.

A horn blared. Then two. Then a cacophony. Not a simple two beat of a *fuck you* but a sustained crescendo of *what the fuck*.

Alarm slithered down my spine. I looked up and squinted through the wet.

A blue SUV swerved past a car, dodged being t-boned by another and careened toward me. Brakes squealed. The smell of burnt rubber laid heavy on the air and drowned out the scent of rain and wet greenery.

I froze, my mind chittering useless noise.

I never felt the impact.

White noise roared in my head.

I opened my eyes.

What was I doing on the ground?

I was crumpled on my side. A pale spill of liquid curved beside me. A single blot of red six feet away. I blinked at it, once, twice, before it came into focus. A shoe. I looked toward my feet, at the black sock on my left foot, the red ballet flat on my right. *My* shoe then. What was it doing over there?

Rain dripped into my eyes. The corn chowder spilled on the ground inched toward me.

Drat. I'd have to clean that up. Littering bad.

Movement drew my gaze up. A woman leaned out of the blue SUV near my shoe, eyes wild, teeth bared in a grimace.

SUV?

I frowned, trying to make sense of it all.

Awareness filtered back through burgeoning pain. Road. Intersection. I should get up. Bad idea, lying in the middle of the road.

I braced my hands against the ground and tried to rise. Pain seared my side and blackened my vision, burning away some of the shock. The back of my throat itched and I coughed reflexively. A metallic taste flooded my mouth and a trickle of warmth trailed down my chin, splattering crimson on black asphalt.

"Thank God." The driver pulled her head back into the car. The engine roared, the tires squealed, and she was gone.

A shout came from somewhere. Irresponsible

bitch. Accident. Police.

A man ran toward me.

Shoe. I needed to put my shoe on.

The sky spun, my vision flooding with rainbow sparkles. I reached out to brace myself against the dizziness and agony bore me down, down through the darkness.

CHAPTER ONE

I woke curled in a fetal position, wet clothing a clammy weight against my skin. My head was heavy, my thoughts airy and indistinct.

Grass prickled at my exposed skin. Something about that was wrong, but I couldn't remember what. I was cold. So cold.

A man was sprawled on the ground beside me. His hand was outstretched, as if he were reaching for me. Long black hair spilled over his back. He wore...

What the hell?

I sat up. A sharp burst of pain on my right side sent stars dancing in my vision. I closed my eyes and swallowed the nausea.

No. No throwing up. Throwing up never made anything better.

I opened my eyes and looked again. He was wearing a silk robe, the kind worn by actors in Chinese historical dramas and we were lying in the middle of what looked like a scene straight off the postcards of traditional Chinese gardens. Craggy boulders and carefully pruned greenery stragetically placed to simulate being in the mountains, complete with a stream trickling just within hearing.

What the everloving fuck?

I must've hit my head. Maybe when I passed out from the impact. This wasn't real. It *couldn't* be real.

Another pang brought bile rushing up my throat. I turned my head and bent forward, bracing myself as I spilled my breakfast onto the grass. Fire licked at all my nerve endings.

More stars flashed as I shifted back into a sitting position. My entire body felt like one huge bruise and my throat burned. I took a deep breath and fought to stay conscious but blackness nibbled at the corners of my vision.

No. Fainting bad. Bad things happened to unconscious people. So far so good. Ish. But there was no guaranteeing that would continue.

A bruising grip wrapped around my wrist and dragged me to my feet, shooting pain up my arm. Up my arm and everywhere else. "Who are you and what did you do to him?"

Agony burned in my side as I hung from his grip. Dazed, I could only stare at the avenging angel who'd jerked me off the ground.

Red hair. Icy silver eyes. Furious expression that turned to stunned disbelief when our gazes met.

Pretty boy. Angry pretty boy.

Shock and trauma hit my stomach like a punch and I couldn't stop myself from throwing up all over him before darkness closed over my head again.

Maybe there were some instances in which throwing up made things better was my last thought before my mind shut off.

CHAPTER TWO

A dull ache throbbed in my side, pulling me from the depths of sleep. Must have slept on myself wrong. I stretched to ease the kinks from lying in one position and froze as the discomfort expanded to straight out pain.

Pain?

Adrenaline shot through my system and I rose to full awareness as memory came rushing back.

Car. Accident. The hallucination involving the Chinese garden and the pissed off angel.

I opened my eyes to darkness. Pure darkness without even gradients of reassuring shadow.

Was I blind?

Blinking fast and hard, I raised my hand to rub my eyes, panic flooding my veins with ice and driving back the muzziness. A ripping sensation spread across my right side and stars flared across my vision, the only light against the black.

A warm hand took mine and lowered it back to my side. "Don't. You broke some ribs and there's significant surface bruising in addition to the internal injuries you sustained. If you must move, do so slowly." The lightly accented voice was husky, deep, and somehow familiar.

Tension eased within me at his velvet tones, responding to the serene authority in his words. The terror subsided but remained in wait.

"Who are you? Are you my doctor? Why can't I see anything? Am I blind?" Panic and nausea roiled in my stomach and a blurry memory surfaced. I'd thrown up on someone. Another impression came to me, the heat of ginger broth and a cajoling voice. *His* voice. Was that why it was so familiar?

He didn't respond immediately and I heard the rustle of paper. Was he consulting my chart?

Careful not to move too fast, I wrapped my right hand around the pendent hanging from my neck, rubbing my thumb over the familiar dips and hollows. Calm seeped in around the edges of the panic and I realized that somehow, even though I couldn't see him, this man gave me the same sense of safety and reminder of being cared for. Absurd, but there it was.

On the other hand, I supposed it wasn't more absurd than a mysterious necklace that didn't have a clasp or anything that would allow me to take it off and that made me feel safe and loved whenever I touched it.

"The blindness is temporary and will go away as your condition stabilizes. Transient loss of sight is not uncommon with head injuries." The absolute certainty in his voice laid my fear to rest.

Transient was good. I could deal with transient.

"How long have I been out?" Fatigue drifted back, tugging at my consciousness.

"You've been asleep for the last twelve hours. Is there someone you'd like to contact?" There was an edge to his question, as if he were fighting back anger. But that made no sense.

Shaking away the thought, I forced my body to relax after a warning twinge arched through me. "No. No one." I didn't want my family to worry and as for my job and friends... both were nonexistent at the moment.

"Not your family? Friends? Your husband, perhaps?" His velvety voice snagged on the word husband and turned rough, his accent deepening. Scottish? But not quite...there was a hint of something else there.

My family? I thought of the chaos that would ensue if my family knew I was in the hospital because of a car accident and shuddered. No, better not to involve them. There was a reason I'd stayed in the lonely apartment even after everyone else had left instead of going home to lick my wounds. My family would want to fix everything and I wasn't quite ready for that yet.

"Heavens, no."

"Not even your husband?" A definite edge to his tone now. Why?

"Mmm? I'm not married." Confusion swirled in my mind for a moment before I realized he must be referring to the temple-blessed ring of jade I wore.

"I apologize for my presumption. I saw the ring and assumed." His voice was smooth again, with an undercurrent of something I couldn't decipher. Relief?

I shook the thought off. Must be my imagination. Or the head trauma.

"My mother gave it to me and that's the only finger it'll fit on."

Exhaustion dragged at me. I yawned, wincing as my side chided me when I raised my hand to cover my mouth. I didn't open my eyes again. The darkness was much more bearable when I had my eyes closed. Comfortable illusions and all that.

"How long before my sight returns? Do I need to give you my insurance information?" Hopefully the insurance would cover it. I didn't want to think about how much a couple of days in the hospital was going to run me but worst case scenario I'd ask for a loan from the parents after I got out. I wouldn't, couldn't worry about it now.

"It shouldn't be too long now, now that you're awake. And no, you don't need to worry about anything," he said, low and soothing.

Sleep called and I yawned again. "All right."

"Would you like to sleep, or would you like something to eat?"

"I'd prefer to sleep, thank you." I didn't want to mess around with eating blind and I wasn't hungry.

"All right."

I snuggled into the pillow. Hopefully I'd be able to see again when I woke up and find out if the doctor's person was as lovely as his voice.

One question surfaced as I drifted off. What sort of hospital smelled like expensive woods and flowers instead of antiseptics?

CHAPTER THREE

G olden warmth spread through me, sweet and thick as honey, and drove back the nightmares. Scowling faces drifted away from me and their accusing words dissipated as awareness returned.

I opened my eyes, expecting to see darkness again. Instead, dark blue gauze billowed overhead.

What?

Forgetting the need to be careful, I sat up fast, only to crumple over as agony seared my side and sparkles danced in my vision.

"Fuh!" I closed my eyes and inhaled slowly through the pain. Gods, that hurt. If there was a button for dispensing more drugs, I was gonna hit it like a truck.

I winced at the image of a blue SUV. Maybe not a truck.

"You're awake." The deep baritone was cold, clipped and...speaking Mandarin.

Coupled with the memory of that blue canopy, I

realized something wasn't quite right. Boston had a lot of Chinese residents, but most wouldn't automatically think to speak Chinese to a stranger, no matter what they looked like.

My eyes snapped open.

I was sitting on a gigantic canopied bed. A trio of copper braziers piled high with red coals gave off a comfortable warmth in the center of the room.

My stomach did a sick flip before flopping. No way I was in a hospital.

Distracted by my surroundings, it took another moment to register that a man held my wrist in his hand.

A stunning man, albeit one reminiscent of a blade. Austerity carved his face, sharpening features that would have been considered feminine on a softer man to predatory menace.

Long fingers lightly bracketed his neck, as if in support or possession and I realized he sat propped up against another man, as if too tired to remain upright on his own.

I looked up and recognition stirred when I met icy silver eyes. It was the redhead, the one I took for an angel. If that wasn't a hallucination...

Fear caught my chest in a stranglehold even as my gaze was inexorably drawn back to the man who held my hand.

Familiarity tugged at me, demanding I recognize him, but my memories came up blank. Pain pulsed at my temples, warning me against digging deeper.

Wincing, I pushed the thought into a box and

kicked it aside. Maybe it was the robe he wore that was familiar, black silk with black embroidery. The robe that the man sprawled beside me on the ground wore.

Was I still hallucinating? Another effect of the injuries? Was it a good sign or a bad one that my hallucinations remained consistent?

I swallowed again and inhaled slowly, staring at the hand around my wrist.

Calm. Calm, Estyria. Deep breaths. Keep breathing.

Warmth spread up my arm from his callused fingers, the heat soothing and calming. Was I imagining it or was it some sort of monitor in the hospital? Maybe I was actually in a padded room, screaming my head off.

"Awake, perhaps, but not conscious," he said, sounding disgruntled. Not exactly desirable bedside manner. On the other hand, who wouldn't want to play doctor with these two, good bedside manner or not?

Lifting my gaze, I looked straight at him and gave him a wry smile. "Does hallucinating but aware of it count as being conscious and cognizant?" Apparently my subconscious liked imperial China and hot men. Who knew?

Russet brows drew together. "You're hallucinating?"

"Since I'm not seeing a hospital and you're wearing robes out of a historical drama instead of a doctor's white coat, I'm going to have to say yes." I turned my focus inward, trying to pinpoint where it hurt.

Aside from the throbbing in my temples, the only other pain came from my side. Wouldn't my head hurt more if I had a head injury that caused hallucinations? Or blindness?

Panic edged in, compressing my lungs. I forced a deep breath, then another, my mother's lessons resounding in my head.

Ice gray eyes narrowed. "You don't know where you are and you think you're in a hospital?" He stumbled a bit over the last word, as if it was unfamiliar.

Ice slipped down my spine at the disbelief and rising anger in his tone. I folded my hands to stop their trembling. Giving in to hysteria only made it worse.

"You're implying I'm not in a hospital? But the man I talked to the last time..." My stomach performed another sick turn.

His mouth compressed as he jerked his head to indicate the other man. "And you don't know him?"

Gods, I wanted to know him, but there was only that sense of familiarity and remembered intimacy. What was it about him that made me want to wake him up and hide in his arms? Where did I get the certainty that I'd find sanctuary with him, even if the sky came crashing down?

I shook my head, fear surfacing despite my efforts to keep my breath steady, as much from my own inexplicable thoughts as from everything else.

His fingers tightened on the other man's shoulders. "No?" His voice was silken, but his tone was filled with danger. "You don't know him?"

I shook my head again, terror rising. "What is going on? Why are you angry?"

Ignoring the pain, I tugged hard at my wrist. Dark spots swam in my vision and agony took my breath away. "Where am I? If you're not a doctor, who are you? Who is he and why is he holding my hand?"

"Sethalor," the redhead snapped and shook him, a hard back and forth motion that jerked his head forward.

That name. I knew that name. But from where?

The man holding my wrist opened his eyes. Dazed, luminous golden eyes with a band of emerald green at the outer edge. He looked confused for a second before his eyes focused on me.

I knew him. I knew those eyes, that look of tender protectiveness. But how? My temples throbbed, adding more pain to terror.

"Shhhh. Calm, Estyria, it's all right. You're safe, Phoenix. Calm before you do yourself further injury."

The doctor with the sexy voice. Except not actually a doctor. But how did he know my name? The endearment he used referenced my Chinese name, no less. Betrayal twined with fear and the edges of my vision went black.

I yanked at my hand, heedless of the consequences, knowing only that I was trapped. Who was this man and how did he know me?

"No. Where am I? Why did you lie to me?"

Vulnerability beat at me, made worse by the inexplicable urge to throw myself in his arms that warred with the infinitely more sensible desire to get away from them.

It hadn't been blindness, temporary or not. They'd blindfolded me, or something.

In one swift motion, he rose from his seat and wrapped his arms around me, holding me still against him. "Estyria. The host of dragons rejoin with the phoenix under the full moon."

I stilled, his words slamming into me with the force of a sledgehammer. That sentence. The one used by my family to make sure that we never went off with someone we shouldn't trust.

Tension drained out of me and I collapsed against his chest, unable to hold myself upright as my bones went to jelly.

His arms tightened and warmth radiated from him into me, smoothing away the jagged edges of pain and stilling the tremors shaking me. He smoothed his hand down my hair, from the crown of my head down to my waist in slow, drugging strokes.

"Who are you?" I asked, my voice husky from fear and fatigue. With the fight gone, I couldn't even rouse myself enough to keep my eyes open.

He stiffened against me, his hand stopping for a heartbeat before resuming. "Qiandai Xiang Sethalor. Do you not remember me, Estyria?"

I shook my head. He smelled familiar too. Bergamot, sandalwood, bay and something unique to him.

"I was in a fever coma years ago and lost parts of my memory. Most of it came back, but some hasn't." Most days I didn't realize what I was missing, my memory like a tapestry with parts worn through and the detail indistinct but the overall picture still decipherable.

Realization struck me like a blow, the knowledge that he was part of what I missed without knowing it. But why? Why did I feel like I had lost something precious, something irretrievable along with and in addition to my memories?

His body tensed further. "Coma?"

"And you haven't made any further inroads into recovering your memories? Don't you care about whom or what you might have forgotten?" That disdainful voice. I'd almost forgotten about the redhead.

I looked over Sethalor's shoulder. "Not when it means excruciating headaches and fainting spells, no, not really. Besides, my mother made me promise to stop when I had terrible nosebleeds every time I tried to force the issue." Brain hemorrhages were no joke. I didn't consider much worth possible death.

On the other hand, if I'd known he was hidden in the depths of my mind, I might not have been able to keep to that promise. Sitting there, sheltered in his arms, I could almost forget the endless questions surrounding me.

The redhead blinked, his mouth going slack for a moment before his eyes hardened and he looked away.

The question couldn't be ignored any longer.

I pushed away from Sethalor's embrace and looked straight at him. "Seth? I'm not sure I want the answer, but where am I?"

CHAPTER FOUR

Sethalor's mouth tightened and his words came slow and reluctant. "You're not on Earth. This is the royal palace of Ziyang, capital of Tavaneth and I am prince regent here. A spell placed on you triggered when you were injured and brought you here."

Royal palace. Tavaneth. The world of all of my mother's bedtime stories. A world of magic, princes, princesses, and dragons.

If this was some kind of reality show prank, it was an immeasurably cruel one. I'd wanted to go to Tavaneth with the sort of devotion and longing another child might reserve for their mother. That longing had never diminished and never went away, only layered deeper as time went by.

Frustration and hurt sharpened my tone. "Bullshit. I might have hit my head in the accident, but surely you don't think I'll buy that."

Despite my words, my mind flashed back to the garden I'd seen earlier. I couldn't explain that, or how a hospital would allow them to make off with someone who'd been in a car accident. What was that about eliminating the impossible? Whatever remained had to be the truth, no matter how implausible.

I shoved the thought away. No. Impossible.

Sethalor's beautiful mouth curved in a humorless smile. "No, *not* bullshit." He backed away, to his seat by the bed. Extending his hand, he turned his palm and fire blossomed in his hand.

Jesus Christ.

My back hit the side of the bed, sending a lance of pain through my side. "Umph."

Sethalor fisted his hand, extinguishing the flame. "Estyria."

He reached out and wrapped one hand around my wrist. Warmth flowed through me from his hand, easing the pain.

I blinked the dark away and was about to pull from his grip when I caught sight of his face. Moon pale to begin with, his complexion was now completely bloodless, his lips ashen. What was going on?

"Sethalor. Break that connection or I'll break it for you." The words whipped through the air like a blade.

I looked from one man to the other, confused.

The redhead took a step forward, hand outstretched.

Sethalor inhaled slowly. "I'm fine, Aedrian."

Aedrian. Somehow I was expecting something more along the lines of Mikhail, Gabriel or Raphael, a name to go with the warrior-angel facade.

"You're *not* fine, Seth. You've beyond over extended yourself." He raised a hand when it looked like Seth was going to argue with him. "If you keel over, I'll bundle her off to her grandparents immediately, regardless of your wishes."

"My grandparents? What connection?" I didn't *have* any living grandparents. My father was an orphan and my mother had always said her parents were lost to her.

"You agreed to be seconded to her protection."

Sethalor and I spoke at the same time.

Aedrian gave me a quick look and   replied in an even tone, "So I did, but I happen to care more about your life. I'll not stand by and watch you destroy yourself just to save her from a bit of pain. She has kin here, both whom are more than qualified to take on the burden of healing her. You've expended far more magic than your body can safely sustain and you know it."

"I have the situation under control, Aedrian."

"I doubt that. You took one look at her and all of your control and logic went straight to Hell."

"Um, hello? Guys?" It was nice and all that he thought I could turn someone's head that thoroughly, but I wanted answers and I wanted them yesterday.

They didn't even spare me a glance, blazing silver eyes glaring into weary green.

"What would you have me do, Aedrian? Should I have sent her to House Xuanyuan and have her awaken alone, wounded and afraid?"

House Xuanyuan? I bit my lip. Surely the name was a coincidence...

Aedrian slashed a hand through the air. "Do not. You'll notice I didn't say a single word of objection prior to this. But I draw the line when you place yourself in danger when it isn't *necessary*."

"I'm sorry, but could you guys have your fight after someone explains what's going on? What do you mean, my grandparents?" I interjected, raising my voice.

"You've been angry ever since I woke. If that isn't disapproval, I don't know what would be," Seth muttered.

"You disappeared without a word. Not a single word to explain what was happening. It was only through the grace of God that I didn't run her through as an assassin when I came across the both of you," Aedrian snapped.

Frustration roared in my ears. I started prying Seth's fingers from around my wrist, knowing better than to try to yank.

"Could someone start explaining before I lose what's left of my mind?" I was on the verge of screaming at the top of my lungs, just to feel like I was doing something, even if it was just venting my aggravation and fear. He was talking about magic. Magic. Like it was obvious and commonplace. And he was talking about killing me like another person would talk about squashing a bug. Whatever goodwill I had toward them went up in smoke.

The redhead arched his brows, his questioning

look just that side of insolent.

Somehow, I knew he was wondering just what I thought I could do to them, a prince who could wield fire and him with his two swords hanging from his belt. Injured no less.

Twisting my mouth in mutual contempt, I returned his flat stare. "You just said that you wanted to kill me when you found me. What kind of person goes around killing random hurt women? Right now, I'm close to seeing you as an enemy who's kidnapped me and who is withholding information from me. I really don't think you want me to act on that assumption." Having two older siblings had taught me to bluff and bluff well. More effective to let them imagine for themselves what you might do rather than give them actual examples they could counter.

Sethalor resisted my attempts to pry him off, a small smile curving his mouth as he studied the byplay between his guard and me. His serenity worried me. Did I overestimate their willingness to keep me safe and quiescent? Or was he also mocking my ability to do anything to them?

I set my jaw.

Aggravation lined the guard's mouth. "I see admitting our care for your continued good health might have been a tactical error," Aedrian said.

"Is this now a battle? Are we enemies? If not, then your only tactical error would be being a heavy-handed prick instead of hanging on to the basic tenets of courtesy and decency."

His mouth dropped open and outrage sparked in

his eyes. "Do you kiss your mother with that mouth? What, are you going to start talking in thieves' cant next? And do pray tell, how have I disregarded courtesy and decency?"

Seth muffled a cough, amusement dancing in his eyes.

I gave him a filthy look before turning back to Aedrian. If he wanted a fight, I was more than overdue. I ran the list of the banned dirty words through my mind.

"You're fucking ignoring my questions. You're discussing what to do with me with someone else like I'm a gods-damned parcel instead of a person with a mind. You clearly dislike me for some reason since your attitude has been nothing but shitty when you talk of or to me. Did you specifically want me to piss off or do you just hate anyone with tits and a cunt?" I was unable to work in motherfucker and cocksucker but the fight was young yet.

Silver eyes rounded, growing increasingly dazed as I spat the words out. "For the love of the gods, woman. You were in the imperial gardens and the *prince regent* unconscious beside you. Anyone else would have killed you for an assassin first and wondered how you got there after."

So maybe he had a point, but I was in no mind to admit it. Admitting he was right would have meant that I accepted the entire circus as real, that I really was in a magical land and everything that entailed.

I slapped a hand on Seth's chest. "Don't just sit there like you're watching a show. Give me some answers. Now." Please gods, let it be a reality show or something.

His expression resigned, he lifted his shoulders in an elegant shrug. "Do you believe me when I say you're in Ziyang? If not, then we're at an impasse since anything else I explain to you will be predicated on that premise."

My eyes narrowed. "Fine. Assume I believe you. Answers. Now."

"You have grandparents here as your family originated from Tavaneth. Your parents were banished from court and they went to Earth but your grandparents remained here because they're custodians to the estate."

I arched my brows, playing along. "There's an estate? They must be fairly well-off. Can you explain why I've never heard of them, ever? And why they've never been in contact?"

"It's verboten for anyone to contact exiles as it's considered an act of treason, and yes, they're fairly well-off." A slight smirk curved his lips, as if he knew I was humoring him and was humoring me back. "As a queen of Tavaneth and mistress of House Xuanyuan, your grandmother holds quite a sizable estate."

Folding my arms, I studied him. Aside from the smirk, his expression was completely serious. "You're playing this completely straight, aren't you? What, is this some sort of reality show or something?"

His shoulders lifted and fell. "I can take you to your grandparents and prove what I'm saying."

A dirty look shot out before I could temper my

expression. "I was willing to trust you based on your knowledge of that phrase and because you seem familiar to me even if I can't remember you, but if you're messing with me about my grandparents, that's a good way to get me started on hating you."

"I'm not lying to you, Phoenix. You'll see." He stood from his seat and extended his hand to me. "But first, you need to change."

I stared at him in disbelief. "What is this, a commercial break?"

"Commercial break?" Aedrian asked.

"Like the intermission between acts of a play," I said, still staring at Sethalor.

Sethalor shook his head. "You can't walk about with your current clothing. It's not only filthy, it's entirely inappropriate for a woman of your position."

"And what position would that be?" I asked mockingly. He really wasn't going to break character, was he?

"A princess and heir to a grand House."

I choked. "What?"

"I did mention that your grandmother is a queen of Tavaneth, did I not?"

"Maternal grandmother," I managed.

"Ah. House Xuanyuan's succession is matrilineal. If your mother had not been exiled, she would have been the next mistress of House Xuanyuan," Seth said.

Aedrian smirked at me.

"And how was I supposed to know that when China has historically been patriarchal? Patrilineal. Whatever."

"Your having your mother's surname didn't tip you off?" The redhead's tone was mocking.

Narrowing my eyes, I shot him the bird. "How about we have a horse trample you, dump you somewhere completely foreign and then see how well you pick up detail?"

Aedrian lifted a shoulder in a negligent manner and grinned at me, sharp as a blade and twice as vicious. "Lass, I've been blooded by two wars. I think my ability to pay attention to detail in difficult conditions is above suspicion."

The urge to stick my tongue out at him was almost irresistible.

Sethalor glanced at Aedrian before giving me a patient look." I know you're confused and upset, but do you want to continue picking a fight with Aedrian or would you like clean clothes and more answers?"

CHAPTER FIVE

I sifted through the clothing Sethalor set out before he and Aedrian left the room. Worry crossed my mind at the way he carried himself, as if his bones were made of glass and he'd shatter with too forceful a step.

Despite that, the man had waved off Aedrian's help.

If Aedrian was to be believed, he'd pushed himself to the limit to heal me.

And then I'd yelled at him.

I pushed the thought from my head, along with the guilt and the fear that I was starting to believe their claims of magic and everything else. The faster I changed, the faster I would get my answers.

Minutes later, I stared at the clothes in complete bewilderment.

They were all silk, all black or red and completely confounding. Some of them seemed to have too many ties, others too few and not a zipper or button in sight.

As I turned them over in my hands, I realized they

weren't solid colors like I thought but made out of shot silk, black woven with crimson and carmine threaded with ebony to create a shimmering effect.

Finally, I pulled out something that looked like a black halter top and a split slip of the same color. Then I reached up to pull my top off.

Breathtaking pain hit me like a ton of bricks and I bit down on my lip to keep from screaming. I was so *over* the whole pain thing, and still no end in sight.

The motion must have pulled at the bruise or something. I tried to raise my arms again and dropped them at the first warning twinge. No dice. There was no way I would be able to change out of my clothing without help.

"Sethalor?"

"Yes?"

"I don't know how most of these go on and I can't really move."

A long silence.

"I'm coming in."

"No! Isn't there anyone else who can help me? There has to be another woman in this place."

Another long silence, punctuated by a long exhale.

"Your presence cannot be revealed. Especially in your current state."

"What? Why?"

"The imperial city is forbidden to all except the royal family upon penalty of death. Even were that not the case, you cannot be seen to be half-naked in my chambers. Your reputation would never survive the rumors."

Imperial city. I had the impression that he was speaking about the imperial palace complex, kind of like the Forbidden City, not an actual city. But who knew? Especially since apparently I had to acquire three more layers of clothing over everything before I could even be seen walking around.

I looked down at my pink peasant blouse and knee length denim skirt.

"I'm far from half-naked." I couldn't resist the retort even as I knew he was correct. The bare arms and low neckline could possibly be excused depending on which era I'd landed in, but as far as I knew, no dynasty had ever allowed women to show their bare calves.

"Courtesans show less skin than you do."

And how would he know? Did he routinely make use of them?

I shoved away the thought, irritated I'd even thought it. He was the regent. He probably not only had courtesans dancing attendance on him but an entire harem of concubines. And it wasn't any of my business.

I set my jaw and envisioned shoving those thoughts into yet another box. None of my concern at all.

"Fine," I conceded.

He came back into the room. His movements were slow and too careful, like every movement hurt. His face had paled further and his lips were bloodless.

"You really don't look fine at all. Do you need to sit down?"

"No."

A low snarl came from the other room at his response.

"Aedrian." Seth's voice was weary, barely louder than a murmur.

The snarling stopped, but the feeling of being prey didn't.

I frowned. There was something they weren't telling me. Something very much to do with me.

"What's going on, Seth?"

When he just shook his head, I raised my voice and directed my question at the other room. "Aedrian?"

Sethalor stared at me, his lips firmed in an obstinate line, green eyes stormy.

A low growl came from the next room, threat rumbling in every word. "If you don't tell her, I will."

I arched both brows at Seth. "Maybe you should anyway. Seth seems to have difficulty with being forthcoming."

The prince sighed. "The effort of healing you was extremely draining, that's all. I will be fine once I've had some rest."

Aedrian snorted derisively. "He should be resting *now*. When a mage uses up their store of magic, if they insist on continuing the spell, their body will burn muscle and bone to fuel it. When Seth woke up, maybe a *shichen* before the first time you did, he insisted on staying by your side to continue the healing and he hasn't rested since. He should be in bed himself, not pushing himself further. You'll recover from whatever bruises remain. If he burns out his magic permanently, that's a different matter."

Icy shock slid down my spine. A *shichen* was about two hours. So he was not only pushing his limits magically, but also physically if he hadn't slept since before I'd woken last. It sounded like the magical and the physical was intertwined, however, so if not attending to one made things worse for the other, that could be a very vicious cycle.

Sethalor had opened his mouth sometime during Aedrian's tirade and closed it again. His breathing was faint and shallow and I got the impression he was fighting to remain standing.

I backed away from Seth. "You should definitely sit down. I can manage the clothing on my own."

"You can't. Not without pulling at the bruise."

Heat slid through my bones and I narrowed my eyes. "You don't need to be touching me to heal me, do you? Stop it."

He shook his head, but the flow of heat stopped.

"You're not going to let it go either, are you?"

His mouth tightened and I knew the answer.

I took a deep breath. "Aedrian could help me with the clothes."

My cheeks blazed hot and my scalp prickled, but the words were said.

Sethalor's eyes widened in surprise and denial flashed across his face. "That's –"

I cut him off. "The only logical thing to do at this point."

He exhaled. "Are you sure? He would be a

gentleman about it, but I would not want you to be uncomfortable."

I gave him a wry look. "All things considered, no offense, but I'm not sure I'm that much more comfortable with you dressing me. At least not enough to make you do it when you look like you're about to fall over."

Pain and hurt flashed across his eyes and his face paled further. "Very well."

Worry sank claws into my chest. "You really really should sit down."

His lips twisted, but he sat down on the edge of the bed. Some of the tension eased in his face and I realized he was expending energy he didn't have just to remain upright.

Aedrian prowled into the room, full of lethal grace and vibrating with barely suppressed rage. "I really don't know whether to commend you on noticing or to dislike you for how poorly you handled that just now." His conversational tone held an unmistakable, underlying edge.

I glared back. He really wasn't helping my nerves. "I'm not sure about the two of you, but I haven't had a man help me dress or see me half-naked since I was a child. So forgive me if I consider it massively uncomfortable and awkward, period, regardless of who does it."

Dark red brows arched. "You mean to say you walk around like that and no man has laid claim to you? What, are the men in your world useless or denser than rocks?"

"Excuse you. I do have a choice in the matter. It's not a matter of some man laying claim to me like sticking a flag in the ground," I said in disgust.

Too late I realized the possible double entendre and bit back a groan.

Silver eyes met green and they both grinned wickedly at me.

"Oh, for fuck's sake, get your brains out of the gutter."

Seth chuckled soundlessly.

Aedrian winced at the expletive. "Not helping your case, lass."

I tapped my toe, my face blazing. "I thought we really cared about my getting out of these clothes."

The redhead's expression sobered. "Yes."

"Would you be more at ease if I left or if I stayed?" Seth asked.

I bit my lip. "Stay, please." *Him* I trusted, however ridiculous it was to do so, but I couldn't shake the thought that Aedrian would get rid of me to protect Seth if he could.

I lifted the halter top and split slip. "I'm assuming these go on first. How should we do this?"

Aedrian took the halter top and made a twirling motion, silver eyes gleaming. "Turn around."

"Okay." In my hurry to evade the amusement in Aedrian's eyes, I didn't realize until I came face to face with Seth's calm scrutiny that turning away from one man meant facing the other.

There was the faintest tug on my blouse before the sound of fabric tearing ripped through the air.

I froze.

The sleeves of my blouse drooped down my shoulders and the torn edges tickled my back as the blouse succumbed to gravity. I crossed my arms, holding the cloth close to keep from flashing him as I spun around, ignoring the twinge along my ribs.

"What do you think you're doing?"

Aedrian slid the dagger into a sheath strapped to his forearm and shook his sleeve down to cover the sheath again, his expression as bland as if he'd just pulled down a zipper rather than sliced through my clothing.

Temper flared at his nonchalance."You can't just destroy my clothing!"

Aedrian gave me a level look, his face set in lines of impatience. "There is no way to remove it without causing you pain. Cutting it off was the only reasonable option."

My jaw dropped. I turned my head to look at Seth.

He arched a brow and shrugged. "Aedrian's right. Besides, it will be simple to replace them should the need ever arise."

I closed my mouth with a snap, imagining flesh between my teeth and turned around again. "Fine, whatever," I gritted.

Hesitant fingertips traced the band of my bra. His fingers slid under the band, his warm touch raising the fine hairs on my arm. Heat rose up my neck and seared my cheeks. I slid my eyes away from Seth's knowing gaze.

"If you cut that off me, I'll kill you. That's really

expensive lace you're looking at." I grimaced as my husky tone ruined my best efforts to keep my words impassive.

He laughed under his breath. "No need. That can stay."

Dark and sensual, the sound slid down my spine and coiled warm tendrils around my core. I shook off the thought of whether he'd bring ruthless directness or tender delicacy to the bed. That supremely inappropriate thought would be why this was a terrible idea.

He reached around me, halter top in hand. "Hold this."

I released the death grip I had on my blouse to take the black silk and fought the urge to cross my arms against the rush of vulnerability. The silk was cool against my skin, in contrast to the blush searing up my body.

Movement caught my attention, Seth's hands tensing from where they were folded in his lap, his fingers slowly curling into fists. Our eyes met and I dropped my gaze to my own hands, white-knuckled against the black silk.

Warmth brushed my neck and waist, butterfly soft whispers of touch as he secured the ties of the halter top. Leaning forward, he picked up a length of red silk, his other arm coming around me to catch hold of the other end and pulled it around my body.

For a moment, I was wrapped in his arms, his scent curling around me. I inhaled and he eased back, the moment broken.

Ribbons were threaded through keyhole openings in the waistband to secure the wrap skirt, his motions graceful and economical. I breathed out slowly, trying to shake off the surreal sense of intimacy.

Aedrian came around and knelt before me, holding the split slip. "Step in."

I stared at the undergarment for a moment before complying. My cheeks were about to explode into flame. Forget that, my entire body was on the brink of spontaneous combustion.

He pulled the slip up and tightened the drawstring, his fingers smoothing the waistband until it settled flat under the skirt.

I trembled under his hands, straddling that line between ticklishness and sensual awareness. Every tug and release of the buttons on the denim skirt coming undone sent shivers down my spine. His movements were deft but unhurried, his composure unraveling mine. It was almost a relief when the denim fell to the floor.

The ties on the skirt had to be readjusted since the bulk of the denim was out of the way and I held my breath throughout.

He stood and reached for the rest of the fabric. A short robe with long bell sleeves went on over the halter top. A thin red gauze overskirt went over the robe and the wrap skirt.

Sinking to his knees again, he wrapped a black sash of whisper-thin silk around my waist, once, twice, three times.

I fought back a shiver. He was close, closer than I'd allowed any other man before. The endless brush of his hands and the devastating intimacy of his heat against me heightened my senses until I felt on the verge of screaming something just to break the tension.

Biting my lip, I looked up and fell into Seth's eyes, the pupils dilated into pools of black. The knowing look he gave me, hot and intimate, made me tremble.

Aedrian held up one end of the fabric he was fiddling with. "Hold."

I did, swallowing hard against the sensual haze threatening to take over my mind.

Sethalor smiled, slow and devastating, the curve of his lips a heated promise.

Placing one hand on my waist to hold the rest of the sash flat, Aedrian twirled the end in his hand so it twined into a thin cord. The heat of his palm burned into my skin, even through the ten million layers of silk he'd wrapped around me. A twinge of pain reminded me to relax against his hold and breathe.

He looped the cord once around my waist before handing me the end. "Hold this." He took the other end from me and did the same with it, finally twisting the corded ends in a complicated knot at my right hip. The result resembled an obi sash with a decorative cord over it.

He trailed a finger along the ends of the sash, tracing its drape against my hip. "You should have a pendant to hold the ends down." His dark gaze was heated, only a thin band of stormy gray remaining.

I wanted to jerk away. If he kept stroking me, intentionally or not, necessary or not, I was going to do something to embarrass myself. Like smacking his hand away.

"The royal colors suit you," Sethalor murmured. He leaned against the bed post, emerald green eyes hooded, the twist of his mouth something I couldn't decipher.

I looked down at myself then back up at him. "You don't sound too thrilled."

"I'm not."

I blinked. "O-kay." Did he want me to ask further? Bringing up the topic suggested he wanted a conversation, but his tone discouraged prying.

"His family was assassinated, probably in someone's bid for the throne and he was nearly killed himself. My guess would be the royal colors aren't exactly happy reminders right now. Lift your foot," Aedrian said dryly.

Shock rolled through me at the bland recital and I nearly missed Aedrian's last sentence. "What?"

"Lift your foot. Place your hands on my shoulders if you need to," he repeated the prosaic words, his expression serene. He held a black silk bootie in his hand.

"Oh." I glanced over my shoulder at Seth, whose expression had turned brooding. Inky lashes veiled his eyes and he didn't seem inclined to continue the topic.

Alrighty then. Let's just throw bombs into the water willy-nilly and then pretend nothing happened.

I rested my hands on Aedrian's shoulders and lifted my right foot. His muscles twitched under my hands, as if he fought the urge to throw me off or move away.

"Gods above, your feet are like ice." Wrapping his hands around my foot, he chafed gently. Long fingers trailed warmth in their wake, rousing nerve endings I didn't know existed.

"She's always had poor circulation," Sethalor murmured.

Aedrian slipped the fleece-lined bootie on my foot, tied the ribbons in a bow around my ankles to secure it and tapped my other foot. "Lift."

Heat of another sort coiled deep in my core as his warmth spread through me. His molten silver gaze swept up and caught my breath.

Could he tell my hormones were rioting? Gods, I hoped not.

I took a quick step back when he set my foot down. "Thank you."

"You're welcome." He stood and moved away. Cool air rushed into the space he vacated and I released the tension in my shoulders.

Just as I thought the torment over, Seth beckoned. "Come here so I can fix your hair."

"Oh." I pulled out the hairstick holding my bun up and shook down my braid. Like I suspected, it was ratty, with strands of hair escaping everywhere. "I can just put it back up in a bun if you give me a comb."

Sethalor slanted me a glance, a sudden chill in his eyes. "Only married women wear their hair up,

Phoenix."

I rolled my eyes. "Does it matter?"

"Only if you want to explain to your grandparents who you married and when," he said sardonically.

"Why would I need to do so?"

"Because you will be meeting them and living under their care for the foreseeable future?" he said with exaggerated patience.

My stomach dropped. "What? Why foreseeable future? Why can't I just go home?"

"I can't send you home. I don't have the means to do so, or I would."

And if the regent didn't have the means, who would? Shit.

"And you're dumping me with people I don't know?"

The corners of his mouth turned downward. "You don't know me."

I froze, having no answer to that. I bit down on my lip.

Ridiculous. Laughable. Why would he keep me around? He was right, I had no claims to him, especially since I couldn't even remember who he was to me. I breathed in slowly and tried to exhale the fear away. No matter that he was the only anchor I had in this world. No matter how I felt. What mattered was what needed to be done so I could go home.

My hands shook. I pulled the hair tie off the end of my braid and started finger-combing the knee length mass to hide the tremors.

Sethalor studied my face and sighed. "You are an

unmarried woman, Phoenix, and the palace is barred to you, remember? You cannot stay here."

I bit down harder on my lower lip before responding. "I understand." And I did, but I didn't have to like it.

Seth arched a brow.

"Really. I do."

He shook his head faintly, but didn't push further. "Come here."

"I'm not a puppy." The words came out harsher than I intended.

I pressed my lips together to keep the avalanche of hurt from spilling out. I wasn't a pet to be dumped somewhere just after I started trusting them. I wasn't a burden. I wasn't a problem to be solved. Shaking my head, I tried to dislodge the thoughts. No. Just breathe out. Let it go.

"No, you're not. Puppies are usually much more biddable and trainable." He took the comb Aedrian extended.

I inhaled. He wasn't going to budge. Might as well get it over with. "Fine, but only because I apparently owe you my life."

He turned me around, but not before I caught a trace of a smirk. "You do know what the usual price for a life is, right? If I were going to demand repayment, I'd hardly settle for your acquiescence to one simple request."

Sethalor's hand wound in my hair and tugged me closer so I was bracketed by his thighs. He ran the comb through my hair in slow, drugging strokes, smoothing his hand in the wake of the comb so he wouldn't pull my hair when he got near the ends.

I closed my eyes, resisting the urge to tip my head back and sink into his touch.

"Are you expecting me to tell you that I do not have anything so valuable as my life to gift to you in thanks and so I must deliver unto you my body that you have so thoughtfully saved?" I asked, my tone mocking. Those trope-tastic lines had featured prominently in half the romance novels I'd read in middle school.

He drew hair back from my temples into two braids and twisted them together into a knot.

"I wouldn't say no to that offer, but I'd settle for your obedience in all things pertaining to your safety and well-being."

My heart, traitorous organ, stuttered. I sucked in a breath. Focus.

"Hairstick."

I passed it to him, our fingers brushing and sending a wave of awareness rippling through me. Like I needed wayward chemistry to muck things up further.

A faint pull, the sensation of wood sliding against my scalp and he dropped his hands. "There. You look as a daughter of a noble House should."

"Not quite. She doesn't sparkle enough; not enough jewelry," Aedrian said.

I raised a hand. "I think we're good." I didn't want to hear them banter, didn't want to sink further into the illusion of safety, of belonging.

Pivoting to face Seth, I looked into his eyes. "Okay. Assuming I believe it. All of it. What else do I need to know?"

CHAPTER SIX

Sethalor led the way out of the bedroom into what looked like a sitting room. Two doors the breadth of a wall opened out onto a garden. A round table holding a porcelain tea set sat in the middle of the room with four stools arranged around it. Silver globes of light glimmered everywhere.

He gestured at a seat. "Please, sit."

The prince waited until I sank down on a stool before moving to sit opposite me.

Aedrian shifted to the door and settled into parade rest, his gaze turning inward, his mouth settling into a severe line.

Seth lifted the teapot from the warming brazier, poured a cup of tea and nudged it in my direction. The scent of ginger wafted up.

I glanced at the cup.

Ginger tea was the bane of my life. It was now at any rate. It was what my mother insisted on pouring down my throat at every opportunity. Moontime? A tall mug of the stuff first thing every morning.

Rumors of a flu going around? A cup both morning and night. Never mind if I were actually sick. Then she poured the stuff down my throat like water. I'd brought the habit with me when I left home and gotten everyone in my social circle into it and now all I could taste when I smelled the sugary spicy scent was bile and betrayal.

"Let's recap: I'm stuck here with no way of going back to my home or family, but I have grandparents here who likely have no idea of my existence who you can dump me on. Easy for you; not so great for me. But what I don't understand is if a spell brought me here, why can't a spell take me back again?"

Having family to fall back on was better than being left to fend for myself, but gods, the whole thing sucked. And why would I have had a spell placed on me to begin with?

Seth shook his head. "I said I didn't have the means to send you home, not that you were stranded here." A whisper of hurt flashed across his eyes. At my mention of going home? "You cannot leave because the moment you arrived here, all borders and portals were closed to you. They will not reopen for you before you submit to the *shenxuan*."

Heaven's choice? That didn't sound promising, especially not when *submitting* was involved. I'd had a bellyfull of it and no more.

"Have I ever mentioned that I don't do submission?"

"You don't precisely have a choice. Tavaneth is a magical land and it is bound to the well-being of its ruler. As the throne is empty and has been for years, the land is dying as a result. The gods are quite invested in finding candidates for the throne. You will not be permitted to leave until you have undergone the *shenxuan* and I know you've heard the stories of what happens to mortals who upset the gods, Phoenix."

I did know. Mortals who disappointed tended to become walking lightning rods. The god of thunder and the goddess of lightning tended to look very poorly upon those who lacked honor.

A shiver ran down my spine and my mouth dried.

I reached for the tea cup, picked it up and set it down again. I wasn't quite desperate enough to drink ginger tea yet.

"So you're telling me I've been drafted and there's no out?"

"First you must undergo the *shenxuan*, which will determine if you are a suitable candidate for the throne or not. Then comes the *tianzhe*, where the ones chosen will undergo further testing. You cannot refuse the former but you can reject the latter."

"Why? How does that make sense?"

"Your choice must be made with full knowledge. You can walk away from a land that needs you, a people that will likely starve without your aid, but the gods require you to do it knowingly. If you leave before the *shenxuan*, the thought that perhaps you would not have been chosen anyway would allow you an easy conscience."

Wonderful. Never let it be said the Chinese gods

were the warm and fuzzy sort. Actually, were they Chinese? I was making assumptions based on architecture and clothing and food cues, but then, Aedrian. What was a redheaded man with what sounded like a Scot's accent doing here? And Seth's English also carried a faint hint of that same accent. So much for assumptions.

I stared at the tea, desperately wanting it to be something else. Preferably something nice and stiff.

"It's ginger steeped in chicken broth, not sweet ginger tea," Seth said.

Surprise pushed aside some of the frustration aching to break free and I sipped at the broth. A note of citrus underlaid the taste of chicken and fresh shitaake mushrooms, all woven through with the familiar grounding burn.

"This is delicious. Thank you." Warmth spread through me, as much from his thoughtfulness as from the spice. Not that he could've known what I now associated sweet ginger tea with, but I'd always preferred savory over sweet anyway. More hints that he *knew* me.

I set the cup down. "If I can just turn down the chance to be what? Empress? Can't I just do that and go home? Why bother my grandparents?"

Sethalor's eyes narrowed in contemplation.

"Brigid wept, you're colder than Morrigan's heart. You'd think a woman would want to meet long-lost family," Aedrian muttered.

My last nerve snapped.

"Stop judging me, Aedrian. You don't know

anything about me. If they cared at all, why don't I know anything about them? I'm twenty-three, yet I've never once heard of them. My parents have never said anything about my grandparents, so I can only guess they're estranged. If so, why should I want to foist myself on them?"

Silver eyes widened for a moment before his expression blanked again.

Seth coughed. "Actually, your grandparents would be overjoyed to meet you. I suspect your parents told you nothing because your mother was banished before you were born and contacting exiles is forbidden on pain of death. I doubt there was a good way to explain that your grandparents lived yet be unable to provide any way of contact."

What was it with these people and death everywhere?

I folded my arms. "Wait. You're telling me I'm required to submit to something to tell me if I can be the ruler of a country that exiled my parents? Seriously? Am I even a citizen if I'm the daughter of two exiles? Shouldn't I be disqualified on that alone?"

And why should I care about this place if we weren't welcome here? I ignored the pang in my heart. Ridiculous, to care if I was wanted here or not.

Sethalor's mouth twisted. "Your grandmother is Xuanyuan Qian, styled Ningxia-ji, mistress of House Xuanyuan and a queen of Tavaneth. The land is bound to the nobility by blood, Phoenix. As her heir and scion, your ties to Tavaneth are undeniable by anyone, much less yourself."

Air went down the wrong pipe and I choked. You've gotta be kidding me.

Sethalor refilled my teacup.

I snatched it up and took a long swallow. "What? I'm related to royalty? I'm related to *you?*" Unreasoning denial filled my throat.

It's not like the Chinese didn't love marrying cousins to each other.

I slapped the thought down. No. Bad brain.

Aedrian choked and Sethalor slid him a warning look. "No. We're not related. The *wang* and *ji* are descended from the generals and advisers who aided the first emperor in establishing his dynasty. They are not part of the imperial family."

I didn't pause to examine the reason behind my relief. "So she's a queen and I'm a what now?" My voice rose in disbelief.

Sethalor nodded. "As her heir, you hold the title of princess. She is referred to as Your Illustriousness and you would be addressed as Your Grace."

Now that I was taking him seriously, what he was saying made my head spin. "Okay. Right. I don't believe this. Why am I her heir? She doesn't even know me. And shouldn't this go to my eldest brother by right of primogeniture anyway?"

"No. House Xuanyuan has always been led by a woman."

"Why me?"

"I don't know how you were chosen to be her heir, I simply know it to be true."

"How do *you* know all this?"

His brows raised into an arrogant arc. "I am an imperial prince, Phoenix. It is my duty to know such things."

My temples throbbed. "Okay. Whatever you say."

Aedrian pulled something from his sleeve and glanced at it before slipping it back into his sleeve pocket. "Ningxia-*ji* has sent notice. Her Illustriousness will be arriving within the hour."

Sethalor stood and extended his hand. "Come."

When did that happen? My grandmother knew of me? I set my palm against his, unthinking, as if it were the most natural thing in the world.

He didn't give me a chance to object or ask questions. His hand clasped mine and the world tumbled away.

CHAPTER SEVEN

The world swirled back into being with an audible pop. Or was that my ears? No matter. My head spun and everything whirled the way it did after too many rounds on a spinning chair. I moaned and pressed a fist to my complaining stomach. I *wanted* to throw up. Preferably on Sethalor, now also known as the instrument of my torment. I closed my eyes, hoping that would help, and forced my breathing to slow. Nope on the closed eyes, but taking a deep breath and then holding it seemed to suppress the urge to projectile vomit.

"Breathe deeply and you'll recover sooner. My apologies. Teleporting us was the only way to leave the palace without detection." Sethalor's voice was soft and wry. It punched into my skull like a twelve-shot hangover.

Sethalor shifted so he took most of my weight and rubbed soothing circles on my back. The scent of bergamot and sandalwood filled my nose and his touch curled warm tendrils in my stomach.

I opened my eyes as the worst of the nausea melted away under his hand. The last I'd felt this much like death involved heatstroke, far too little food and three bottles of rice liquor between three people. The thought of teleportation being a real thing didn't help in the slightest.

I kicked the thought into a box. If I let myself fall down the wormhole of wondering how it was managed, I'd run screaming.

Sethalor stepped back, his hands falling away when I braced my palms against his chest and stood upright.

I looked around now that the world had settled down.

We stood in front of two massive red doors. A black plaque with *Xuanyuan* lettered in gold paint hung above the entrance.

Awareness whispered across my senses and the hair on the back of my neck rose. I turned my head.

Aedrian stood behind us, naked blade at the ready, his expression intense.

A shiver slid down my spine. "Um. Is that really necessary?"

Silver eyes slanted me an icy glance. "He is the regent and an imperial prince. You are a princess. By all logic, neither of you should be going anywhere without a full escort. Yet here we are, one of you about to cast up your accounts, the other wraithlike from magic drain, and with one sword between the three of us. It might as well be a ready blade."

Someone wasn't happy. Then again, was he ever?

I stepped closer to Sethalor.

"You know full well that there would be little reason to kill me now that I am not in line for the throne, Aedrian." Sethalor's voice was calm, almost conciliatory.

Aedrian's mouth thinned and he jerked his chin at the door. "Knock, so we can get in out of the open."

The prince gave a faint shake of his head before reaching for the bronze door knocker. The dull thud echoed through the night.

Long minutes later, just as my stomach was starting to squirm at the wait, the door swung open.

An old man stood just within the threshold, long silver braid falling forward as he bowed. "Imperial Highness. Lord McKenna. You are welcome." He studied me for a moment and a soft smile curved his mouth. "Especially since you're escorting the little miss."

I stiffened. The term was both honorific and endearment. Things were simultaneously getting more surreal and more believable by the moment. But why would this old man even know of me, much less known enough to recognize me on sight?

"Phoenix, this is Wei *bo*, seneschal of Xuanyuan House." Sethalor tipped his head to the old man.

I nodded, uncertain of the courtesies expected and more than a little curious as to how Seth knew my grandparents and their butler to call him by that honorific.

Uncle Wei? Sethalor had to be more than passing familiar with my grandparents and their household.

Uncle Wei led the way around the decorative wall that blocked outsiders from seeing directly into the grounds. The estate was a *si he yuan*, a quadrangle home in the traditional style: A house with four wings surrounding a courtyard and connected via arcada and roofed stone paths.

"Wei *bo*, have your master and mistress arrived yet?"

"No, Imperial Highness, but they should be arriving within an incense stick's time."

Incense stick's time? I racked my mind for my history lessons. About fifteen minutes then, perhaps twenty. Possibly even thirty, depending on all sorts of things.

We passed through an arched doorway bisecting the front wing of the house and into the gardens. The main house would be on the other side of the courtyard.

Holy batman. This wasn't a courtyard. Not the way I usually thought of the term at any rate. It felt like we'd stepped into a fairytale forest.

Sethalor and Aedrian fell back to flank my sides as my steps slowed.

Golden globes lit the paved stone path. Wind whispered through the greenery, carrying the fragrance of night blooming flowers. Water burbled and fell somewhere nearby. The night was quiet but alive around us.

Unexpected tears pricked my eyes as an inexplicable pang of longing pierced my heart. It felt like...coming home. How, when I had never seen the place?

We took another turn and a building came into view. Intricate lattice-work covered the top half of the wooden walls, allowing light in, while oiled paper kept the elements out. Stone steps at the end of the path led up to the roofed hallway that connected the wings of the building to each other, a series of arcada designed so the inhabitants could appreciate nature without being inconvenienced by inclement weather.

Uncle Wei strode up the stairs and threw open the doors. "After you, Little Miss."

More golden globes were set into the walls for illumination. Two scrolls of calligraphy hung on the wall directly opposite the door, the characters fluid like wind and sunlight on water and completely indecipherable.

Two chairs sat beneath the scrolls, carved in geometrical latticework patterns so they resembled thrones constructed of delicate lace. A round wooden table with four wooden stools carved in a similar fashion was set in the middle of the room.

Uncle Wei didn't follow us into the great room. "If you have need of anything, Xuelan will be just outside the door."

He bowed and closed the doors after us.

Aedrian stood by the side of the door, hands laced behind his back.

Sethalor sank onto one of the stools, resting one elbow on the table and propping his chin on his fist. Perhaps it was the lighting, but he looked paler than before.

Or was it the teleportation? And then, I'd felt terrible immediately after but he'd touched me and I recovered so quickly... Almost like magic.

I nibbled at my lip, debating whether or not to say something. I hadn't forgotten how protective Aedrian was of him but it wasn't like I wanted him to keel over either.

"How much of your memory did you lose?"

I startled at Aedrian's question.

His face was still and watchful, his eyes intent.

"I'm not sure. Most of my memory loss seems to be centered around the two years before, so years fifteen to almost eighteen are pretty much a blank, but the rest is patchy in ways I don't understand. I can still quote reams of the poetry we memorized as children, but I can't remember any of my birthdays. I forgot some of my family, but not others, and what I do remember has odd holes and blurred images."

"Who did you forget?" Sethalor asked.

"Kendrick and Katherine. They weren't too happy about that." They'd sulked and said that I wasn't getting any presents for a decade.

Sethalor sat up straight. "But of course you remembered Kieran and Estella."

His words reverberated through my skull, tripping off sparks of pain. Agony sliced through my heart. A vise clamped down on my brain and squeezed.

Pink elephants. Pink...

I reached for the mental image, the circuit breaker my mother had come up for me.

Too late.

Darkness wavered around the edges of my vision as the pain turned excruciating. I threw out a hand to break my fall, knowing I was going to wake with more bruises.

CHAPTER EIGHT

Voices drifted over and around me, pulling me back to consciousness. I fought it, clinging to the state before full awareness. My temples throbbed and there was a metallic taste in my mouth. If I rose too soon, it would bloom into a full blown migraine.

Just. Stop. Talking.

The third time my name came up, I gave up. There was no ignoring the fact they were talking about me.

Warmth and a soothingly earthy scent surrounded me. Leather, sun dried linen, and the faintest hint of musk. Guess someone caught me before I did my faceplant. I kept my eyes closed as I tried to figure out who had me. Probably Aedrian. I wasn't sure how I felt about that. Maybe he didn't dislike me as much as I thought he did, if he cared enough to keep me from slamming into the floor. He wasn't anywhere near me when I went down, so he must've expended effort. Or was it to spare Seth?

"But if she doesn't remember them..."

"Shh. She's awake."

Busted.

I forced my eyes open.

Aedrian sat cross-legged on the floor, cradling me in his arms. I was curled up in his lap with my cheek resting on his chest. Seth sat beside him, facing me, his back braced against the base of the chair. His lips were bloodless and he looked worse than before. I didn't know that was even possible.

"How do you feel?" He reached for my hand.

I pulled my hand away and tucked it into my sleeve. "No. Don't touch me."

Sethalor flinched. His hand dropped. Aedrian tensed under me and I got the impression he wanted to throw me out of his lap.

"You look like shit. Keep your hands to yourself, boyo, before Aedrian kills me to keep you safe."

Aedrian's muscles relaxed.

Gritting my teeth, I stood and weaved toward the nearest chair. Inhaling slowly, I resisted the urge to think about those two names and what they might mean. The echo of Seth's voice sounded in my mind and I shoved it away. No. Not now. Not that any time was a good time to start a nosebleed.

Aedrian unfolded from his position on the ground and held out a hand. "She's right. You can't give her anymore unless you want me to carry you out of here."

Sethalor gave him a look, but took his hand and let the redhead pull him up, immediately sinking down on the chair behind him.

Aedrian didn't return to his post by the door but stood directly behind him, as if waiting to catch him if he faltered.

The casual trust and intimacy between them made my nose sting. I bit my lip, blinking away tears. I wanted that. I craved that easy give and take of devotion so much it felt like I was pulling myself inside out with want.

Reaching for the jade pendant around my neck, I wrapped my fingers around it, tightening my fist until I could feel every carved detail against my skin. Remembered sensation brushed over my skin, phantom arms wrapping around my shoulders, the barest puff of air over my head as if someone laid a kiss there. I swallowed my tears, closed my eyes and sank into the wish until I could almost feel the warmth of the embrace.

I was loved. I was going to be okay. I was cherished and wanted and it would all be okay.

"Her grandparents are going to ask questions."

Disgruntled at being shoved out of my happy place, I opened my eyes and stared at Aedrian. Why was he stating the obvious?

The redhead huffed out a breath. "It's going to be a mess if you faint with every other question they ask about your family and it seems like there's no particular logic to what triggers the headaches and what doesn't."

Seth cocked his head. "Or is there?"

It sounded almost as if he knew something.

Seth stared back at me, his gaze limpid but

unrelenting.

"No." I wrapped my hand tighter around the pendant. "I don't know what is dangerous territory and what isn't. One of the worst episodes was when someone asked me if I'd ever thought about what I'd wear to my wedding. Another bad one was when mom asked me if I wanted anything for my birthday."

Gold streaked across his eyes and Sethalor tilted his head, his expression contemplative. "I see. For tonight we can simply tell them the truth. I found you in the royal gardens, injured. The healing drained you and you need your rest. Anything else can be discussed tomorrow."

"Much as I also enjoy avoiding my problems and hoping they go away, realistically, what's going to change between tonight and tomorrow that would help the situation?"

"I think the headaches may be magical in nature, not physical. Your grandmother would be able to verify this."

Shock slid through my veins in an icy rush. "Why would you think that? And why would we discuss it tomorrow?"

Inky lashes came down to veil his eyes. "I have some notion of what memories you're missing and the possible reasons why you lost them. If I'm correct and your grandmother needs to lift mental bindings from you, it would be best if you rested beforehand. Your mind and body has already been through much and release of the bindings will be injurious."

"Those two names you mentioned..." I shied away

from thinking about them, but even the edges of memory hurt. A fleeting smile floated up from the depths of my mind. A familiar voice. Then the painful throb of warning.

He shook his head. "Don't. Not now."

"But why would the mention of wedding plans trigger the headaches?" I bit my lip. "And if they're magical in nature..." If my mother came from this world...

The door opened and a woman stepped into the room.

I rose to my feet in surprise, relief and anger washing over me. "Mom?"

CHAPTER NINE

She moved toward me and I realized my mistake. Not my mother. But it wasn't just wishful thinking. She could pass for my mother's twin. I stared at her, barely noticing the man at her side.

My father called my mother his peony, lush and aristocratic, but this woman with her black hair knotted up and striding toward me with a warrior's grace resembled an orchid, elegant and untouchable. The clean lines of the royal purple tunic and wide-legged pants she wore furthered that impression. A single spray of plum blossoms, embroidered in silver, climbed up her pants leg, the only decorative concession.

"Is that my grandmother?" I threw Seth an incredulous look.

"Magic." He shrugged, a small smile curving his mouth.

Of course. What *wasn't* magic?

She hesitated as she approached.

I stilled, nerves trembling in my stomach. What

did she see? Did she believe Sethalor when he said I was their family?

My grandmother stopped in front of me and raised a trembling hand to cup my face. Tears glimmered in her amber eyes. "Child."

Her hand dropped and she turned to Sethalor, dipping down in a formal courtesy. "Your Imperial Highness. I apologize for my disrespect, but I am barely able to credit my eyes." Her gaze returned to me without waiting for Sethalor's acknowledgment and she reached for my hand. "My grandchild."

Breath left me in a relieved rush. Sethalor was right. I was welcome here, at least.

"*A-mah*," I said, using the more intimate term for grandmother.

She answered with a brilliant smile.

The man beside her bowed. "Your Imperial Highness. Lord McKenna. Thank you for returning our pearl." He cleared his throat and took a step closer, his voice turning firm. "*Our* grandchild, Xiaoqian."

I raised my gaze and looked into my grandfather's eyes, my breath catching and swelling in my chest. The tip-tilted eyes I'd inherited.

Realization clasped me by the throat as I noted the too-full bottom lip beneath a perfect bow and the nose that flared a bit too much beyond aquiline. This was the first time I'd seen a familial resemblance and the first time I realized how much it bothered me that I didn't resemble either of my parents or my siblings.

I bit my lip to keep the tears back. And he referred to me as their pearl.

"*A-gong*," I said, squeezing the words out through the tightness in my throat.

He cleared his throat again. "What is your name, child?"

"Xuanyuan Fengxun Estyria."

Grandmother's eyes narrowed thoughtfully on me. "Feng xun. Are you the phoenix who searches or are you what the phoenix searches for?"

Grandfather's brows raised in turn and he glanced at my grandmother. "Not your father's surname? Then that means..."

Sethalor lifted my right hand so my sleeve fell back to reveal my wrist and the hollow jade bangle snugging it.

"Yes, she is the scion and your heir."

A telltale stream of warmth flowed up my arm and I tugged my hand from his grasp, breaking the connection.

I glared at him. "Stop that."

Distracted by his surreptitious healing, I didn't realize the implications of his gesture until my grandmother caught my hand in hers and traced the bangle, a thoughtful look on her face.

"Wait. This means something?" Carved out of a solid piece of snow jade and then hollowed to display the delicate filigree of flowers and vines, I knew that the bracelet was rare and probably priceless, but I wasn't aware of its symbolism.

I fingered the pendant around my neck. Did that have meaning as well?

Grandmother nodded. "Yes, this is the symbol of

Xuanyuan House and is given to the heir."

"But I've had it for forever." I could rotate the bangle around my wrist, but only just.

A strange smile quirked her mouth. "You've had it since birth, if I am not mistaken. Every girl child born to a Xuanyuan is offered the breast or the bangle once they've opened their eyes. She who chooses the bangle becomes the heir."

"Maybe I just wasn't hungry enough?" I muttered.

My grandparents exchanged a look and my grandmother's smile deepened. She traced the bangle with her forefinger again. It glowed faintly before it separated into two pieces and fell into her waiting hand.

A bright burst of pain arrowed through my chest.

Sethalor caught my elbow as I staggered and Aedrian surged forward, hand outstretched.

This was getting far beyond old.

I sucked in a deep breath and firmed my knees.

Alarm spread across my grandmother's features. Lifting her hand, she touched the pieces to my skin and they immediately flowed over my wrist, becoming whole again.

The pain eased immediately and I breathed out. What the hell just happened?

Worry darkened my grandfather's eyes. "What happened, Qian?"

Aedrian's hand dropped, but he took another step closer.

Seth's hand tightened on my arm. "That wasn't normal, was it, *shimu*?"

She shook her head, her face pale. "No, it isn't. Usually there is only mild discomfort if the bangle is removed. It is a physical tether of the heir to the land, a binding if you will." She touched my cheek. "I only meant to demonstrate that the bangle chooses its owner as well. It would not have become whole again at the touch of any other. I regret having caused you pain, even unintentionally."

I wrapped my hand around the bangle, unable to keep from making sure it was on my wrist and solid.

The regent swept me a quick glance, beautiful mouth tightening. "Speaking of uncertain magics and bonds... I suspect that someone has tampered with Fengxun's mind. However, it might be best if we did not try dismantling the spell for the time being."

My grandparents tensed, their gazes whipping to Sethalor's icy green eyes.

"Why do you think so?" asked my grandfather, his voice cold.

"She has amnesia. What's strange is that she has blinding headaches if certain things are mentioned but not others. I'm led to believe that a block has been placed on her memories."

My grandmother's eyes narrowed. She laid her hand on my forehead, her eyes closed and she started murmuring under her breath.

Waves of cold heat spread from her hand over my scalp and penetrated into my skull. The throbbing which had mostly died down flared up again with a vengeance and my knees buckled from the sudden onslaught of pain.

Sethalor caught me against his chest, strong arms tightening around my waist.

Gods-fucking-damn it. These people needed to let me know before pulling shit like that.

My grandmother's voice came through the barrage, flat with contained emotion. "I'm going to remove it now. I didn't think a mere probe would affect her thus, but as it clearly does, I do not wish her to go through this twice." A soft hand caressed my cheek. "Brace yourself, Granddaughter, there may be some pain."

I would have laughed if I could have managed it. Some pain? My world was nothing but pain. Had been nothing but pain since that thrice-damned SUV started the whole nightmare.

Fire seared through every synapse, a fiery web of pain that overlaid my entire body. I bit down on the scream boiling out of my throat and bucked in Sethalor's grip.

A grunt escaped him and his grasp turned bruising as he staggered back against the force of my convulsion.

Flames. Incredible pressure inside my skull. My ears popped with a wet sound as all sensation disappeared. The world spun dizzily around me before winking out.

So tired of that ... happening...

A warm hand smoothed over my forehead and

siphoned the pain away. The scent of warmed sandalwood and patchouli told me who held me in their arms.

Seth.

I opened my eyes, wincing against the light. Emerald eyes looked down at me, relief clear in their depths. Tension ebbed out of him.

"You're awake. That's good." My grandmother's voice came from beside me.

Turning my head, I met identical looks of concern from my grandparents.

I sat up from where I had my head pillowed on Seth's thigh. The movement made stars flash across my vision and the world spun lazily around me. A hand clamped down on my shoulder, steadying me. Aedrian. He moved out from behind Sethalor, bent and easily lifted me to my feet. Setting me on my feet, he kept one arm wrapped around my waist to pin me against his body and reached out to Seth.

Sethalor's mouth twisted in a wry moue, but he accepted Aedrian's hand, rising to his feet with a grimace of pain.

My grandparents stood as well, their eyes intent upon us, their expressions grim as they studied us. My grandfather, in particular, looked at us as if we were bugs under a microscope.

Aedrian hooked one of the stools over with his foot and pushed me down. "Sit." He gave Seth a sharp look. "You too, before you fall over." He nudged Seth onto the chair beside me.

Grandmother took the seat opposite , her

expression apologetic. "I really must apologize, again, Fengxun. Much to my chagrin, I didn't expect the spell to react that way to a simple probe. I merely wanted to ascertain if what the prince said was true, with no intention to dismantle it. It appears the spellcaster really didn't want anyone tinkering with it."

I nodded, choosing to keep silent. I wasn't a big fan of how she'd just...done things. To me. Without asking. Or even warning.

"Will she regain her memories now?" Seth asked.

"There is nothing obstructing your retrieval of the memories now, but it's not so simple as that. The mind is a delicate thing; it isn't a box you can simply dip into at will. I wouldn't be surprised if your mind has already been trained to flinch away from remembering because of the pain. I would suggest not pushing, as much as you might want to, at least for a week or so, perhaps longer. Your brain needs to heal from the bruising. Beyond that, your mind needs to be able to learn that looking for memories doesn't have to bring pain."

I nodded, covering a yawn with my hand. Fatigue battered at me now that the pain was dying away and I was one blink from dozing off.

Grandmother gave Sethalor a flat stare. "Your Imperial Highness, I think we have much to discuss."

My grandfather nodded as he seated himself beside my grandmother. "Not the least of why you have not told us of Fengxun's existence before today." His eyes narrowed and his next words were silk-smooth and lethal. "Especially since you are bound to her."

I stared at them, my brains full of cotton batting, their words drifting in one ear and out the other. Weights pulled at my eyelids, warring with my need to know what was going on.

Sethalor sent my grandfather a look of pure aggravation. "It would have pleased me greatly if you hadn't seen fit to blurt that out," he gritted out.

Grandmother folded her arms, her eyes turning cold. "And why not?" She slanted a look at me and her voice faltered. "It seems Fengxun is unaware of this as well. How is this?"

"You may be a grown man and regent now, but I am still your teacher and I can still thrash you if I need to, boy," my grandfather said.

Aedrian coughed.

Seth sent him a filthy glare before hissing out a sigh. "You and your wife may be my teachers, but I think you both need lessons on being discreet." His voice lowered, the velvet tones lethal. "I had my reasons, not least of which is that your granddaughter has amnesia, doesn't remember me, narrowly missed death and has been tossed into a world and circumstances completely foreign to her. When, pray tell, should I have informed her of this? Before or after trying to keep her alive? Or when trying to persuade her that she hadn't lost her mind and that we weren't trying to dupe her?"

My grandmother blinked. "Ah, so you do care for her. I was wondering, since the bond is incomplete.

Yet you still haven't explained why you haven't spoken of her in the last five years."

Aedrian snorted out a laugh before quickly muffling it into a cough.

Palming his face, a low growl issued from Sethalor's throat. His other hand clenched and unclenched, as if resisting the urge to throttle something. "She wasn't here and wasn't coming here. What was there to speak of? Should I have mentioned in passing that I happened to be bound to your youngest granddaughter, but so sorry, I had no idea where she might be or what she might be doing?" he gritted out.

Her eyes widened before narrowing again, her mouth opening as if to say something, then closing with a snap.

My grandfather wrapped an arm around his wife's waist and drew her back a step. "Dear heart, you might want to stop plucking at the tiger's whiskers before he takes a bite out of you."

She flicked him a glance. "Weren't you the one who threatened to thrash an imperial prince?"

"Yes dear, but you'll notice I stopped before he started issuing death threats."

"He hasn't yet."

"Body language, dear. Body language. Our beloved protégé is one word away from strangling you."

Aedrian outright laughed. "Seth, I think the women of House Xuanyuan just might be your nemesis."

"Must be," Seth snarled.

I blinked and blinked again, vaguely aware that there were whole seconds between the rise and fall of my eyelids. Their voices buzzed around me, words I heard but didn't fully understand.

Her brow set in a contemplative pleat, my grandmother's gaze flickered between us before catching my eye. "Fengxun needs her rest. We will discuss more on the morrow. Fengxun, I will have Xuelan take you to your rooms and attend to you. Have you eaten? Perhaps you should eat before you sleep."

I shook my head, mute. Sleep fled as panic surged at the thought of having to sleep in this foreign place, with people I barely knew, even if they were family. I curled my hands into fists and shifted closer to Sethalor, twining my fingers into the folds of his sleeve.

Warm fingers covered mine, unwound my hands from the fabric and rubbed warmth into me. "*Shifu, shimu*, may I escort Fengxun to her rooms?"

My grandparents exchanged a glance.

"With Xuelan and Lord McKenna in attendance, I don't see why not," my grandmother said.

CHAPTER TEN

The rooms assigned to me were in the east wing of the house, where the heir of the House traditionally resided in Chinese culture. So much so that the heir to the empire was commonly referred to as the master of the East Palace.

I clung onto the bits of trivia I knew, bits of flotsam to keep me from drowning in all the unknown around me.

The east wing was arranged in a similar fashion to the main house, constructed in a quadrangle with three suites and a sitting room surrounding a courtyard of its own, connected to the main house by a moon gate and the ubiquitous arcada.

Xuelan pushed open a door and stepped to one side, waiting for me to go in.

I stared at her, my mind blanking. Sweet of face and willowy, I couldn't tell if she was a teenager or about my age. Her gaze was curious and direct, a small smile curving the corners of her mouth despite the lateness of the hour.

She seemed nice, but.

I hesitated in the arcada in front of the bedroom and looked up at Sethalor.

The wry smile on his face twisted further before he sighed, laying a hand at the small of my back. "I won't leave until you've fallen asleep, if that's what you want."

"Please."

A slow exhale escaped him. "How you bring me to my knees." His hand exerted gentle pressure on my back, nudging me forward. "Go. Let Xuelan help you prepare for bed and I'll sit with you when you're done. You should have a hot soak, but perhaps not tonight. You might fall asleep and I don't think you want Xuelan attending you in the bath."

I shook my head, too tired to speak.

Xuelan extricated me from the ten million layers of silk and brought me a basin of hot water with a towel.

I couldn't do much more than wash my face and hands, but I refused to let her sponge bathe me. *That* was far too strange and well beyond my ability to cope.

She bundled me into a plush nightgown that fell to my ankles and chivvied me into bed, saying she'd let Sethalor know I was appropriately covered.

The duvet held the scent of herbs and I pulled it up, snuggling into its folds. Aside from having a vanity and chest of drawers, the bedroom was very similar to the one I'd woken in, what felt like an eternity ago.

Sethalor walked into the room, looked around

and pulled the vanity stool over to my bedside. Aedrian followed, silver eyes alert despite the fatigue etched around his mouth. He returned to the doorway and settled into parade rest after making a turn around the room to check the windows and what was presumably the bathroom.

Sethalor leaned over and brushed the back of his hand against my cheek before drawing back and sitting down. "Sleep."

I closed my eyes. Except for the sound of soft breathing, silence filled the room. Minutes later, the stool creaked and fabric whispered. My eyes snapped open, anxiety pushing away sleep.

Grave emerald eyes met my gaze and his mouth compressed. "I said I wouldn't leave until you slept."

I bit my lip.

He sighed. "You have a distinct breathing pattern when you are sound asleep, Phoenix. I've woken you from enough naps to know the difference."

It didn't matter. My heart wavered, unsettled. He was the only familiar thing in this new world, in the midst of endless revelations. I held out my hand. His mouth twisted before he wrapped long fingers around mine and tucked our entwined hands under the covers.

A feather-light caress, like a benediction, brushed over my forehead as I fell into sleep.

I woke to a shadowed room, the dark alleviated

only by pale moonlight. There was no one else and for a moment bitter pain jagged through my chest. Unreasonable as it was, I wanted them there, even Aedrian.

The moon called, promising companionship if not comfort and I slipped out of the room, taking the duvet with me.

A small waterfall flowed from a formation of rocks designed to look like a mountain, complete with bonsai growing from its crevices. I curled up under the comforter on the stone bench beside the pool and tipped my head back to look at the full moon overhead.

Countless travelers had taken solace in the moon over the years, knowing it would eventually come full again. They took comfort in being under the same moonlight as their loved ones. No help for me since for all I knew, it was a completely different moon from the one I grew up with.

I sighed and huddled deeper into my blanket. So many things made sense now in retrospect. The bedtime stories. The archery and martial arts lessons. Riding training. The mental games my mother played with us. It was as if she knew we would need the skills one day. But why would we, if she were in exile? Did she think there would be a pardon?

"I'm not sure what I did to deserve this, but I think you might have a terrible sense of proportion," I told the sky. They said the gods never gave you more than you could bear, but at the moment I had my doubts.

The moon didn't respond.

The back of my eyes prickled and my nose stung. I tipped my head back further and widened my eyes to hold the tears in. Crying didn't help. It never did and the accompanying headaches would just be another problem to deal with. Oddly enough, the logic only made me want to cry more. Biting down on my lower lip, I blinked furiously.

A flash of white caught my eye. I turned to track it and came face to face with a cat. A really large cat, about the size of a fat Maine Coon. It looked like a snow leopard but it had sharp tufted ears like a lynx. Fluffy tail lashing the air, it kept deep blue eyes pinned upon me. A red cord peeked out from its fur around its neck and a transparent crystal dangled from the cord. It stepped closer, sapphire eyes narrowing.

I blinked and a single tear escaped.

Before I could swipe it away and pretend that never happened, it flicked its tail over my cheek, sweeping the moisture away.

Stunned, I stared at it.

It sneezed at me before deliberately turning its head away.

I could take a hint and it was enough not to be the only breathing thing in sight. I pulled the duvet up around my shoulders and head and leaned against the back of the bench. Exhaustion dragged at my eyelids.

The soft caress of the night wind, surrounded by green living things, also helped. I needed a swim in the worst way, but this would do. I breathed in slowly and exhaled. In some ways, it was soothing to know there was nothing I could do. Nothing I could change at the moment to make things better. It was all out of my hands, at least until tomorrow.

A weight leaned against my side and a low rumbling purr resonated through my bones. I pulled down the blanket. The cat had curled up on the bench beside me with its tail draped over its nose.

I pulled the blanket back into place and let the soothing vibrations lull me to sleep.

CHAPTER ELEVEN

My grandparents were already seated at the round table in the great room when I walked in.

"Sorry, am I late? I'll try to be faster next time." I covered a yawn. It had taken longer to get ready than I was used to, even with help, particularly since I was distracted by the question of why I was nestled in the bed when Xuelan came to wake me, the cat nowhere in sight.

My side barely complained when I was moving around and I suspected Seth had come back, found me in the garden, and slipped me some more healing before tucking me back into bed. Hopefully he wouldn't look worse after a night's sleep than before he left.

Grandfather put down his cup and shook his head. "No. We just sat down."

"I wasn't sure what you liked, so I had the kitchen make a little bit of everything." My grandmother's faint smile carried a hint of chagrin.

I understood why when the dishes kept coming out.

Each dish was no larger than the size of my palm and held about four bites each. Even so, they covered the entire surface of the table by the end. There was enough food to feed at least three more people.

"Thank you. You really didn't need to. What if we can't finish all this food?"

My grandmother laughed. "Oh, don't worry about that. Your grandfather can eat at least half of this on his own."

I blinked. "Really?"

He set down his chopsticks and turned his hand palm up. Fire bloomed in his palm, a perfect fiery lotus.

My breath caught.

He closed his hand. "Fire is one of the more costly elements to control and so we fire mages tend to consume quite a bit of food."

I exhaled slowly. Freaky fire shows first thing in the morning. I couldn't decide if it was completely cool or if I should be sitting in a corner whimpering about how my world had broken around me.

"You said 'we'. So *A-mah* is a fire mage too?"

She nodded. "Yes."

And so was Seth.

I waited a beat. "So I have magic too?"

A look of surprise crossed her face. "Of course."

Of course.

I sighed.

She said that as if it were one of Newton's laws of

physics, something incontrovertible and inevitable. Whereas I was one wrong breath against rocking myself in the corner, hands over my ears, and singing to myself to keep the world out.

She passed me a bowl of rice porridge. "Your mother is the daughter of two fire mages. Even allowing for your father being a mundane, magic should be a strong presence in your blood. And I have my doubts about him having no magic."

"Oh. What sort of magic do I have?"

Not fire, something in my mind whispered.

I tried not to pay attention to the voices, but I agreed. Fire was nice and all, but I didn't want it to be my element.

My grandfather arched his brows at me over his bowl. "You should know, Fengxun. What element soothes your spirit and rejuvenates you?"

"Water." I loved the water. I'd gone to a landlocked state for college and thought I'd shrivel and blow away with the wind. I pushed off the mental image. Thinking about myself with magic wasn't really working well for my heart rate at the moment.

"Just as well that water is your element. Fire is a harsh mistress. Without sufficient power to fuel the magic, fire can consume an unwary mage," my grandfather said.

Grandmother nodded. "But that is not to say that it is simply a matter of how much inherent power the mage has. It is also a question of how much power the mage can channel. How open a mage is to the elements and the universal flow is just as important as the well of raw power they were born with."

Grandfather pushed the rest of the white-fish at me and scraped the last of the preserved tofu into his bowl. "Take the imperial prince, for example. He has immense power by virtue of his birthright, but he is almost completely closed to the world around him. He should not have been nearly as drained as he was but for his stubbornness."

I searched his face, but his expression remained bland. "How do you know him anyway? He seems familiar with you." And he called them *shifu* and *shimu* yesterday, if I remembered correctly.

"We were tutors to the imperial princes. We've known His Imperial Highness since he was still toddling around his mother's garden."

I frowned. Disbelief bubbled up around a knee jerk burst of rage. "Wait. He exiles your daughter and then asks you to tutor his offspring? What kind of..." I choked back the *sadistic mess* on the tip of my tongue and settled for trailing off.

He lifted his right shoulder in a shrug that didn't quite make it to casual. "The imperial princes showed signs of being fire mages and the emperor wanted to make sure they made it to maturity with their minds and bodies intact."

I held up a hand. A headache started up at my temples. "You mean that just being a fire mage can kill you? Not that you had to do something reckless or wrong?"

Grandmother nodded. "Yes. It is especially bad for men. All that hot blood and *yang qi*, you understand."

My grandfather slanted her a glance. "Keep casting that in my face, wife, and I'll remind you of it the next time you throw a chair through a window."

She made a moue. "You deserved it."

He arched a brow. "For looking at a tavern wench a second too long? I'll remind you that we wouldn't have caught that assassin if I hadn't been on guard."

"On guard for a nice set of tits."

I choked, not expecting to hear that word from my grandmother. A chunk of fish went down the wrong pipe.

She reached over and pushed my tea closer to me.

I downed one cup and poured another. Tears welled up from coughing.

"Now look what you've done. You've gone and scandalized the child." My grandfather's tone didn't sound so much chiding as amused.

Grandmother sniffed. "I'm certain her mother has said worse in front of her. A dog doesn't change its habits of eating shit."

I gave up. I put down my tea before I snorted it out my nose and laughed. She was right. My mother routinely said similar things around us. She said if the ancients saw fit to saddle us with idioms like that, there was no reason we shouldn't use them. And if people were going to behave badly, there was no reason to gloss over their sins with pretty paper.

"You didn't sound happy with Sethalor, *A-gong*."

Amusement slid from his face and his mouth turned grim. "I'm his master and teacher. If he's going to insist on killing himself, I'd rather not be known as the man who taught him how to wield magic. Heavens know that I never taught him to be so stubborn."

That wasn't the tone of a man out to protect his pride. It was the sound of a father worrying about a beloved son.

Grandmother laid her hand over his and squeezed. "I'm sorry."

He shook his head. "Heaven's will, Fengxun. He lost his entire family to assassins. He was betrayed and nearly killed himself when he came back to pick up the pieces. Then the gods refused him the throne. A weaker man would have broken. I suppose I should be grateful that he only refuses his connection with the land."

The reminder of reality killed what amusement I had.

I poked at my bowl of porridge, my appetite fled. "Heaven's will? Sethalor said something about that."

Their faces sobered and they exchanged a look.

My grandmother set down her bowl and folded her hands. "Yes. The *shenxuan*, when the gods choose candidates for the throne. I'm afraid you cannot avoid that."

"Sethalor said something to that effect." I spun my bowl in my hands, feeling uncomfortably like I was prying. "What do you mean he was refused the throne?"

My grandmother's lips compressed. "Actually, we don't know that. All we know is that the mantle and crown didn't descend when he woke from the fever when it should have passed to him as the last member of the imperial family. It is possible he rejected the land first, considering his unwillingness to open to the earth's energies."

"He did mention that the land is tied to the ruler and that it's dying. Is that true?"

Grandfather tipped his head. "Yes. The drought shows no signs of easing. Here in the capital, we feel it less harshly because the city sits by where two rivers meet the sea, but further out west, people are starving. The ground is so dry that no seed will germinate and when they do manage to coax seedlings with careful irrigation, it takes only one dust storm to destroy hope."

A sharp pain pierced my heart. I pressed the heel of my hand against my chest.

"And it's not going to get better?"

Grandfather shook his head. "Not unless a new ruler takes the throne and feeds the land."

That didn't sound creepy at all. "What do you mean, feed?"

"The ruler is bound to the land. The earth is as their flesh, the rivers their veins and what nourishes one feeds the other."

"Um. If one is dying, isn't that kind of dangerous for whoever becomes emperor?"

"It can be, but usually the royal consorts will share their energy to replenish the emperor," my grandfather said, with an odd look at my grandmother.

My brows shot up. "Wait, you mean there's

actually a reason for the emperors to have like three thousand wives?" They had to be kidding me.

Grandmother snorted. "Hardly. Even when the land is in dire need, if the consorts were strong mages, five or six would more than suffice. Even if they were all mundane, ten or twenty would do. More than that is simply lust."

"Also, every House has a hoard of magical energy that the scion can pull from at will. Depending on how strong the House is and how entwined Scion and House is, additional consorts may not be strictly necessary," my grandfather said with an arch look at my grandmother.

A sly smile curved her mouth. "Indeed."

"Wait. What are you referencing?"

"The ruler holds the country as a whole, like the brain and heart ruling the body. We, the queens and kings of Houses govern demesnes within the country, much like organs within the body. Your grandfather is a strong mage, equal to me in magic, which is why our lands have not yet felt the effects as strongly. However, even if our personal abilities were limited, we could draw upon the cache of power maintained by House Xuanyuan for generations."

I frowned in concentration. "But, then shouldn't the imperial house have a magical store as well?"

"Yes, which is why the country has been able to do as well as it has been for so long. However, it's been years and Tavaneth isn't a small country. The damage will also grow exponentially as desertification encroaches and the remaining water needs to be used to keep our people alive rather than toward irrigation. If I guess correctly, we may have another three years, maybe four before the drought dries the great rivers entirely," my grandfather said.

The pang dug in harder, sinking talons in my heart and clawing. Wincing, I pressed down harder.

"Besides, Sethalor has shut himself off from the country and I suspect that affects how much he can maintain the land. It could be three years, it could be much less," my grandmother added.

My grandmother patted my hand. "Don't worry, Fengxun, it is unlikely to come to that. The gods will find a candidate soon enough."

"If it's been years, what makes you so optimistic?"

Her gaze was calm and knowing. "Someone will answer the call. Eventually the cry will become so overwhelming that there will be no evading it, even for one of no magical ability. In the interim, we will maintain the balance for as long as we can."

"Even for someone without magic? Can someone without magic become ruler?"

She nodded. "Of course. As I said, how open one is to the magic is just as important as whether one has the magic. A canal does not have to have water of its own, it need only be open to bodies of water. The second king of Tavaneth had no magic of his own, but his consort was a sorceress and it worked out well enough."

"When is the *shenxuan*?"

"It is your choice. When you are ready you will present yourself to the gods at the ancestral altar and they will judge you then."

"What does it involve?"

Grandmother spread her hands in a helpless gesture. "They say the gods walk through your mind and soul with you, but I do not know what that actually entails."

"You mean I need to go ask them to come rummaging through my brain?"

She slanted me a glance. "Yes."

Great.

We ate in silence for a while as I tried to process what I'd learned and what I'd seen.

"Why were my parents exiled?"

Grandmother set her bowl down and sighed. "There was a confluence of factors, but perhaps the real reason was because the emperor felt betrayed by your mother. They grew up together and I think he always assumed that she would be his empress when the time came."

"Suffice to say she didn't want to. Not wanting to merely be first amongst many was part of her reasoning, but more importantly, their notions of how best to rule a country diverged when they were young and became mutually exclusive when they grew older," grandfather interjected.

"Then your father appeared as if sent by the gods, Yalian fell in love and that was that. Perhaps the emperor would have been willing to let her go for the sake of their childhood friendship if she hadn't made it clear by her actions that she found him, his governance and in extension his country lacking,"

Grandmother said.

"Speaking as a man who had to tutor the brat, I have to disagree. Even if Shangguan Yunji had never appeared, she would never have married him and eventually their relationship would have soured. To a certain extent Yalian thought he was holding the country hostage as some sort of lure to entice her into marrying him and that only furthered her disgust of him. She was never able to dissemble well when she knew right was on her side and eventually he would have tired of her disrespect."

Grandmother glanced at my grandfather before looking back at me. "I think you're right. At any rate, when your father suggested returning to his native world, Yalian was more than happy to go and experience it for herself. She told the emperor what she intended and that she was going to marry your father and he flew into a rage, telling her that if she left, she would never be welcome back again."

Studying the serenity of their expressions, I tilted my head. "You don't seem too mad at the emperor. Why not? He cost you your daughter out of sheer spite."

A bitter laugh escaped my grandfather as he shook his head. "It's been more than three decades, Fengxun. At this moment, I've lost my daughter for far longer than I've had her. We've had ample time to come to terms with fate."

"She was eighteen when she left," my grandmother murmured, a catch in her voice.

And my mother had just celebrated her forty-eighth birthday. Damn.

"Sorry. I didn't mean to imply you didn't care."

He waved the apology away. "No need. The first decade was the hardest. We found fault in everyone, including ourselves. If I had been a better teacher. If Qian had been more careful to impress upon her the necessity of catering to an emperor's will. If we hadn't been so sure that the emperor would be understanding, would at the very least grant us grace because of the relationship between our Houses. If we had claimed her lost rather than admitting that she was gone to your world. All these should haves and more."

He looked like he was about to say more, but a knock came at the door. "My lady, His Imperial Highness sent word that he will be arriving within an incense stick's time and asks that you not meet him at the door. His Imperial Highness will meet you in the customary place."

My grandparents exchanged a look before they rose.

"That would be the solar. Come, we will await him there," my grandfather said.

"He is impatient," my grandmother murmured.

"Yes. It is a good sign," he agreed.

"Why?"

They bent identical looks of surprise on me but it was my grandmother that answered.

"He has not shown much passion for anything since he woke. He goes through the motions but he has not truly lived for years. It is good to see some fire in him at last."

Recalling the pain and darkness in his eyes, I pressed a hand to the twinge in my chest.

CHAPTER TWELVE

y jaw dropped when I saw the solar, ethereal and magical in the morning mist. Composed entirely of frosted glass, it looked like a spun sugar greenhouse. Delicate bamboo blinds that could be rolled up or down for degrees of privacy shielded the large picture windows. Sheer green gauze curtains were drawn at the moment, just thick enough to blur the features of whoever sat inside, but not enough to block the morning light.

There was an area just inside the door for shoe removal and storage, with the rest of the hardwood flooring raised up off the ground. Furs and rugs covered the floor, with cushions for seating surrounding a low table. A silver dome rested in the center of the table.

I toed off my soft boots and stuffed them onto a shelf. My grandparents walked straight in and I realized that they'd been going around barefoot the entire time.

"Should I not be wearing shoes?"

"Ah. Guests usually wear their shoes in the public rooms. In rooms that are reserved for the family, it is expected that we follow custom and go barefoot," she said.

"You noticed that the rooms and wings of the house are connected with arcada?" he asked.

I nodded.

"All the paths that are covered with roofed hallways are cleaned twice daily and are considered to be part of the home."

He caught my glance at my shoes and shook his head. "Those are indoor slippers."

"Oh." I wiggled my toes in the fur. "Aren't you cold?"

She laughed. "Of course not, as fire burns hot in us. Besides, it is second nature for us to shield against the elements now. You will learn to do so as well, once you harness your magic."

Not if, but once I harnessed my magic. Her casual confidence that I had magic and that I would use it shook me.

A soft susurrus interrupted my next question of when. The air vibrated and shimmered a second before Aedrian and Sethalor appeared.

My grandparents rose to their feet and bowed. "Imperial Highness. Lord McKenna."

Unfolding to my feet, I followed their lead and bowed.

A slight frown gathered between his brows. "Please, be at ease," Seth said.

We sank back to our seats.

Aedrian knelt by the door, sword across his thighs.

I fluttered my fingers at him, not wanting him to feel left out, but not sure of myself or protocol.

Silver eyes brightened and he inclined his head slightly.

Sethalor folded to the ground in a single elegant motion, dark green eyes scanning over me before he faced my grandparents.

To my relief, he looked fine. Still pale, but his lips had the faintest tint of pink, which was a good thing, right? Considering that my bruises looked half-healed and it no longer hurt to move normally.

"It is unnecessary for you to bow to me, as you well know," he said softly, but with a unmistakable edge of command.

My grandmother shrugged. "It has been more than ten years since your edict, Imperial Highness. Pardon me for saying so, but as fickle as imperial decree can be, it is better to err on the side of etiquette."

Seth folded his hands, his eyes chilling to chips of green ice. "What are you about, *shimu*? If this is about the bond, that is not for you to pass judgment on. If not, how else have I offended for you to chide me so?"

Grandfather raised both brows in faint reproof. "She is our granddaughter. How is it not our business?"

Bond? Something surfaced in my mind. They'd mentioned that the night before but I hadn't been paying attention. Then someone said something about love...

"Um. Am I missing something here?"

Sethalor held up a hand. "First, we will speak of the *shenxuan*."

His absolute tone carried the unmistakable weight of power.

My grandparents bent their heads and I realized it was the imperial prince and the regent who just spoke, not the man who'd held my hand so I could sleep.

"I thought I didn't have a choice about the *shenxuan*."

"There isn't one. However, there are things you need to know and I'm certain you have questions."

"How exactly *does* the *shenxuan* work?"

"The gods walk through your mind and decide your worth. From most accounts, the candidates fell asleep and had a dream they couldn't remember upon waking."

"That doesn't sound too complicated. What's the big fuss about discussing it first?"

A sharp smile curved his mouth. "You must decide whether you will accept the gods' choice within twelve hours of the *shenxuan*. If you are chosen and you choose not to abide by their decision, you will be sent home immediately and you will not be able to return. Unlike the exile set in place by my father, this banishment cannot be lifted by any other than the gods."

An involuntary, pained sound came from my grandmother. My grandfather shifted and took her hand in his, murmuring something in her ear.

I blinked. "Harsh."

The edge in his smile went razor thin. "Everything has a price."

Shock rippled through me and I stilled. Where had I heard that before?

Everything has a price. The price of having, daughter, is knowing you might be called upon to give. Sometimes you will need to give more than you have. The true measure of a person is whether they give what is required rather than only what they can spare.

It was my mother's voice, but when did we have that conversation and why?

Sethalor continued, "When you make the decision to commence, you will begin the purification process. This will take three days. You will not allow meat, wine, or spices other than salt to pass your lips for two days and fast for the third. You will bathe before presenting yourself at the altar on the fourth morning. The *shenxuan* usually lasts no longer than from dawn to dusk, with most experiences being much shorter than that. You will know if you have the gods' favor at the end as it usually manifests as a physical mark, often upon the countenance."

Involuntary tattoos? Talk about submission. And fasting? Oh fun.

"So what you're saying is that if I get chosen and I turn it down, I'd probably never see my grandparents again."

"Would you submit to the yoke of the throne instead? Agree to carry the burden of ensuring the well-being of all who live upon your lands? Will you second your life and all your descendants to the crown? Consider your choices carefully, Phoenix."

I narrowed my eyes. "I'm not sure if you're trying to scare me off or guilt me into staying. Isn't it hubris to worry about this now? I might not get chosen. If it's been five years and the gods haven't found someone they liked yet, I doubt I have much to worry about."

"Just letting you know where you stand, Phoenix. Better to think about it now rather than scramble for a poorly-made decision when it is upon you."

The dirty look I was giving him turned filthy. "If you're giving me all the information, then what was that about a bond? And what happens to my being heir to my grandmother if I'm excommunicated by the gods?"

"The Xuanyuan estate will revert back to the crown if there is no heir."

"Even so, you should not allow that to sway your decision. Choosing whether or not to devote your life to something of this magnitude should not be done out of obligation or guilt," my grandmother interjected.

"About that bond..." I prompted.

Sethalor closed his eyes briefly and sighed. He looked around the table, meeting my grandparents' gaze in turn before looking squarely at me. "Lend me your right hand."

I reached across the table.

He extended his hand and pressed it to mine, palm to palm. Entwining long fingers with mine, he murmured a soft word under his breath.

Warmth flared up my arm from wrist to elbow.

Sethalor raised our joined hands so our sleeves fell back.

I gasped and my grandparents echoed the sound, with my grandfather following with a low curse.

Golden lettering shimmered the length of our forearms. Not like a tattoo; golden light shone forth from under the skin in no language I'd ever seen. It had the sinuous flow of Arabic but the individual characters resembled ancient Chinese pictograms.

Taking in a slow inhale, I kept my tone as even as possible. "Can someone please explain... what the hell just happened?"

"Your soul and mine are bound and this is a physical manifestation of that bond."

"But it appears to be incomplete," my grandfather said.

Seth flicked a glance at him and traced a finger over the markings on my skin, where there was a stutter in the liquid forms midway to my elbow. "Here? Yes."

I tensed as a burst of heat coiled in my stomach at his touch.

I raised a finger. "Can we stop talking about this like it's commonplace and like I understand what's going on? Because I don't. How are we bound? Why are we bound?"

"You loved me once. That's why and how we're bound." His voice was bland, as if he were commenting on the weather.

Once? And he loved me? What about now?

"But it's incomplete? Why?"

"Need you ask? You don't return his love, therefore the bond is incomplete," Aedrian snapped. At some point in the conversation, he'd turned around from facing the doorway to watch us.

Didn't I? His presence filled a hole in my soul I never knew existed until we met again. I wanted to hear him laugh, to be the one to make him laugh and erase the sorrow from his eyes.

But to think that was absurd, wasn't it? Some kind of Stockholm Syndrome or whatever caused by the circumstances. Why *would* I love him when I barely knew him?

"That's not how the god-given bonds function, actually," my grandmother said. "For one thing, the bonds would have dissolved completely if she did not, in some fashion, return his affections. For another, the bonds usually do not set unless the heart is completely and irrevocably committed." Her mouth curved in a strange smile. "The bond between you, Lord McKenna and the imperial prince, for example, appears to be quite sturdy. For the bond between he and my granddaughter to have this sort of interruption is highly irregular."

"Is there anything about the magic around me that isn't irregular? And do these bonds usually manifest as light shows?" I snapped.

"No, dear, you seem to be quite the special one. Usually the bonds appear as tattoos do. I've never seen ones to glow like this," my grandfather murmured.

My grandmother's words penetrated and I whipped my gaze to Aedrian's shocked one. "Wait, these two are bound too?"

"Why yes." Grandmother's gaze panned from Seth's face to Aedrian's and back again. "You didn't know?"

She blinked, but the look in her eyes was one of sly amusement rather than confusion. "I suppose you also didn't know that there's two strands to the bond between the commander and the prince? I wonder why that is."

CHAPTER THIRTEEN

C urled up on the bench beside the pool, I huddled under a blanket and stared at the waterfall. I'd retreated to my rooms after my grandmother tossed down that particular nugget of information and everyone went weird. Seth had said something perfunctory before poofing off. Without Aedrian. Who'd paled and hared off, presumably after Seth. Although how he was supposed to find someone who could poof around when he wanted to be alone was a bit beyond me. Then again, Grandmom had said they were bound too, so who knew?

I wrapped my arms around my shins and pillowed my cheek on my knees, closing my eyes.

My world was unrecognizable to me. I thought it had shattered before, with what happened with my job and my friends, but apparently it had fragmented long before that and what happened a few weeks ago only further scattered the shards.

Suddenly, however, being dumped by my boyfriend for not being enough, and then subsequently dumped by his friends who also happened to be my bosses didn't seem as monumental as I thought before.

A bitter laugh bubbled up. *I* felt broken, my thoughts muted by pain and disbelief. The quiet weighed so heavily the boxes in my mind didn't even rattle anymore. What I'd learned and the size of the choice before me dwarfed whatever I'd put away in them.

Could I really just leave and go back to Earth, knowing I'd be turning my back on a demesne generations of my family had bled and sacrificed for? It wasn't even a question of long-gone ancestors and what they had done to be granted a House and title. My grandparents could have chosen to liquidate their estate and gone into exile with my parents, but they hadn't. They chose to respect the responsibility of overseeing the land and the people who depended on it, even knowing it might mean they'd never see their only daughter again, even knowing that they couldn't carry the responsibility forever. It could have all been for nothing, but still they stayed.

Grandmother said the kings and queens held the land for the crown. Presumably, whatever burden was attached to the crown would only be exacerbated if the demesne reverted back to the throne.

Could I live with myself, knowing that I wasn't just refusing to help but that my decision was probably going to make things worse? No longer the vague guilt of eating well while children starved elsewhere, but the gut-wrenching knowledge of being the direct cause of suffering.

Something soft and furry touched my hand.

I opened my eyes.

The cat sat in front of me, eyes solemn, so close I saw the striations of ice blue surrounding the pupil. It leaned in and brushed its cheek against mine with a soft chirp.

It was bigger than I remembered. I'd thought it about the size of a lynx the night before, but with it staring at eye level, I revised my estimation. It was at least the size of a young tiger.

A prodigiously fluffy tail whipped around its body and tapped me on the nose. The sound it made this time carried a note of demand.

I leaned forward and put my arms around its neck, ready to retreat if it looked like my advances weren't welcome.

Mrip. A purr rumbled through its chest and it moved closer, curving its tail around my waist.

I closed my eyes again and breathed in the scent of snow, pine, and mint.

"I'm going to stay." My stomach rebelled as I said the words, nausea boiling up my throat, worse than any stage fright, but it felt right. Nothing other than my family waited for me back on Earth and once a new ruler took the throne, it would be easy enough to ask for a pardon or a favor that allowed us to visit.

Another rumbling purr and the pressure on my waist increased.

"I'm glad someone likes that idea because I'm absolutely terrified."

It nuzzled its cheek against mine again and chirped.

"Why do it then?"

My fingers convulsed at the unexpected voice and the cat made a grumbling sound. Looking up, I met Aedrian's silver gaze.

Startled by his appearance, I missed the meaning behind his words at first. "Why what?"

"Why stay?"

I gave the easiest and simplest response. "It's the right thing to do."

"Is that all?"

"Do I really need much more of a reason than that? Does anyone?"

"Are you an angel or a fool, to jump into the lion's maw with neither knowledge or training?"

I rubbed my cheek against the cat's fur and sighed. "I studied political science in college, with a minor in Chinese history and politics because I had some idea of being the change I wanted to see in the world. I didn't pursue it further because of various reasons, but I wouldn't say it's a complete suicide mission." Just, you know, most of one, but I didn't need to give him more ammo to work with. Neither did I need to admit that I didn't think there was any chance I'd be chosen.

The commander stared at me, his eyes stormy, a cynical curve to his mouth. "You're a dangerous one, aren't you, little siren?"

"What?"

"They say sirens don't always breed true, but when they do..." he murmured, studying me with that cool, sardonic gaze.

"*What?*" I repeated. Was the man on crack?

"You're saying all the correct things with all the appropriate emotions, but I can't forget what you did to him with your betrayal. What I can't imagine is *why*. Was it because he never told you he was a prince? Was your family and your life too much to give up for a mere third son? If so, then your change of heart now makes sense."

The cat's tail lashed against the ground, a low rumble starting in its chest.

My mouth fell open. Was the man for real?

"You really don't think much of me, do you?"

He shrugged. "You broke a good man, one of the finest I've ever known. Should I celebrate your presence, knowing that?"

Judged and found wanting. Again. Pain and anger raked poison into old wounds. "You don't know me. You don't know what happened," I choked out the words, tears stinging my eyes. And what did he mean, that I broke Seth?

"Neither do you, which I find rather convenient."

The cat snarled at him, the rage-filled sound rumbling into a clear threat.

I bit down on my lower lip, refusing to let the tears fall. "Do you suspect me of having somehow orchestrating the accident too? Placed myself in mortal danger so I could come here and play Daji?" Daji, the concubine who brought a king and kingdom to their knees with her beauty and malice. I didn't know whether to laugh it off and thank him for the roundabout compliment or scream.

His fist came up to rest on his sternum and he averted his gaze. "I thought him a fool, but I didn't realize how easily a man can get entangled in your net. Even now, knowing what I do, your tears... they make my heart tremble."

Stumbling to my feet, I dashed my hand across my eyes and headed for my room. I didn't need to be listening to this. It wasn't flattering, wasn't romantic, wasn't anything but abuse.

"Running away, little siren?" His mocking voice snapped the last thread of restraint holding all the aggrieved rage back.

I rounded on him. "Yes. I'm running away. That's exactly what I'm doing. But you know what? At least right now I'm running to something bigger than myself. The truth is that I don't have a life to give up back on Earth. No friends, no job, no one who wants or needs me other than my family. So why would I say no to staying when something here needs me? I know the pain of being abandoned, of being considered trash and I would never do that to another." I darted past him, knowing I was on the verge of a complete meltdown.

Strong fingers closed around my wrist and tugged me back with enough force I collided into his chest.

Pain radiated out from my side and I gasped, more tears welling forth. Not healed enough, apparently.

Aedrian cursed under his breath and took a step back. "I apologize. I didn't mean to..."

Something butted into him, shoving him against

me to press hard against the bruise on my side.

I gasped.

"Brigid take it, cat."

I sucked in a breath, trying to will myself calm but the pain and frustration refused to subside. A howl clawed its way out of my throat and I gave in, keening until my throat burned and I ran out of breath.

Another muffled curse and then I was swung up into his arms and cradled against his chest.

"Hush. Hush, darling. I'm sorry. I shouldn't have..."

The rising wave of grief and fury drowned out his voice. No. No. I didn't want to hush. I wanted to scream until all the pain vanished, to shriek my innocence at the heavens and demand recompense for my hurts. I hadn't, couldn't when everything first started falling apart and now the idea of having to shove it all back made me sob harder. And he didn't get to call me darling. He didn't get to throw awful accusations at me and then try to brush it all aside with sweet words.

My strength ebbed out with every tear until I couldn't even hold myself away from him, much less push him away. A throbbing headache set up behind my eyes and nose, pulsing in time with the ache in my ribs. I drew in a shuddering breath, hiccuped and sobbed again.

What right had he to judge me? What right had anyone?

Fingers trailed through my hair, smoothing soothing lines down my back as he kept up a low rumble of soft, lyrical words in Gaelic. Interspersed were soft repetitions of *sorry* and *hush*.

"Gods below, Aedrian." Seth's voice, holding a note of appalled surprise.

The muscular body under me tensed. I squeezed my eyes closed, gasping for breath, needles digging into my eyes, but I couldn't stop.

"Poor darling. Shhhhh." Seth's voice dropped to a soft croon.

Gentle fingers cupped my jaw, tilted my face up and traced a cooling line from the corner of my right eye to the end of my eyebrow before doing the same on the other side. He feathered a kiss between my eyes and the pressure behind my eyes eased.

I opened my eyes, my vision blurry from my swollen eyes and the tears that kept falling.

Sethalor crouched beside us, emerald eyes dark and lines of pain etched around his mouth. "Shhh, darling."

"Can't. Stop." I gasped out the words.

"Do you want me to make it stop?"

I nodded, unsure what he could do, but more than ready for whatever help he offered.

He brushed away my tears with his fingers. "Sleep, my heart. Sleep and heal."

My eyes closed and I fell into welcome sleep.

CHAPTER FOURTEEN

I knelt in front of the altar at the foot of the goddess, watched the incense drift up in lazy plumes of smoke and waited. Rows upon rows of ancestor plaques looked down on me from behind the white jade statue of the goddess. *My* ancestors. Talk about performance anxiety.

Anxiety sharpened by not having seen my grandparents, Seth, or even Aedrian in the three long days since I'd woken from the sleep Seth placed on me and repeated my willingness to submit to the *shenxuan*. The first two days, my meals had been silently placed on a stool in front of the door to the small meditation room off the side of the *lingtang*, the hall of ancestors. The third day, nothing but a pitcher of water and a note from Sethalor reminding me that I still had the choice of backing out. I'd sat on the narrow bamboo bed and traced my fingers over and over his words, until I fell asleep and was woken by the girl sent to take me to the bathing chamber. Not Xuelan, oddly, but I couldn't spare the brain to think

112

about why that was.

Were there really true choices in the world?

It didn't matter now. I had made my decision and I was going to abide by it.

As per custom, I wore a simple white shift and nothing else. My hair hung loose, the tips pooling on the ground. I shivered, cold from nerves and fasting. My stomach had long since stopped grumbling, knowing nothing was forthcoming. The faintness, however, persisted.

Grandfather's voice rang in my mind, remembered words raising a shiver down my spine. *The gods walk in your mind and deem you worthy or nay.*

There were many things in my brain I didn't particularly want anyone, much less the gods, rifling through. No help for it now.

I pressed my palms together, closed my eyes, and bowed my head. The thick earthy scent of the incense wrapped around me and my head went light, as if I would drift away on the smoke. Tension ebbed out with each breath, the incense curling deep within me, my thoughts emptying with each exhale.

Cloth whispered in the dark quiet and I raised my head to see a woman standing before me. She wore a white cloak over white robes, the hood pulled up so only the tip of an elegant nose and crimson lips showed.

Golden light shimmered around her. Nothing so brash as glowing. It was more like she gathered the light around her, leaving the rest of the room in darkness.

I pressed my forehead to the ground, breath sawing in and out of my lungs. Up until that point, I'd been able to stay detached from the concept. Gods. Magic. Something greater than myself taking control of my life.

Her presence was a physical pressure against my skin, compressing my breath, my flesh and blood. No way to hide from the thought now; no neat little box to stuff the enormous into.

"Xuanyuan Fengxun Estyria. Raise your head."

Her voice, deeper than I anticipated, vibrated through me, down to my bones. The words reached deep within me, catching hold of my heart and soul.

She raised her hands and pulled the hood back. Dark eyes stared at me from a classically beautiful face, unearthly eyes, with stars glimmering in her irises. She wore her beauty like a skin, something to shield mortals from the true extent of her otherworldliness. I wanted to look away, but I couldn't. Her eyes drew me in and I fell, swirled into an endless sea of stars.

When I could see again, I knelt alone in space, surrounded by boxes and the stars. They shivered and I knew they weren't going to hold. Panic rose and expanded as I realized I couldn't move. My muscles remained lax, no matter how hard I tried. They vibrated harder and a muffled sob tore out of my throat.

The boxes weren't going to hold and somehow I knew they were the mental boxes I'd been shoving things into so I could cope.

Why would you want them to? Why contain and compartmentalize yourself when that detracts from your power? Amusement colored the goddess' question, even indulgence, her voice resounding in my head this time rather than manifesting as sound.

The largest trunk exploded. The metal chains holding the lid down snapped like embroidery floss. Wood shards flew everywhere, setting off the rest. Boxes went, one after another, like popcorn in a hot skillet. I couldn't look away, couldn't block out the roar of my mental defenses going down.

The force of the explosions pushed and shoved at me, finally gathering into a whirlwind of debris. Screaming faces appeared in the winds, their open mouths revealing jagged teeth. They snapped at me, tearing ribbons of cloth off as they spun past until I was laid bare.

The last of the safeguards fell. Memories and emotions moved in for the kill. A sharp pain struck me at the base of the neck and burgeoned to encompass my brain and then my entire body. Every inch of me burned, every breath I took felt like inhaling fire.

The goddess appeared in front of me and looked down at me. She smiled and laid her index finger between my brows, extinguishing the flames. *Grow strong, little phoenix. I have replaced your shields for now, but you cannot hide behind them forever. Not if you intend to fly.*

Her ice cold hand brushed over my eyelids, closing my eyes and I passed out.

A bell tolled, rousing me from my reverie. I felt woolly-headed, as if I'd had a fitful nap that proved more draining than refreshing. Prickles raced up from my toes when I wiggled them and my limbs were heavy and clumsy.

I looked up.

Orange and red stained the sky outside, the fiery colors of sunset rather than the softer shades of dawn. I glanced at the incense. Less than an inch remained of the twelve-hour coil I lit before settling into place.

A creak as the door opened, then the sound of quiet footsteps. The hairs on my nape raised as Sethalor's presence wrapped around me and joy bubbled up before I reminded myself of his conspicuous absence before I went into seclusion.

I'd thought he cared, at least enough to be a friend, but apparently not. Yet another of my misjudgments when it came to people.

Perhaps he was upset I forgot him. Perhaps he resented my chance at the throne when it should have been his. Perhaps I'd changed in his estimation and not for the better. Perhaps...a million perhaps and not a one something I should be dwelling on. I should have known better than to expect, to anticipate, simply on the basis of his kindness.

"The *shenxuan* is over."

I turned to face him, collecting my thoughts, careful to keep my expression serene and tone light.

"I gathered. When do I get to know my grade?"

He stood over me, his face cast into shadow. "No need to wait. You've been chosen."

"What?" That fast?

Sethalor pulled a mirror from the sleeve of his robe and held it up in front of my face. "Look."

My lips parted in surprise. Three crimson petals marked my forehead, in the space right above the point between my brows. It looked like a flower had landed on my forehead, just so, a lily blossoming where my third eye would be. I knew, logically, that he'd mentioned something like that, but to see it actually happen was eerie.

"The mark of the goddess, a show of her favor." His mouth twisted, as if in pain or rejection of the thought.

I traced the pad of my middle finger over the mark. It was smooth, the coloring an even crimson, like a birthmark.

"Okay. Will it go away when this is all done?" I latched onto the inane, desperately trying to keep the freakout at bay.

He slipped the mirror back into his sleeve and shrugged. "I do not know."

A whisper of panic surged up my spine. I took a deep breath, stuffed it down, and sat on it.

"Okay." It wasn't ugly. The deep red stood out, striking against the soft ivory of my skin and the black of my eyes and hair. In fact, it looked right, as if it had always been there, just waiting to be uncovered.

His eyes narrowed. "You're taking this well."

I really wasn't. The now-familiar headache pounded at the inside of my skull. But if I started screaming, I'd never stop.

He turned away and reached for the incense sticks. "If you wish, we can commence the ceremony for rejecting the *tianzhe* immediately. This time tomorrow, you can be back in the bosom of your family. We simply need to –"

Bitterness blossomed at the tip of my tongue at his urgency. Even if he no longer cared, did he have to act like he couldn't wait even a moment longer for me to be gone? Especially since I would never be allowed back once I took that step.

"No. I'm staying." The words sprang out and I hadn't intended them, but they sounded right somehow. I truly hadn't thought there was a snowball's chance in Hell I would be chosen, but now that I was, I had to go through with the rest.

His hand fell and he whirled around, shock and horror flashing across his face. "What?"

"I'm staying," I repeated, confused by his reaction. It wasn't resentment or jealousy behind his reaction, but something else, something like...fear?

Emerald eyes went luminescent, gold flaring out in a wave from his pupils and I flinched back from the rage and pain in his face.

"Why would you agree to this?"

"Agree to what?" I asked, confused by the note of disgust in his voice. Surely he wasn't talking about the throne.

"Undergoing this. To the possible responsibility

of taking the throne to a country you owe no allegiance to."

"It is the right thing to do." The headache intensified and sent my stomach into revolt. I took a deep breath and willed the nausea to subside.

A long-fingered hand wrapped around my nape. Soothing warmth spread through my head and the drumming dulled. Heat traveled down my spine to my legs, the numbness receding in its wake.

"Thank you."

His hand dropped away as he turned from me. "The right thing to do? For whom? For what? In whose name?"

I rose, unwilling to have that conversation on my knees.

"You were the one who told me that it was the duty of the noble-born to submit to the will of the gods."

"If I remember correctly, I also said you could reject the *tianzhe* that comes after the *shenxuan*."

"Do you just want me gone?" I asked, unable to stop myself.

"I want you as far away from here as can be reasonably contrived."

Sorrow and pain welled up. Did the very sight of me upset him that he didn't want me around? "Look, I'd guessed that you're not my biggest fan right now, but I'm sure we can manage to stay out of each other's way while I'm here."

Incredulous, he spun back to face me. "What?"

"You're the regent, so I guess we'll have to work

together for now, but we don't need to spend much time together if you really hate seeing me around. And if I don't get the throne, which I doubt I will, then we can go back to being strangers." An edge of bitterness slipped out despite my best efforts.

I just couldn't reconcile his actions, couldn't understand how the man who'd never once tried to contact me and who left me to deal with everything alone for the last three days could be the same man who'd treated me like even a paper cut on my finger was a lash upon his heart when I first arrived.

Reason told me that there was nothing he could've done. My grandparents had been very clear. No visitors allowed while I was in seclusion. Probably even his note was pushing things. But still. He could've been there when I'd woken up, shame-faced over how I'd broken down in front of him and Aedrian. We could have spoken before I started the cleansing ritual.

"You think I don't want to see you? That's what you think this is about?"

"Ummm. Yes?"

"No. I don't want you here because I don't want you anywhere near that deathtrap people like to call a throne. It's taken my family, my life, and everything else I hold dear. I will rain fire on this world if it takes you as well."

Air congealed in my lungs. My eyes widened and I had the urge to back away. He didn't look like there was any hyperbole in his words. Scratch that. He looked on the verge of burning the world down. That whole raining fire thing? I could see him, bathed in flames, screaming to the sky for vengeance. It was so vivid, the pain so tangible I almost believed it memory rather than imagination.

"If you hold the crown, you will be bound to the land. Your life and health will be linked to the earth. The country has been starving these past five years without a ruler on the throne. Can you even begin to imagine what it might leech from you if the mantle should fall upon you?"

Not really, no, but I didn't think it a good idea to admit it.

The pain and rage in his face wrenched at my heart. I reached out and curled my hand around his wrist. "Seth."

He closed his eyes and bowed his head. "This is my fault." The words were torn, his voice rough with fury.

"What? How is this your fault?" I stepped closer and he let out a shuddering breath.

His head came up. The hatred in his face stunned me. "Do you know why all this is necessary?"

I shook my head.

"It's because I didn't want it. I didn't want the crown because I loathe everything it represents. Everything that's been taken from me has been in its name. And now it will have you too. Gods. I thought someone else would take it, someone who wanted it and then I could be free of it, but no. It had to be *you*."

"Don't. Please." I reached out and cupped his cheek in my free hand. "It's fine. It'll be fine." I spoke the words but not even I believed myself. But regardless of my own doubt, I had to try. Even if watching him tear himself apart made it hard for me to breathe.

"I thought I could escape it, maybe I'd have a chance at happiness once I was free of it. I never wanted you near it." His eyes closed in defeat. "The gods mock me."

Realization dawned, bright and painful. He was waiting for it all to go away. That was why he hadn't come to find me, hadn't sent someone to bring me to Tavaneth.

My grip tightened on his wrist. "Seth," I sighed his name. "What would you have done if I hadn't waited?"

His eyes opened, luminous with grief and rage. "Your happiness and safety are paramount. My heart stopped once when I thought you dead and that was enough. Losing you would have been a small price for keeping you safe, even if you found joy with another."

I didn't even know where to start, rising anger pushing back the pain. "So you're telling me that if I hadn't lost my memory, I would have spent the last five years not knowing if you were dead or alive?"

His eyes hardened. "My own heart, technically you broke faith with me first."

"What?"

"When I was to return to Tavaneth, you agreed to come with me. You never came."

"And you never thought to come find me?" I suspected, but I needed to know for sure.

"Seeing as I was then attacked and left for dead, you'll have to pardon my absence."

My heart stopped once when I thought you dead.

"Right." I sighed and let my hands drop away. An entire airline's worth of luggage to sort through and nowhere to start. "Where do we go from here? What do you want from me?"

He pivoted and walked away, his words trailing softly in the air between us. "I don't know myself, now that the gods have seen fit to torment me further. Barring the impossible, I'll settle for keeping you safe. Let your grandparents know I will be by later to discuss the situation. I have some contacts that might be of help." His words were cool, his tone colder, as if it was another man who'd just laid his soul bare.

The door closed behind him and I turned to look up at the statue of the goddess. "I hope you know what you're doing, because I certainly don't."

CHAPTER FIFTEEN

My grandmother's eyes narrowed on my face when I walked into the great room. My grandfather's lips thinned before he exhaled long and carefully. They sat at the round table, the ever present tea set sending tendrils of fragrant steam into the air.

I'd taken the time to shower the incense smoke from my hair and grab a quick bowl of soup before meeting my grandparents. It didn't look to be a quick or easy conversation, especially not with Sethalor's disapproval involved and I needed a bit of fortification after an entire day on my knees.

Grandfather bowed his head for a moment and pressed his fingertips to his mouth. "I see that the goddess has made her will known."

I nodded. It still didn't feel real. At all. "I suppose so. Sethalor said he'd be by later."

Grandmother inclined her head. "I would be surprised if not. We will wait for him to discuss battle plans."

"Battle plans? Is it so bad as that? Doesn't having the mandate of a goddess count for anything?"

My grandfather sighed. "It will keep you safe from outright murder, yes. It will not buy you allies amongst the court nor ensure the loyalty of your courtiers." He flicked a glance at my grandmother. "It also won't smooth the path between you and the imperial prince."

The rabbit hole kept getting deeper and I was beginning to despair of ever reaching the bottom. I took a deep breath. The things I didn't know were going to kill me. I just knew it.

"Brilliant. And no one thought to warn me of this beforehand. Why did I think this was a good idea?" I said, only half-joking.

"Amusingly enough, wasn't I just asking you that very same question?" Sethalor's dry voice came from the doorway. It was ragged, as if he'd screamed his throat hoarse.

I whipped around.

He and Aedrian stood at the door. They bowed in unison.

Seth strode forward and took the seat beside me. "I apologize for my tardiness. Shall we begin?"

Aedrian stayed in guard position at the door, face blank, his gaze a roiling liquid silver.

"Does the itinerary involve my running in circles and screaming, and or, telling me all that I need to know before throwing me into a battle zone? If not, might I strongly suggest the latter? I can live without the former, but at this point I feel I'm overdue for my allotment of hysterical fits."

"Allotment? What sort of parameters does this allotment involve?" Aedrian's tone was wry, his intimation clear.

I gave him a toothy smile. "I get a sizable share for every near-death accident. Then I get an allowance for each major life-changing experience. Then there's the quota for every single time my worldview and paradigm of the universe is blown wide open." I tapped my finger on my lower lip. "Gee, all that and I haven't even gotten to my monthly ration of hysteria just for bleeding from my uterus."

Grandfather coughed.

Grandmother smirked. "I have weapons and straw dummies in the practice yard, Fengxun. I can also give the mannequins the face of anyone you would like to eviscerate. In the meantime, I can promise that we will be much more forthcoming with information." Her expression turned apologetic. "I'm sorry we didn't think to mention that there would be complications. We have played this game for so long that it seemed self-evident. I have to admit we also made the decision to believe you wouldn't be chosen."

Right. Fuck me for being a naive child. When was there ever *not*?

I bit back a sigh. "Okay. My bad. So now what? Intel, please."

Seth poured a cup of tea. The scent of jasmine rose into the air. "I have contacted Riordan. He will come as soon as he can and render what aid is necessary."

My grandmother folded her hands with a small

smile. I knew the look, that of a teacher quizzing a beloved student. "What do you think will be necessary?"

His stare was cool and contemplative. "The other candidate for the throne is Helena Hauville."

I frowned. That sounded like a French name.

A furrow marred my grandfather's brow. "Two women. The court will be beside itself."

"Yes. I suggest allowing Riordan to pose as a third candidate. It would serve as distraction and decoy. If need be, he will also be another line of defense should any think of rebellion."

"The gods will allow that?"

"I think yes since we would be deceiving mortals, not the gods. I will speak to the high priestess on the particulars, but I cannot imagine that they would want to see more chaos than necessary. There will be mayhem at the announcement that two out of three candidates will be women, but much less than if we told them their only option was to be ruled by a woman."

I tapped my finger on the rim of my teacup. "How will this make things better in the long run if ultimately, there's going to be an empress?"

"The *tianzhe* is a period where the candidates preside over court and weigh in on the decisions made there. It is a chance for both the court and potential ruler to gain an appreciation of how they will or will not function together. I expect that the imperial prince's hope is that the members of court will be swayed once they have a chance to know you and Princess Helena."

Seth inclined his head at my grandfather. "Yes."

"But why is it even a problem? Grandmother is the head of our House and it sounded like there were other queens of Tavaneth. I thought that meant the patriarchy wasn't going to be a problem."

My grandfather lifted one shoulder, the gesture both wry and dismissive. "History spirals and cycles because people like their biases. There hasn't been an empress in generations, and only two in the history of Tavaneth before this. Most will take that to mean the gods find women lacking, ignoring that House Qiandai has historically been mostly blessed with sons and not daughters. No daughters have been born to House Qiandai in generations either, but many like to see that as another indictment against women rather than a flip of Fate."

Sethalor turned his head to me, his eyes going cool and hard. "You will face enough opposition as is; we will not speak of the bond between you and I. Do not mention it to anyone outside of this room."

"I wasn't going to anyway, so okay." I frowned. "Do you mean opposition or do you mean danger?"

"I mean both. It will be no benefit for your name to be linked to mine."

Because he didn't want the throne? Or because of other reasons? I couldn't help but wonder how the court took his relationship with Aedrian.

"All right. But isn't your relationship with my grandparents common knowledge?"

"They are my former teachers and I owe them

respect, but nothing else in the eyes of the court. We will not give them any reason to expect more."

"Okie-dokie then. Any other orders you wish to give, oh my lord and master?"

"I'll keep you apprised if I do."

I decided against informing him that I was being sarcastic.

"Lord Hauville has many allies in the court and he has always coveted the throne. It will be a great coup for him if his daughter takes it."

Grandmother sent him a bland look. "Is that your desire?"

"It hardly matters as I don't think the gods care very much for my desires. I mention it because Hauville was acquitted of suspicion in my family's deaths, but I have my doubts."

"It would be excessive, not to mention foolhardy, for him to move against us before the *tianzhe* is over," my grandmother said.

"He has compatriots who might be willing to take the fall for him, provided enough motive. It would be easy to amass incentive with the weight of the throne behind him."

A shiver ran down my spine. "Super."

Grandfather reached over and patted my hand. "Don't worry, Granddaughter. We are more than capable of keeping you safe."

"I would offer you a contingent of palace guards, but I'm uncertain where their loyalties lie."

Grandmother sighed. "We appreciate the intent, Imperial Highness. In the meantime, House

Xuanyuan is not without defenses."

My grandmother's tone was bland, almost dismissive, but Seth must have heard something I didn't for those dark green eyes flared with frustration. "I apologize. I have been...remiss about sweeping out the vermin."

"And now you are not the only one who might be bitten by a stray viper," she said tartly.

His mouth quirked in a humorless smile. "Believe me, I regret that more than you can imagine."

"Hauville has his cohorts, but they are not the entirety of the court. What other factions are there?"

Seth flashed my grandmother a sardonic look. "I'm no longer in the classroom, dear teacher. No need to quiz me."

"Yes, but Fengxun needs to know. Indulge me, if you will."

"There are the royalists, who support the throne no matter who takes it. They comprise perhaps a fourth of the court. I do not know how useful they will be, as they tend to be rather hidebound in their way of thinking. As you will see, unreasoning devotion cuts both ways. There are Hauville and his cronies, of course. I expect that he may have as many as half the courtiers in his pockets. Some of them may be swayed should the candidates display competency, but it is likely gold will speak louder to them and Hauville has rather a large supply of that."

Grandfather tilted his head, a smirk playing around his mouth. "As if House Xuanyuan could not buy and sell him twice over."

Seth went on as if he didn't hear my grandfather's comment. "The remainder will likely wait and see which way the wind blows. They have sufficient integrity not to simply fall in with Hauville but they are not the vanguard by any means."

I raised my hand. "What's wrong with Hauville and if there's something wrong with him, how is he still a lord?"

Seth's mouth compressed and my grandparents exchanged a glance.

"Hauville is a king of Tavaneth, so he can only be deposed in case of high treason or premeditated murder. As I said, nothing has ever been proven. Aside from my personal distaste for him, he is not known for his mercy or just handling of those in his demesne." He moved his shoulders in an elegant shrug. "A thief is a thief and receives the same sentence of having a hand lopped off or sent to the mines for hard labor, regardless of if it's a man with a penchant for other people's jewelry or an orphan who decided to steal rather than starve. His taxes are high with no leniency and he only paves those roads useful to him."

In short, a rich douchebag who made his fortune off exploiting the poor and defenseless.

"Okay. So we really don't want him influencing policy and helping set laws. Got it."

"In short, yes. He also undermines the power of the crown by building his militia and demanding more autonomy over his demesne. I would not be surprised if he has thoughts of insurrection."

"Does this mean we don't want Helena to take the

throne because he might try to puppet her?"

His mouth tightened. Rage simmered between us, made the more chilling by how still he went. He gave me one long narrow-eyed look and I remembered that he didn't want me anywhere near the throne. He didn't want Helena on the throne for practical reasons but with me as the only other option...

I dropped my gaze and stared at my teacup, turning it in my hands just so I had something to do other than look into his pain-filled eyes.

He stood. "I do not think there is anything else that needs discussion. At least not urgently. The rest can wait, I believe, until we have more information."

He rose and bowed slightly to my grandparents. His gaze stuttered when it swept over me and I realized he was avoiding the mark on my forehead.

"I will see you at court tomorrow. Good evening."

I watched him walk away, distracted by the fluid grace of his movements. Gods above, the man was gorgeous.

My grandmother cleared her throat.

I turned back to my grandmother's knowing smile and my grandfather's narrowed gaze.

"Fengxun?"

"What?"

"Is there something we should know about the situation between you and the imperial prince?"

Spreading my hands, I shrugged. "I have no idea and I'm not thinking about it."

What I didn't want to admit to myself, much less anyone else was that, beautiful as his words were and as much as I wanted to believe him, I couldn't. His emotions carried the force of a tsunami when unleashed, which was frightening enough, but the ease and speed with which he sublimated them under that mask of cool control terrified me.

Perhaps Seth loved me, but the person he fell in love with was a girl I didn't remember and who I likely bore very little resemblance to. Certainly he didn't seem to want to care for me now. Adding in the strange byplay between him and Aedrian and I couldn't allow myself to believe, to hope.

Keeping my voice light, I changed the subject. "So. About court. How does it work?"

C<small>HAPTER</small> S<small>IXTEEN</small>

We stood outside the front door, waiting in the predawn cold for...something. My grandparents had said I would be taken to the palace, but didn't have any more details than that. I suspected Sethalor left orders I was to be woken up at oh-fuck-o'clock and brought to the gate and nothing else.

Typical.

I pulled the hood of my cloak up and tucked my hands into my robe's sleeves, missing the heavy warmth of the cat. As usual, it'd slept at the foot of my bed, but instead of disappearing before I woke, that morning it'd walked me half-way through the courtyard to meet my grandparents before vanishing.

Impatience scratched at me and I fought the urge to tap my foot. It would have helped if I'd known what, exactly, I waited for.

A palanquin appeared at the end of the street. The dark wood of the palanquin's riding box was carved in elaborate, lace-like patterns. Red paper lanterns hung from the four corners, and crimson silk curtains obscured the door.

"Is it just me, or is that palanquin moving on its own?" Creepy.

Grandmother nodded. "It is a temple palanquin."

"You know that doesn't answer anything, right?"

"It didn't sound particularly like a question, Fengxun. The temple palanquins are powered by the magic of the gods."

"Oh. Okay." Better, but still creepy.

The palanquin stopped in front of us and lowered to the ground, eerily silent.

She settled her hand at the small of my back and nudged me forward. "Go on. It is perfectly safe."

My grandfather snorted and my grandmother jabbed him in the ribs.

"Not helping, *A-gong*. I'm already kind of freaked out already."

He cleared his throat. "Your grandmother is right. There is no danger in that palanquin. Only in what lies in court," he muttered the last, and I couldn't tell if he'd intended for me to hear or not.

Grandmother jabbed him again.

"Ahem. Don't fret, His Imperial Highness will be in court as well. He won't let the jackals eat you alive."

She sighed in frustration. "Husband, just hush."

I took a slow breath and exhaled. "It's fine, *A-mah*. Forewarned is forearmed, right?" And I loved my grandfather the more for worrying about me rather than being excited. Not that *anyone* was excited in a good way.

Her answering smile was wry. "I suppose that is so." She glared at my grandfather. "Although a certain someone could still stand to learn to keep his mouth shut."

I took a deep breath and walked forward before my grandfather could make more snide comments.

Due to the openwork carving, the inside was bright and airy. A padded bench seat upholstered in blue silk hugged the back wall, a small bronze foot warmer tucked underneath.

I sat, careful to arrange my silk skirts and robes so they wouldn't wrinkle.

The palanquin rose with an almost imperceptible hitch and I wondered if it was deliberate. A human touch added so I would have some idea of what was going on.

Lulled by the smooth sway of the palanquin, I rested my cheek against the wall and let my mind drift. A million tiny wings fluttered in my chest, spurring my heart rate and made it hard to breathe. I closed my eyes and slowed each inhale and exhale.

The swaying stopped and the palanquin came to rest with a small jolt.

I sat frozen, not sure what I should be doing. Should I step out or remain in the palanquin?

"Her Grace, Xuanyuan Fengxun Estyria." Sethalor's voice came from outside the palanquin, the sound deeper than usual, the resonance echoing in my bones.

Was that an order to get out of the palanquin, or was he just heralding my arrival?

The curtain lifted after a moment. Well, that answered that.

Sethalor stood framed by the opening of the palanquin, resplendent in black robes sashed with crimson silk. A throne of black wood sat behind him, carved in intricate openwork, with two dragons curling down from the back rest to form the hand rests and two phoenixes perched on the back, beaks raised in song and wings outspread.

He held out his hand, somber-eyed and grim.

A stray thought came unbidden, and I gave him a wry smile. Emerald eyes widened slightly in surprise before his mouth curved in rueful response.

In olden China, when the bridal palanquin, or the *huajiao*, arrived at the groom's house, he would be the one to raise the curtain, the first to lay eyes upon his bride after she left her childhood home. His hand would be her support out of the *huajiao* and thereafter.

I shoved the thought aside and took his hand, performing a small courtesy once I'd stepped clear of the palanquin. "Imperial Highness."

Sethalor laid his other at the small of my back, turning me, and murmured, "Do not reveal any weakness."

The palanquin disappeared with a pop and I looked out onto the court. It took all my fortitude to keep my expression serene, greeted by that sea of stony faces. Looked like the lords of the court were indeed none too happy about my candidacy.

Rows of men stood arrayed before the dais, the rows bifurcated by the long red carpet leading from the dais to the double doors at the end of the audience chamber. Fifty faces stared at us with varying degrees of consternation and shock, their countenances pale against their black court robes. Black robes with black sashes, heavy bands of red and gold embroidery hemmed their long flowing sleeves, providing the only color. The sleeves draped from the wrist to near their knees, with the lords at the front of the room boasting thick bands of embroidery that covered most of their sleeves. The lords near the back wore thinner bands that were mere fingers thick.

I took a deep breath and met their stares head on. If I could appear before a panel of my peers and professors to defend my dissertation, I could deal with a crowd of cranky old men.

The twin doors swung open, the four guards at the door bowed, and another unmanned palanquin floated through the doors, up the red carpet, and stopped at the foot of the dais.

Wonder what the populace thought about unmanned palanquins moving through the city? Was magic common enough here that they were used to it? Or did the same magic that propelled them also keep them from sight?

I thought Sethalor would greet her the way he did me, but he didn't move.

"Her Grace, Helena Hauville."

A low rumble of quiet dismay traveled through the ranks. Seemed like they weren't super thrilled with this candidate either. The thought was comforting. At least it wasn't just me they objected to.

Not that misogyny was much better, but at least it wasn't completely personal.

Without the pressure of everyone's eyes on me, I breathed easier and things I hadn't noticed before came into focus. There was a silver-haired lord who had green eyes in the front row and another lord with hair closer to reddish brown than black.

Seemed like this court was much more open to foreigners than I originally assumed. There were lords with ebony skin and others a tawny golden brown. I wondered what their last names were, if Hauville wasn't the only lord with what I'd consider a foreign name. It made sense though, if magic allowed for swifter, more reliable travel. It would be interesting to see how this place differed from the China of my history classes. I knew that ancient China traded extensively with other countries, but as far as I knew the courts didn't welcome large numbers of foreigners into their ranks.

A slim white hand brushed aside the palanquin curtain and the most beautiful woman I'd ever seen stepped out. Golden hair framed a flawless face showcasing emerald eyes, classic aquiline features, and a tiny crimson mouth. A crimson vine with three leaves wound up to her temple from her right earlobe, serving only to further accentuate her beauty.

Sethalor shifted closer, his robes brushing against mine, ostensibly to allow her space upon the dais. However, his fingers brushed mine in a comforting movement before he folded his hands behind his back.

She was tall, only half a head shorter than Sethalor,

who I estimated at near six two. Helena glided the two steps toward us and curtsied to him, regal and elegant, princess to peer. She nodded at me before turning to face the audience.

She was the picture of a queen, elegant and commanding without being self-conscious. Much like Sethalor, she looked as if she were bred and raised for this sort of stage. Helena appeared perfectly at home standing in front of a full court of powerful men, her expectation of respect and obedience clear in the way she surveyed the room.

In contrast, I wanted nothing so much as to disappear.

Another palanquin floated in.

"His Grace, Riordan Byrne."

The murmur this time was more of relief than trepidation.

I barely restrained a snort.

Those hidebound men were relieved to hear a masculine name, were they? I'd thought their reverence for the gods would have spilled over onto the gods' choices, but apparently not. It was probably a very good thing Seth had thought to bring in Riordan.

The hand that raised the curtain this time was similarly slender and pale. He brushed aside a stray wisp of his shoulder length blond hair as he uncoiled to his full length, sapphire blue eyes narrowed as he gave me a quick once-over. Three crimson stripes slashed across his right cheekbone, bringing to mind the claw marks of a cat.

He strode forward, bowed to us in turn, and spun on his heel, casual arrogance in every clipped movement.

I smoothed out my brow with effort.

Sethalor took a step forward, "Lords and ministers, these are the candidates for the *tianzhe*. Look upon them and know them well, for they hold the mandate of the gods and shall be regarded as myself in all matters of the court."

I held back a shiver. All matters? They certainly were giving us enough rope with which to hang ourselves.

A man stepped out of line and bowed, clearly waiting permission to speak.

Sethalor nodded at him, "Lord Zhao."

"My lord, might I suggest delaying the *tianzhe* until more candidates can be found?"

"To what purpose, Lord Zhao? "

"It is clear, my lord, that the women have been allowed their candidacy only because there is a dearth of qualified candidates. As such, it would perhaps be better to wait for more candidates to be chosen."

Anger flared in my stomach and burned away my nerves. I gave him a flat stare.

Douchebag, your misogyny is showing.

"Lord Zhao." Sethalor's tone was patient, his words carefully even. "Do you mean to say that you suspect the gods of only choosing the women because there needed to be more than one candidate for the *tianzhe* and that you do not believe them to be actually qualified in the eyes of the gods to sit the throne?"

"That should be more than clear, Imperial Highness. They are women, after all."

Wow. That wasn't subtle at all.

I bit the inside of my cheek. I wasn't about to make things more difficult by speaking out of turn, but I now had a goal and a mission. As much as it was possible to do so, I was going to make his life a living misery.

Another lord stepped out of line and bowed.

Sethalor exhaled, not quite a sigh. "Lord Lai."

"My lord, I would second Lord Zhao's motion."

"What is your objection, Lord Lai?"

"Her Grace Xuanyuan Fengsun is the daughter of Shangguan Yunji and Xuanyuan Yalian, is she not?"

I fought to keep my expression bland.

"Yes, and what of it?"

"The princess is the daughter of rebels and grew up on another world -- aside from the question of where her loyalty lies, there is the issue of her never having learned about our world and having no knowledge of how to rule. Despite her best intentions, can we truly trust that she will be a good empress for Tavaneth?"

Huh. His objections were actually reasonable rather than just misogynistic bullshit. Except, how did he know who I was and who my parents were?

"Lord Zhao, Lord Lai, are you presuming to know better than the gods? It is clear by the signs upon them that they are favored by the gods. These are not the marks made by gods who have reservations about their candidates."

"Your Imperial Highness..."

"Your Imperial Highness..."

Sethalor raised a hand, cutting them off. "Need I remind you the consequences of waiting further? The rains have stopped and the rivers are drying. Unless you have better reason than you have laid out thus far, I do not think the priestesses will agree to a delay in the choosing."

The silver-haired lord with the green eyes stepped forward, his bow just this side of what courtesy dictated.

"Weiyuan-*wang*?" Sethalor's shoulders set.

"Imperial Highness, forgive my forwardness, but much as you may personally feel guilty for the current state of the country, you cannot allow that to color your decisions. Lord Lai raises pertinent points and I agree with him that it may be wise to wait and see if there is another candidate before commencing."

Ouch. Burn. He didn't just stomp on Sethalor's sore points, he tap danced on them with soccer cleats on. Interesting how he chose to sabotage Sethalor though. I expected him to say something on his daughter's behalf but clearly his game went deeper.

"I think you all forget yourselves." Sethalor's voice snapped out like a whip, icy cold and emotionless.

"The candidates have been chosen by the gods. Tradition dictates that the *tianzhe* starts the next day, with no delays. The current state of matters may indeed be my burden to bear, but I will thank you not to persuade me to add to my transgressions. If any of you wishes to gainsay the gods, then you may petition the gods on your own. If they admit your appeal, then you may bring it to court with proof of the god's will. Barring that, we will begin as intended."

Lord Lai looked suitably chastened, bowing and retreating to his place without another word, whereas Lord Zhao looked as if he were about to spit nails, sketching only the most cursory of obeisances before stepping back. Weiyuan-*wang* studied Sethalor for a moment more, a faint smile tipping his lips before he inclined his head and resumed his position.

"Is there anything else to report?"

The lords looked at one another, some clearly encouraging their colleagues to speak up via much eyebrow waggling and pursing of lips, but none stepped forward.

"Court is adjourned."

The rows of men bowed as one, then filed silently out of the room.

Helena Hauville turned and curtsied, "Good day, Imperial Highness, Your Graces."

She walked down the dais, across the room to the right and pressed her palm against the wall. A panel of wall swung outward, revealing a door, and she stepped out of sight.

Sethalor murmured, "You will also use that door when you leave the audience room. We do not enter and leave via the main doors with the lords for security's sake."

I glanced at him. "You don't trust your lords?" Gee, I wonder why. I had no doubt at least four of them wouldn't hesitate to shank me should they find me alone in a dark alley.

My sarcasm went right over his head. His eyes turned cold, his expression blanking. "Power can be a very dangerous thing, Phoenix. You never know when someone might be willing to kill for it."

I barely resisted the urge to roll my eyes at him. "That was Helena Hauville's father, wasn't it?"

"Yes. Georges Hauville, styled Weiyuan-*wang*."

Riordan Bryne spoke up. "So, Phoenix Princess. We meet at last."

I angled my head and narrowed my eyes. "You know me?"

He tipped his head at Sethalor. "I've heard of you from our boy here."

Sethalor looked around, mouthed a few words, and flicked his fingers.

A shimmering bubble sprang up around us, the air compressing with a faint pop.

I raised my eyebrows at him.

"Aural shield."

"Right. Of course." I infused my words with as much sarcasm as I could muster.

He got it that time.

He quirked a brow. "Still not a morning person, I see."

I narrowed my eyes at him. "No. Not at all."

"Then I'll make this fast so you can go home and have breakfast. Riordan will escort you to your grandparents. You will allow this without fail, even if they are just outside the audience chamber. You and I should interact as little as possible in public, so if you have any messages for me, relay them to Riordan. Should anything happen in court, unlikely as this chamber is triple warded and shielded, go directly to Riordan, hide behind him and follow his directions to the letter. Am I clear on this?"

Defiance flared up once before I squelched it. There was nothing I liked so much as giving men who thought to order me around hell. I'd always joked Kendrick learned his legendary charm by cutting his teeth on my sharp temper. Certainly he realized very early on he'd catch more little sisters with candy than not. This, however, was no game.

"All right."

His gaze turned intent and his mouth softened. "So pliable. Should I worry about crossed fingers?"

I rolled my eyes. "I'm not a reckless teenager with an overinflated sense of invulnerability anymore, Seth, and I don't have a death wish. If people pull out the swords, I'll duck behind Riordan and use him as a meat shield."

"I'll hold you to that, Phoenix." He bowed slightly, turned on his heel, and left. Right through the shield, which shimmered and wobbled as he passed, but held. Amazing, that.

I stared after him. He certainly wasted no time getting away, this prince of strange signals and mixed feelings.

I turned to Riordan and forced a grin. "So. I hear you've volunteered yourself up as a human shield. Do tell me what prompted you to do that?"

"It would be any man's honor to shield such an

exquisite face and lovely form from any ills that might befall the unwary. Rain or sleet or arrows, I'm your man.

I blinked slowly at him. "You're a flirt."

"Guilty as charged, Princess."

The gleam in his eyes never faltered, and I felt my smile shifting to something more genuine in return.

"Tell the truth. You're just here because you love stirring the pot."

An exquisitely slow and elegant shrug. "My love for meddling in the kitchen may be well documented, but it doesn't preclude any of my other loves." He flashed me a sultry look from under his lashes. "Like that of making a profession out of trailing along behind a gorgeous creature such as yourself."

Another man hiding behind a mask.

I caught my sigh before it could escape. Who was I to talk about masks and avoidance? I'd chosen oblivion over pain, after all. I was many things, but I tried not to be more of a hypocrite than necessary.

CHAPTER SEVENTEEN

"Lord Riordan Bryne to see you, Your Grace." I looked up from my scroll and blinked. I wasn't expecting him. Riordan had handed me off to my grandfather just outside the audience chamber and walked off, saying something about needing to speak with Aedrian. I'd thought I wouldn't see him again until the next morning.

A teenage girl wearing a maid's uniform stood inside the moon door of the garden, gently rounded cheeks alight with a blush. A star-struck glimmer lit her eyes and her breathing came soft and fast.

Oh dear. I knew the look.

The cat sat up and made a derisive noise, its tail lashing the air.

I stroked its ears, whispering *"be nice"*, and it sniffed.

I frowned. "Should I go meet him?"

"I would never dream of making a lady walk to me, my dear." Riordan walked in and flashed me a brilliant smile.

The maid looked like she was about to swoon at his words, her hand fluttering up to rest against her throat.

I sighed even as sympathy welled up for her. There was just no recovering from an onslaught of charm like that.

"Stop trying to make the girl swoon at your feet and tell me what you're about."

He arched a brow and laid a hand on his breastbone. "Me? I would never."

"Bullshit. I'll bet you keep a silent tally of how many girls go starry-eyed over you and review them each night before you sleep instead of counting sheep."

He heaved a pathetic sigh. "Is it so terrible to aim to bring some beauty to this cruel world?"

"You're making it sound like it'd be a crime against humanity if I tried to bruise that pretty face." I paused for a beat, ignoring his incredulous look. "No, never mind, you'd just get girls tripping over themselves to comfort you. I guess I'll have to settle for ignoring you. That'd be worse, wouldn't it?"

He tossed his head back and laughed. "Ach, lass, you're something alright. Little wonder you've managed to bring Aedrian and Seth to their knees at last."

Aedrian and Seth? On their knees? My memory obligingly reminded me of what happened the last time Aedrian knelt at my feet.

My cheeks warmed, but I kept my gaze steady on those cool blue eyes. "Hardly. I doubt those two so much as bow to anyone."

"Perhaps not to force. But to love? The strongest man bends where his heart falls."

"Love?" I laughed.

Seth, perhaps, but Aedrian? Any reasonably discerning person could see that Aedrian only had eyes for Sethalor. What game was he playing?

Golden brows arched. "You don't believe me? Why not?"

"Aedrian may be in love, but I'm fairly certain it's not with me. Besides, we met, what, less than a week ago? I hardly think he's ready to fling himself at my feet in that short a time."

"Ah, but a *coup de foudre* requires but a single heartbeat."

"Perhaps, but still. Not with me."

Sensual lips curved in a faint smile. "Interesting, that you do not believe me."

I shrugged.

He laughed. "Fair enough, darling. Now, for the real reason I came here.... Seth wanted me to let you know that he will be dropping in today. He won't be arriving via the front door to be announced, so stay alert."

I raised a brow. "In other words, don't take a bath or anything I might not want interrupted."

"Indeed."

He bowed. "And that discharges my duty. I will see you anon, Your Grace."

He turned.

That was it? It was baffling, and worse, boggling.

Did Seth and Aedrian have literally no one else they could trust to bring that message? What sort of snake's den had I landed myself into?

"Wait." I walked around to face him.

He gave me a quizzical look.

"That's all? You came here, just for that one sentence message?"

A grin spread over his face. "Are you inviting me to tea, Your Grace?"

I waited until the table was laid out with tea and a variety of delicacies and we were alone before I started pushing. "Why did you really come? I don't believe it was just to tell me that."

He gave me a questioning look.

I shook my head. "Don't even play coy with me. What are you trying to do?" Why would he toss Aedrian into the mess? It made sense for him to say something about Seth, but the commander?

A smile curved his mouth but his gaze chilled. "What makes you think I have specific intentions?"

"Riordan. I doubt you give someone so much as a smile without an agenda, much less information like that."

The smile deepened. "What a thing to say. Perhaps I was so overcome with your loveliness that I let control over my words slip."

My eyes narrowed as I sat back to study him. Despite the flirtatious smile, those sapphire eyes were cool and intent.

I decided to try another tack. "How do you know Sethalor and Aedrian?"

He leaned back and folded his hands, mimicking my pose. "We fought in a couple of battles together."

"Wars?"

Lifting his shoulders in an insouciant shrug, his smile gained a sharp edge. "I can't recall the specifics. After all, one war is much like another to a mercenary, so long as I'm paid in the end."

"Ah, how much is Sethalor paying you for your aid and discretion then?" I asked mildly.

A gleam came and went in his eyes. "Enough."

"Riordan. If you want me to believe that you have a weakness for women, enough to let things slip that you shouldn't, then you should perhaps babble a bit more."

"Perhaps, but you see, my dear lady, tales of bloodshed would only taint your perception of me. I would hardly want that. If you asked me something else, such as whether your countenance rivals a rose, I promise I would make a better show."

"Why admit to being a mercenary then, if you wish to keep my good opinion?"

"There is flattery and then there is lying, my dear lady."

Picking up a dumpling, I placed it in my mouth, chewing to cover the fact that I didn't quite know how to continue.

Riordan lifted his cup to his lips, limpid blue eyes serene.

"Tell me of your home country. Is it far away? How is it like and unlike Tavaneth?"

"Airelan?" His face softened. "It is nothing like Tavaneth. It is a land of lush green and an abundance of water in all its forms, with a pixie beneath every leaf and witches dancing in the mist."

Airelan? Ireland? I racked my brain for the Irish phrases I'd memorized when I thought I was going for a semester abroad.

"Céad míle fáilte." A hundred thousand welcomes. I'd been warned that the true Irish never used it, but it was the only thing I could pull from my mind at the moment.

His head snapped back in surprise. "An bhfuil Gaeilge agat?"

I lifted my hands and shook my head. "No, I don't speak it, actually. I just know some phrases."

His eyes narrowed. "You're quite the bundle of surprises, Your Grace."

I shrugged at him. "You keep your secrets and I'll keep mine."

Tawny brows shot up and his expression turned contemplative.

Ireland, eh? So he wasn't from Tavaneth. I did wonder about the accent underlying his words.

Tapping my fingers on the table, I cocked my head in thought. "What is the year, Riordan?" There was little use asking what year it was in Tavaneth because if it was anything like ancient China, the calender reset with each new ruler, but presumably Europe or its equivalent would be using one more similar to what I was used to.

"According to which calendar, Your Grace?"

I closed my eyes for a moment in frustration. Foiled again. "Fine. Do you have steam engines yet? Automobiles? Have airplanes been invented yet? Airships? Bicycles? I suppose this isn't really worth asking, but has man set foot on the moon yet? How are wars waged now? With firearms and horses or--"

"Whoa. Halt a moment." Riordan raised a hand, eyes sharpening.

Resisting the urge to bounce in my seat, I closed my mouth on further questions. The more I asked, the more questions tumbled into my mind.

"We have steam engines, yes, but they tend to be the amusement of rich men. I know not what automobiles are, or airplanes, but I have heard of bicycles, from across the strait in Faransi. I have also heard of an eccentric nobleman in Deauzilan who flies about under a large balloon that he calls an airship. As for the moon, mages have attempted to reach it for as long as mages have been able to fly, but none have survived to tell the tale. As for how war is waged, why would you wish to know that, Your Grace?"

Seemed like my mercenary had quite the prodigious memory and mind for rumor and detail.

"Why not? It seems knowing a bit about how warfare is conducted is useful for someone in my position. Also, knowing what weapons are used will allow me some idea of how far science has come in this world, although I can see already that it's not going to give me any accurate sense of time."

"How do you mean?"

I indicated my clothing and the house. "Everything I've seen points to this being sometime, somewhere in the Tang dynasty, but steam engines and airships are from a much later date in time in my world. I suppose I should have anticipated that magic would change things, but now I'm not only adrift in space, but also in time, with no way of finding my bearings."

"Is that important? Is it not enough to simply live each day as it arrives? You're far too fair a lady to worry about such things." He smiled, but it was clear his attention was elsewhere.

"Tsk, Riordan. You're not even trying." I shook my head. "At any rate, it is important because many things depend on timing and knowing what is available and what isn't. Knowing your opponent is half the battle, as you well know."

"Indeed, granddaughter," Grandmother said, entering the garden. "Now, if you wish, I can help with at least half of that equation: helping you to know yourself."

Riordan stood and made her a low bow. "Your Illustriousness."

She gave Riordan an uninterpretable look. "Lord Bryne. If you'll excuse us?"

Grandmother waited until he made his leave before turning to me, her expression thoughtful. "Be wary of that one, Fengxun, he is not as he seems. In that vein, I would suggest not allowing yourself to be placed in a compromising situation. I know that your world is different, but do not forget that there are very different rules here."

"You don't think he's trustworthy?"

"In all ways but in matters of the heart, Granddaughter."

What was it with today and everyone wanting to talk about my love life? "I really wouldn't worry about that. But as for different rules -- would I be forced to marry if I got caught entertaining gentleman callers without a chaperone or something like that?"

Her jaw tightened and she shook her head in slow negation. "No, but things would be quite different should someone attempt to compromise you. In that case, rest assured it would end in nothing so civilized as marriage. The best he could hope for would be a swift death."

I flinched. "What? Is is likely someone would try that?"

"Unlikely but not impossible. You are a princess, possible candidate to a throne. With House Xuanyuan at your back, they would not dare force but there are those who might attempt seduction, aphrodisiacs or spells to cloud your mind."

A shiver raised all the fine hairs on my arm.

Her tone gentled. "Be careful, Fengxun. Take care in who you place trust and who you allow close. Lord Bryne may be trustworthy, but not all will be."

I nodded.

"Now then, I thought you might want to learn more about your magic."

CHAPTER EIGHTEEN

Grandmother looked up, closed her hand on the ball of flame, stood, and curtsied. "Your Imperial Highness."

My concentration broke and the sphere of water I was trying to spin in my hands splattered all over my hands and the table.

Damn. I was just getting the hang of it too.

I dipped a quick courtesy, almost too fast to be considered rude, and muttered, "Your Imperial Highness."

Then I went back to trying to shape water.

It'd only taken me a couple hours and the better part of my grandmother's patience, but I'd finally managed to move from creating stationary shields to manipulating projectiles.

The rational part of my mind informed me that was good progress and I had no reason to whine about it. Very good progress. Magical, even.

Bad jokes aside, magic was all about intent, about bending imagination and will to conscious thought and all the meditation and visualization stuff my mother had put us through was finally finding practical use.

My mouth twisted. If I let myself think about how very *deliberate* my mother's plans for us turned out to be, I'd start screaming. So I wouldn't think about all the things she'd insisted that we learn and just... focus on holding water in my hands.

Still, good thing we were in the gardens. Although I still privately thought we could have had the magic lesson in the bathroom once we'd figured out my element was water.

"No need to stand on formality, *Shimu*."

She inclined her head. "What brings you here, Imperial Highness?"

Ignoring them, I focused my thoughts on drawing out the wet from my clothing. I pulled the water into a ball in my palm and dropped it in the basin in the center of the table before turning my attention back to them.

He reached into his sleeve and pulled out a round mirror about the size of my palm, strung on a silver silk cord with elaborate knotwork. A mermaid and merman carved in ebony formed the frame for the double sided mirror, every feature and detail exquisite.

She arched her brows. "A mirror, Imperial Highness? Is that appropriate?"

What was wrong with gifting a mirror? Much as I tried to remember a custom or tradition, I came up blank.

He passed it to her with both hands, his motions careful. "I thought it prudent considering the situation."

Her brows drew together as she inspected the mirror, "I see. Very well then."

She handed it back to Sethalor, giving us a wry look. "Do you need a chaperone, Imperial Highness, or shall I allow you some privacy?"

"I would appreciate it if I were allowed words alone, *Shimu*, but only on your forbearance."

Her lips twitched. "You have it and my trust. Make certain you do not abuse either."

I waited until she turned the corner before arching a brow at him, "So what did you want?" Despite my best efforts to brush off what Riordan had said earlier, I couldn't keep heat from rising to my cheeks.

A challenging arch of his brow answered, "Is that any way to speak to your regent?"

"I thought we were dispensing with formality."

"That was for your grandmother, who is my teacher and therefore tradition dictates that I respect as my own mother."

I tapped my foot. "Right. Did you want just the one curtsy then, or two to make up for my insolence?"

He shook his head ruefully. "Neither. It would behoove you to be more cautious in the future, however. As Lord Lai has demonstrated, the walls have ears. It would serve no one well should you be accused of contempt of the lords or of the court."

"Let me guess, threat of death again." Come up

with something new, why didn't they?

"Contempt of a lord can carry a sentence of anything from thirty slaps to the face to a public caning. Either would leave you discredited and likely bedridden."

"Gee, you're making this all sound so wonderful." A teeth-chattering shudder ran through me.

He sighed. "This is not your world, Estyria. It is better if I woke you to that fact now rather than later. My influence is limited, especially with the *tianzhe* commencing, and there is only so much I can shelter you if you purposely set out to inflame."

"You have such faith in me." Was he judging me based on how I'd acted since I arrived, or was he expecting me to behave a certain way based on the girl he knew?

His eyes narrowed at my caustic tone. "Estyria, I know you. You do not suffer fools well and the court is filled with them. Do not antagonize them."

"Don't worry. I'm not a teenager anymore." Guess that answered my question. He wasn't seeing me. He was seeing someone else through me. I bit down on my tongue and breathed through the hurt.

He closed his eyes, tipped his head back, and exhaled slowly.

His eyes opened, his face went blank, and he rolled his shoulders, releasing the tension riding there. "Let's try this again.

"It was very worrying how much Lord Lai appeared to know. It would appear that your grandparents have at least one servant who is either disloyal or less discreet than desirable. I have the utmost faith in your ability to be discreet in court, but you will need to remember that you are under close scrutiny at the moment and you will likely have no privacy for the foreseeable future. Even after we find the person or persons responsible, it would be best if you were circumspect at all times."

His serene response made me feel like an overreacting bitch. Even if he was expecting someone else, it wasn't his fault and he'd been nothing but careful of my safety and well-being ever since I'd landed in his lap. Probably literally, all things considered.

Besides, to be fair to him, I *had* been rude. I knew I should've addressed him properly.

I hissed my frustration, ending with a huff at the knot of tangled grief and anger in my chest. "All right. I'm sorry. I didn't mean to be a bitch about it. I'm just...overwhelmed." And grumpy. And confused. Thanks to one Riordan Bryne.

His lips thinned and I could see the thought almost as clearly as if he'd shouted it. If I was overwhelmed now, how was I going to cope with what came later?

He didn't vocalize it, however, and I was grateful.

"I would like to show you something."

"The mirror?"

He placed the mirror between us on the table. "Yunya, if you please?"

The surface clouded before clearing to reveal a girl's face. She blinked dark eyes at us, an impish smile curving her mouth, lending a fey air to elfin features. "Yes?"

I sat back with a thump on the stone seat.

"Phoenix, this is Yunya, mirror spirit to our family. She will serve as amanuensis to you."

"Amanuensis?" I managed to wheeze out.

"She will record all that passes in court, look up pertinent cases and laws, and assist you in other research and correspondence you will need to attend to."

So like a paralegal of my own.

My mind spun and I caught at the only thread I could see.

"Is that even allowed?"

She winked. "Why would it not be? I would not be providing you with anything that you could not find out yourself. Besides, it is only to the realm's benefit if you were made as familiar as possible with the various laws and precedents."

"Yunya, if you could ring her grandfather's mirror."

The image of Yunya faded from the mirror, the surface clouding over, then my grandfather appeared in the mirror, seated at a table.

He rose from his chair and bowed, "Your Imperial Highness."

"*Shifu*. At ease, please. As you can see, I'm showing Estyria the functions of mirrors."

Grandfather resumed his seat. "I do see. I was intending to present her with a mirror today, but my lady informed me that you had already anticipated that need."

Seth inclined his head. "I thought it would be helpful for her to have a mirror spirit to aid her."

Grandfather's face turned thoughtful, his gaze flicking to my face before focusing on Seth again. "Yunya? She will accept Fengxun?"

"Yes." His answer was curt, bordering on the edge of a warning.

"I see." His eyes were sharp, but his tone was gentle, "We do not challenge your claim, Imperial Highness, but be aware of what your actions pronounce. You do not wish for rumors to spread before you can announce your decision yourself."

Seth exhaled slowly, tension bleeding out of his shoulders, and made a bow. "Yes, venerated teacher."

Grandfather chuckled. "If you do not have any more need of me, I shall beg pardon."

"Farewell."

My grandfather disappeared and Yunya's face took its stead.

"Yunya, if you could retrieve the records of the genealogy of House Xuanyuan."

The mirror's surface wavered and then writing started scrolling. Lines upon lines of names, connected by lines and branches, the words smaller than I could read.

"You can ask Yunya to enlarge the words if you wish, or search for specific words."

I looked at endless lines of names going back countless generations, feeling a bit dizzy, and caught upon a stray thought. "It looks like my family wasn't very prolific. Most of them didn't have more than one or two children. Isn't that rather unusual?" Another way in which this place differed from Earth.

"More than likely partly due to who is in your family tree. Most supernaturals do not tend to have many young in exchange for their longevity."

I froze. "Supernatural?"

Wry amusement arched his brows. "Did you think you were anything else, with your command of magic?"

Well, when you put it that way...

"Oh." But my mother had more than two children.

One long finger traced the names up through the branches. "Your father is very much human, and that no doubt helped with how fertile your mother managed to be. However, at least the last two generations had fewer children due to choice rather than genetics. Your grandmother was quite independent in her youth and she only accepted her duty when it was near too late. Your great grandmother's husband died when they were very young and she never remarried. My own father only managed three children, even with his consorts and ladies."

Near too late? My grandmother looked barely older than my mother was.

A genuine smile curved his lips at my questioning look. "I would not dare to tell you the truth behind your grandmother's age, so don't ask. You'll have to trust my word."

He tapped on the mirror again. "Yunya, I wish to

compose a message to my mirror, please."

The mirror turned opaque, the surface looking like the stationary I'd used before and he used his finger to write upon the surface. The characters flowed as if from a brush, the calligraphy free form and gorgeous, but I couldn't recognize the writing.

"What are you writing?"

"This is the ancient language. I merely wrote your name."

I narrowed my eyes. That looked like far too many letters to be my name. And that word looked like the character meaning imperial. "My name?"

"All your names and titles. Yunya, send."

The message dissolved, as if ink into water, and disappeared.

"Message sent and received," she said.

"That should be the basics for now, Estyria. Yunya should be more than happy to show you the rest as becomes necessary."

"Indeed I would, it would be my pleasure." Her face popped up again.

"It would be best if you kept Yunya at your side always."

"Always?" Surely there were times when a little more privacy was desirable.

"She is very discreet."

His eyes met mine and his grin turned sly. "Believe me, there are things Yunya would prefer not to be privy to."

"Believe me, I've more than learned about when to be present and when not to be."

"What was that about my grandfather asking if Yunya would accept me or not? And what was he talking about when he mentioned actions and decisions?"

Man and mirror exchanged a glance.

Yunya tipped her head. "Most mirror spirits are bound to a single person. I am unique in that I am bound to a family, the House of Qiandai to be precise."

"So, why?"

Her eyes swept to Sethalor and Yunya's expression flickered before she mouthed "goodbye" at me and disappeared.

Sethalor flicked his fingers and the aural shield sprang up. "You and I are bonded, Estyria. As such, you can be considered part of House Qiandai. If others knew that Yunya is willing to accept you as part of my House, they might assume that an alliance was made."

"And we don't want that," I said, testing.

Long lashes fell to shield his eyes. "No. We don't. It is safer for you that way."

"What about Aedrian? Grandmother said you were bound to him too. So this mirror should work for him as well, right?"

His shoulders tensed for a moment. "Yes, I suppose he would be considered part of my House as well, should he wish to be recognized as such."

"Is the bond that you and he have the same as the one we have?"

Something dark surfaced briefly in his eyes before he lowered his lashes again. "God-given bonds can occur between siblings and brothers in arms just as easily as between lovers. Not being a mind mage like your grandmother, I cannot say for certain, but I can't see why it would be different."

"What do the bonds do anyway?"

"They permit the bonded to speak to each other's minds and they can be used to monitor the bondmate's well being. With the deeper bonds, it allows one bondmate to share the pain and wounds of the other, to avert what might otherwise be a fatal injury."

"So what does it mean that our bond is incomplete?"

"I don't know. There isn't any precedent for it."

"Special. That's me." I sighed. I could do without being special. The mirror caught the glint of afternoon sun and reminded me. "Why did my grandmother look so odd when she saw the mirror?"

The look in his eyes was enigmatic. "Mirrors are traditionally used as a betrothal gift."

I blinked "Right. So you just happened to have this spare mirror lying around?"

"No." Pain flashed across his face before he raised his hands and scrubbed them abruptly across his face. He breathed out slowly, emotion bleeding out of his expression as he exhaled. "I cannot do this right now. I beg your pardon."

He stepped back and disappeared.

Godsdammit. Me and my big mouth. Again.

I sank down on the stool and swallowed hard against the tears pricking behind my eyes. His pain tore at me, made worse that I knew I was a source of hurt for him.

I was being too careless with him, with our past. Sooner or later I would have to stop using my lack of memories as a reason to stab him in the back. There was no excuse. Not my strange sense of comfort around him. Not the coping mechanisms that my therapist had deplored. Not even that he was willing.

I knew too much about what kind of willing love prompted and it wasn't always a beautiful thing.

Closing my eyes, I slowly expelled all the air in my lungs, using the exercise to focus and remind myself of the situation.

A warm weight leaned against me, soft fur wrapping around my wrist as the now-familiar purr rumbled against my ear. Sinking my hands into the cat's fur, I reminded myself once again of the truths I had.

Not mine. Not my burden to bear. Not my man to comfort. Nothing I could do to help that he'd accept. The best I could do was to be more careful.

So why did I want to keen heartbreak to the sky?

CHAPTER NINETEEN

I slipped out of the servant's entrance, concentrating on being as unobtrusive as possible. I'd noticed as a young child that I could move around in plain sight unnoticed if I held firm the thought of being invisible. Maybe it was some form of magic. Maybe it wasn't. Either way, I needed to get away, away from everything in my grandparents' home that spoke of luxury and wealth, all reminders of duty and honor.

The guards stared straight ahead, oblivious.

Success.

I kept my walk to a brisk and officious pace. I'd been caught once or twice when I started gloating too early.

The need to swim simmered in my body and made my muscles twitch. There was no one to talk to, no one sufficiently uninvolved in the current mess. The worst part was I wanted to talk to Sethalor. I wanted to wrap myself in his embrace, let his heartbeat pace my breathing, and have it all out.

Delirious, deluded, and despirited. I was losing control and falling and there was no safety net in sight. The only person I trusted with myself was also the last person I could ask.

The street gradually widened, hawkers lining the sides, and opened onto a market square. More hawkers selling their wares on blankets, costermongers with their carts of fruit and vegetables, and stalls selling everything from food to scrolls to jewelry.

People thronged the impromptu market place, haggling, singing out their wares, browsing, and -- breaking vases over a thief's head.

In one corner a vendor had a small metal pool of tiny fish, selling hand-nets of bamboo and paper to children, allowing them to take home what fish they caught. In another, a vendor sold sticky clusters of sugar-shelled strawberries, the sweet scent of caramelizing, melted sugar wafting on the breeze. A hawker turned skewers of lamb over a fire, the fragrance of rosemary and cumin mingling with the smoky richness of wood smoke. A hijabi with a rack of brightly patterned silk scarves. A girl with a sign saying...

I jolted to a stop, a finger of ice sliding down my spine and lodging in my stomach as I read the clumsy lettering on the piece of paper.

Mai shen zang fu.

She was selling herself to pay for her father's funeral.

Swallowing back the nausea, I stood, frozen,

watching how she knelt there, head down, a plain straw mat beneath her knees the only protection from the stones beneath her.

In the bustle of the market, she was ignored, shunned even, the gazes of passersby sliding over and around her, their footsteps making a wide circle around her, as if poverty and death were contagious.

Wonder what the grandparents would say if I brought her home and asked for help?

I bit my lip, caught between wanting to help and frustration that I didn't actually have any means in this world. What rights I had were on sufferance only and it wasn't like I had any money or any way of getting money or any authority or anything useful. On the other hand, it wasn't quite like you could pay for a woman the way you paid for a bunch of bananas, even if I did have money.

Or could you, here?

Trapped in my misgivings, I stood in the shadows watching her, outrage and helplessness churning in my stomach.

Two men stopped in front of her sign. They laughed, pointed at the sign, and started shoving and slapping each other in that particularly entitled way, obviously more than a little tipsy.

They wore richly embroidered robes, and the dye job of their clothing was clearly superior to the faded garments of the poorer folk. Deep hunter's green and sapphire blue overrobes -- they stood out like peacocks amongst sparrows.

Should I grab the girl and run and sort it out later?

"No! Please!"

Her low cry solved that particular question.

I dashed forward, noting how the passersby went from circling around her to outright scuttling away. Even the hawkers who were forced by space constraints to share the side of that street with her hurriedly bagged up their wares and scurried to other corners of the market.

Blue robe turned to his companion, mouth twisted in exaggerated mockery, "The poor darling is frightened, she says."

Green robe raised a brow, "Didn't she say she's willing to sell herself to bury her da? What, isn't a man allowed to test the wares before he buys them? Xia Sanlan, look at that sign again for me."

Blue jerked a thumb at the sign spread out in front of her, "Nah, says so right here, Zheng Jian. The little woman's just a bit shy."

I stopped just behind them, uncertain. The odds didn't favor me. Not when everyone else in the marketplace seemed determined to ignore what was going on.

Zheng Jian bent down and lifted her chin, stroking one hand over her cheek, "Now then, sweet thing, why don't you come home with us? We'll take real good care of you, if you know what I mean." He nudged Xia Sanlan with his elbow and chuckled lasciviously.

"Please, no. Just leave me alone, please." She jerked her chin from his grasp. Tears rolled down her cheeks.

My gut seized. I could go. They hadn't noticed me

yet. I could go back for help. I could turn around and...

"Why you ungrateful--" Zheng Jian grabbed her again. This time he dug his fingers into her flesh, ignoring her pained whimper.

There wouldn't be time. It looked like they would rape her in the streets if they wanted to and everyone else would just let them.

I swallowed the knot of pure terror in my throat. "Let her go. Please."

Their shoulders stiffened before they turned to face me as one. Zheng Jian didn't even release her, just twisted around, dragging her along with him.

"Why lookie here, here's another chickie." Xia Sanlan grinned at me. He took a step forward. "Why, did you also want a chance at this?" He flipped aside his robe to reveal the trousers underneath and grabbed his balls. He gave them a meaningful heft, the gesture salacious and mocking.

Gorge rose in my throat.

"Please leave her alone. She said no."

He stared at me and licked his lips. "Well, well, looks like someone's jealous. Don't worry, lovie, there's more than enough of big Zheng to go around. Besides, she's got something to sell and I've got a yen to buy. Nothing wrong with that at all." He absently shifted his hand to press the girl's face into the side of his thigh. She tried to wrench away, but he cupped her head in his hand and shoved her harder against the bulge in his pants.

Rage overcame terror. He was all but forcing her mouth against his crotch in the street. The angry words spilled out before I could stop myself. "She doesn't want to sell to you. Why don't you go find someone who will?"

Xia Sanlan stepped forward, his face darkening with rage and menace. "Shut up, cunt. Run along if you don't want to play, but don't start trying to spoil our fun here."

The girl shoved Zheng Jian away from her and tore her face away from his grasp. "Please! Don't leave me."

Zheng Jian's eyes narrowed and an ugly glint flared to life before he casually backhanded her so hard she hit the street.

She didn't move. Blood trickled out from under her.

Utterly taken aback by the sudden descent into violence, I froze in horror, my stomach turning at the sight of her blood seeping into the flagstones.

"Look what you've done now. You've cost us a pretty bitch so I suppose we'll just have to take you instead. You happy now?" Xia Sanlan stepped forward and reached for me, grabbing my arm and dragging me towards him.

Thrust out of my dazed state by the revolting feeling of his moist hand against my skin, I used the momentum of his pull to step into him and punched him in the throat as hard as I could.

Thank the gods for martial art lessons.

Xia Sanlan made a horrible gurgling noise and grabbed his throat with both hands, staggering backwards.

"You vicious bitch." Zheng Jian spat at me, lunging for me with both hands outstretched.

I kicked him in the balls, hard. He let out a loud oomph, turned bright red then ash pale, and crumpled to the ground.

"Who's the bitch now?" I kicked him again in the stomach for good measure. His hands fluttered, as if undecided whether to protect his stomach or his groin. He let out weak retching noises.

The girl lay sprawled on the ground. I crouched down beside her and patted her cheek gently. "Are you all right? Can you move?"

She remained motionless. The wound on her forehead bled into a grotesque mask across her face.

"There she is! Get her!"

I whirled around.

A group of men in servant's livery ran towards us. Xia Sanlan pointed in my direction, apoplectic rage on his face, hand wrapped protectively around his throat.

Damn. This wasn't going to end well.

Four men, not counting Zheng Jian and Xia Sanlan, against two females, one of who was clearly down for the count. Zheng Jian was already uncurling from his fetal position and I didn't want to think about what would happen if he called for reinforcements as well.

Then a light rain started to fall, soothing and calming, a reminder of my magic.

I looked at the heavens, swallowed, and pulled power, hard and fast. It cramped, and I tasted blood in my mouth. I took a breath, rationing the power out the way I would unwind a spool of thread, imaging the power tricking out in a slow but steady stream.

The rain swirled around me, slowly forming into a sphere. I tried to focus on it becoming impenetrable, a globe of currents carrying sharp shards of ice to repel the men.

One of the men backed away, "She's a witch. You didn't say she was a witch." He fully backed to the end of the street before turning tail and running.

Another of the men gulped, then adjusted his balls for maximum testosterone boost and stepped forward, "Pffft, it's only water."

Despite his brave words, he didn't walk straight into the shield, but stretched out his hand to test it.

"Arghh!" Blood tinted the shield a pale, pale pink and he clutched his hand to his chest, blood dripping from between his fingers. The ice had shredded his fingertips, ribbons of skin and flesh hanging off of bone.

My knees went weak. Bile filled my mouth.

Now wasn't the time to feel squeamish.

Forcing my gaze away, I concentrated on holding the shield, my grandmother's voice resonating in my mind. *Remember, it is your will that shapes the water. It is an extension of you. Hold your will steady and pull from your core.*

"Uh. We're outta here." The other two men looked at him, then at me, and ran.

"You worthless pieces of shit! Get back here!" Xia Sanlan called after them, his voice ravaged.

I clamped my hands to my stomach, trying to breathe through the pain of what felt like someone trying to carve my uterus out with a blunt wooden spork.

You're not used to magic, so be careful not to overdo it. There is ample time for practice. You must stop when it starts to be painful to draw power.

Zheng Jian staggered to his feet. "We'll just wait her out. I know her kind. Sooner or later she'll run out of power and then we'll have her." He laughed, malice threading with pain in the sound.

"Oh yeah. I want her. I want that bitch bad." The wounded guard stared at me, his voice vibrating with rage and hate.

"You can have her when we're done with her." Zheng Jian flicked a glance at him, then turned back to stare at me.

I clamped my teeth down on my lower lip, determined to bleed out first before I let the shield fall.

Sorry, A-mah. I'd rather face whatever consequences came from abusing magic than let that girl and myself get raped.

"If there's anything left." Xia Sanlan stared at me hungrily, his cackle bordering on the insane.

I closed my eyes, focusing on extending what little power I had left.

"What did you say you wanted to do with her?" Sethalor's voice, soft and lethal.

My eyes sprang open.

Sethalor. Thank the gods.

He stood behind them, hands folded behind his

back, his eyes blazing with an unholy light in a too-pale face. Aedrian held twin swords aloft at his side, the promise of death in his eyes.

The three men glanced back at him, but didn't react, clearly thinking he was one of them.

Zheng Jian reached down to cup his crotch, snatching his hand back with a hiss as he encountered abused flesh, "I want to beat her bloody for what she did to me. Then I want to spread her and fuck her until she bleeds."

Xia Sanlan nodded, his eyes intent with a fanatic's gaze, "Until she bleeds and bleeds and bleeds."

I closed my eyes, dizzy with revulsion and power drain. If the guys were going to play white knight, they'd better do it fast, before I passed out.

"I thought so." Sethalor moved forward with deadly intent. "Aedrian, put away your swords, they don't deserve to bleed on your steel. Make sure they don't rise again."

Zheng Jian turned around, outraged. "Who the hells are you?"

Sethalor only smiled before he kneed him in the groin, then shoved his palm into his nose. Zheng Jian went down like a ton of bricks. Sethalor shoved his limp body away and Aedrian moved forward, booted heels meeting joints with sickening crunches.

Xia Sanlan spun around at Zheng Jian's burbled scream. "The hells?"

Sethalor kicked him in the stomach, jerked him close when he was bent over retching and kneed him in the nose. He released him to sag at his feet, then casually stepped on his balls and ground his heel down. The high pitched scream went on for a stomach-wrenching eternity before it cut off abruptly.

Aedrian moved to block off the guard's escape. He sheathed his swords in one fluid motion while kicking out. One foot caught the guard in the groin, the other hit him in the solar plexus and he went down with a faint gurgle.

Sethalor looked at me and snapped, "Drop that shield before you do yourself irreparable injury, Estyria."

It took effort to drop the shield. I had tied it to my will and my breath and it was hard to persuade myself that the danger was truly over.

Water vapor drifted away on the breeze. I slumped forwards, my only thought that of the relief from pain.

CHAPTER TWENTY

Sleep receded enough for remembered adrenaline to hit my bloodstream like a freight train. I opened my eyes and blinked woozily at my bedroom ceiling. My bedroom? The memories slammed into me. The girl. Seth. Aedrian.

I bolted upright. Nausea roiled in my stomach and my vision went black. More memories flooded in to fill the dark. The men. The blood. The way shredded flesh looked.

My breath hitched. I panted, the oxygen in the air suddenly nonexistent.

I pulled out a mental box and started throwing all my thoughts in it. I didn't pause to examine, didn't stop to do anything more than acknowledge they existed before locking it away.

"You're awake."

I blinked away the haze and turned my head. I inhaled, slow, and exhaled slower.

Sethalor sat by my bed, a scroll in one hand, a porcelain cup in the other. A small ball of light hovered beside his shoulder, just enough to read by, but not bright enough to disturb my sleep. The now familiar sheen of the aural shield glittered around us.

"Seth. We have really got to stop meeting like this." I tried to summon up a smile and failed. "I thought you weren't allowed in my bedroom. Where are my grandparents? Do they know? What happened to the girl?" My voice rose and my words came faster at the end despite my best efforts.

"They went to sleep earlier after the physician pronounced you well. The girl has been settled in one of the guest bedrooms. She has not woken, but the physician said it is a healing sleep."

"Are they mad?" I asked, hesitant.

"Of course. I had to explain arriving at their doorstep with two unconscious women, one bleeding like a stuck pig and the other their long-lost heir and beloved granddaughter. It's fortunate that my association with your grandfather goes back quite some years or he might have taken a sword to me when he saw you senseless."

I flinched at the harshness in his voice.

He reached for my hand and raised it to his lips, folding a soft kiss into my palm. "To sneak out of the residence like that, without taking even a maid with you, you are truly begging for a spanking." Despite his sharp tone, his touch was careful and soothing, his hands gentle, and I saw his words for what they were. A distraction.

His scent wrapped around me, warmed patchouli, cedar, and leather. His presence pushed away the jagged edges of my mind, calming and soothing.

Tears stung my eyes. I couldn't keep my lip from quivering. It was so close. Too close. I'd never been that near violence before, much less such visceral violence.

Or have you?

Ignoring the voice, I shoved that thought into the box, kicked the box into a dark corner and turned the lock on everything. No. Not now. I wouldn't deal with this now.

There was a small voice that asked *when* and I ignored that too.

He moved to sit on the bed. Strong arms hauled me up and over into his lap.

I curled into his arms and sniffled back the tears. "How did you know where I was?"

His body was tense under mine. "Yunya mirrored me. Also, I can hear your thoughts on occasion. It is part of the bond and what allowed me to find your precise location."

Oh. That didn't sound so great if I wanted to verbally abuse him but since it saved me from rape and worse, I wasn't going to complain.

"Can I turn it off when I want to call you names?"

"Just remember that you are technically part of my family before you start cursing my antecedents." His tone was deliberately teasing, his words light, but his body vibrated with remembered rage.

Seth stroked my hair for a few more moments before he spoke again, restrained violence and fury spilling into the air between us.

"If I hadn't come, what would you have done? Died alone in that square, with no one the wiser?"

I swallowed hard. "I didn't know. I thought it would be safe. I thought no one would know me and so they'd leave me alone."

He leaned his forehead against mine, his eyes closing. "This isn't your world, dear heart. It isn't as safe and it's made much less so when you fight despite not knowing the rules of engagement."

I pushed him away. "Should I have just allowed them to carry her off and rape her?"

Brilliant gold eyes narrowed. "If you had brought a guard, you could have saved her without placing her in any danger. For that matter, if you had told them you were the granddaughter of Ningxia-*ji* or a member of the regent's household, they would never have dared to lay a hand on you. Even if you had claimed to be a princess, that might have done some good."

"That's... that's revolting. What about everyone else who doesn't have the protection of your name? Should they just resign themselves to being brutalized?"

Sethalor tightened his embrace, and his hand combed through the loose fall of my hair, releasing the scent of osmanthus into the air. "Stating that you had a safer method of achieving your aims doesn't mean I support rape. Don't push me away, Estyria. I need to be certain of your safety. It took years off my life when I saw you standing in the midst of blood and violence, pale and shaking from the use of your magic."

If he hadn't shown up when he did...

An involuntary shudder slid down my spine. I tucked my head into the curve at his neck, and placed my palm over his heart, allowing the steady beat of his heart to lull my senses.

"Is this sort of thing usually allowed? Men able to take women on the streets, with no one to stop them? Is there no law, no morality that prohibits that?"

"No, but there are always those who believe themselves above the law. Happily, these particular men will be quite thoroughly disillusioned of that idea. They have been sentenced to hard labor in the desert for their crimes."

"Don't you guys have a police force or something like that?"

He sighed. "Something like that. The magistrates have their thief takers, bounty hunters, and watchmen, but they do not quite serve the same function as your police. Those who have a complaint can take it to the magistrate's hall and appeal for justice. Unfortunately, this system ceases to function when the offender in question is the magistrate's son."

"Why isn't there a police force?"

He stiffened, his breath catching in his throat, his hands stilling.

Shit. This wasn't another one of those trigger questions, was it?

"To create a new force within the current system would require the monarch's seal. As regent, I head the court and work within the confines of established law and precedent, but I cannot create new laws or branches of government." His tone was even, his voice expressionless.

"Huh." My eyelids got heavier with the prosaic turn of the conversation, sleep a siren call I couldn't resist.

Then again, why resist? I was safe and warm in Seth's arms.

"Estyria. What am I to do with you? I can't keep you safe from yourself." He nuzzled against my hair, his voice deep and low, a thread of sound winding around my heart.

I forced my eyes open, the weight of my eyelids dragging them closed almost immediately, swimming through the morass of sleep to force blurry words out, "So sorry. You don't need to though."

"I've been thinking, while waiting for you to regain consciousness."

"S'dangerous, thinking."

"...requests...saving your life...promise... " His voice came from far away, the words slow and blurry.

"Mmmm..." I turned my face into his chest, my thoughts coming through molasses.

"I'm going to take that as assent..."

Sleep claimed me and drowned out the rest of his sentence.

"Estyria, wake."

I rolled over, half debating ignoring him when my

stomach growled so hard it clenched.

Ow. I flopped onto my side and peered at Sethalor, sitting again at the table with a scroll. "I'm surprised you're still here. What was that about the rules again?"

"Saving your life for the second time seems to have granted me a certain amount of leeway." His voice was just this side of sarcastic.

"Right." I held out my arms. "Please?"

The box rattled and shook from the closet in my mind. It knew I was awake.

His eyes darkened to near black, but he rose and came over to the bed.

I shifted so I could wrap my arms around his neck and twined my legs around his waist. I pressed my face into the curve of his neck and took a deep breath. The familiarity of his scent settled my mind.

He curved his arm under me to support my weight. "Are you all right?"

I shook my head. His presence suppressed the box but I knew it was still there, waiting.

It'd been one nightmare after the other towards the end. Dreams in which zombies chased me, where I had to take them apart with an axe into ground meat before they'd stop chasing me. Dreams in which something unknown was chasing me and I somehow knew that I couldn't kill it, unlike the zombies, so I could only run. Run past endurance, when my breath was rich with the taste of iron, until the stitch in my side expanded to full body pain.

"What time is it?"

"It's about an hour before you need to leave for

court. I woke you late because I thought you needed the sleep. Also, I have to talk to your grandparents."

"At oh-fuck-o'clock in the morning?" Only someone used to the ridiculous schedules that court involved could call being woken at four in the morning late.

"I need to let them know that Aedrian has been officially seconded to your guard and that he will be with you at all times."

It was funny how there was a line of before and after. Before, I would have bristled at the calm assumption that he could assign me a guard without consulting me. Now, I just buried myself deeper in his scent and nodded. I'd deal with the question of whether Aedrian wanted to guard me or not later.

"All right."

Tension drained out of him. "No fight?"

I mumbled against his neck, "I'm really not reckless and brash. What makes you think I want to go anywhere without a guard now that I know what lies outside these walls?"

His sigh ruffled my hair. "I didn't want that for you, Phoenix."

"Where's Aedrian anyway? I'm surprised he's let you alone for so long."

"He's otherwise occupied." His voice was soft and lethal, bringing forth the memory of the man screaming under his boot. "He'll return in time to escort you to the palace."

I shivered, as much because of remembered horror as because I found I couldn't feel sorry for whatever happened to the men at all.

Who was I?

Furthermore, what was I turning into?

CHAPTER TWENTY-ONE

I rushed through my ablutions, got dressed, and then gulped down my breakfast with near unseemly haste. Sethalor shook his head at that last, but I noted he'd set aside my bowl of porridge to cool before I showered.

My grandmother stood at the doorway to the great room.

I slowed when I saw her, uncertain of what she would say.

"Estyria. Be at ease." Seth reached for my hand and drew me to his side.

I gave him a wry look. "That's easy for you to say. You're not the person in trouble."

My grandmother's face was drawn and sharp grooves marked her mouth. She scanned me as I approached and the lines eased in her face. Her bow and greeting to Sethalor was perfunctory, something I hadn't seen before.

"Granddaughter."

I tried not to wince at her stern voice.

"Yes, *A-mah*."

"You will do me the courtesy of taking at least one guard with you whenever you leave the residence."

I flinched. "Ah. All right." Looking around, I didn't see my grandfather. "Where's *A-gong?*"

A dangerous light flared in her eyes and her expression turned cold. "He's otherwise occupied. I expect you'll see him later."

Ah. That didn't sound good. In that mafia-esque taking care of business euphemism way.

Sethalor cleared his throat. "*Shimu*. With your permission, I would like to officially second Aedrian to Estyria's protection."

Only the slightest flare of her eyes gave her surprise away. "Lord McKenna, Seth?"

Surprise flashed across his face at her familiarity before he bowed. "Yes."

"House Xuanyuan thanks you for your grace, Imperial Highness."

Huh. Formal again. Seemed like my grandmother was really taken aback by his offer.

Placing a hand on my lower back, Sethalor shifted and turned me so we faced the path to the front gate.

Aedrian's form detached from the shadows in the garden and moved into the light. He strode over, every movement suffused with an easy grace. He stopped four feet away and bowed, his blood-red braid sliding forward with the motion.

Icy gray eyes gave me a quick once over before meeting my gaze squarely. Expression cool and professional, the dangerous look in his eyes raised the hairs on my nape. He gleamed against the backdrop of his starkly utilitarian black robes, which were sashed and edged with more black.

Stepping forward, I caught his hand and pulled. "I need to talk to you. Alone."

Dark red brows raised, but the man was unmovable.

Understanding, I looked over my shoulder at Seth. "Seth. That okay with you?"

The imperial prince tipped his head at Aedrian. "He's seconded to you, which means he answers to you and only to you."

A wry look crossed the redhead's face.

I tugged on him again and this time he followed me to a side-path so we were shielded from the prince and my grandmother.

"You don't have to do this if you don't want to."

"This?"

I sighed. "Look, you've made your feelings about me more than clear, so I'm not really sure why Seth wants you to guard me, but I'll talk to him about it. I just wanted to make sure that you weren't going to be chewing nails in the meantime."

Dry amusement curved his mouth. "*I* requested to be seconded to your protection. Seth didn't ask."

I blinked. "What?"

His smile deepened to genuine humor. "If that's all, perhaps we should rejoin them?"

Completely thrown, I nodded and followed him back.

"Satisfied?" Seth asked.

Not quite, since I had no idea what crack Aedrian accidentally got his hands on before he volunteered to guard me.

The men exchanged a look and something occurred to me. "I hesitate to ask, but what did you get demoted from?"

Aedrian's brows shot straight up, the ice in his eyes receding for an instant before the mask slid back.

"Fengxun."

I ignored my grandmother's chiding tone. "What? You can't tell me that this is a promotion, or even a sideways shift for him."

Seth sighed deeply. "Aedrian is the commander of the palace guard. Not was. Is."

I whistled. "That's quite a demotion. I'm really sorry. Are you sure you don't want me to ask him to ruin someone else's life and career?"

"Is. Not was," Seth repeated.

His eyes glinted with humor. "It is my honor to be seconded to your service, Your Grace."

"Are you sure you're not just saying that because he's standing right there?"

"In that case, perhaps you should ask when he isn't standing two paces away."

I shrugged. "Just did, remember? All right. Fine. Just remember I gave you an out and if you're going to resent anyone, you should be peevy at him for ruining your life, not me."

My grandmother's mouth twitched, amusement touching her face for the first time that morning.

Sethalor rolled his eyes. "Consider me suitably repentant." His face sobered. "You must always keep Aedrian at your side, Phoenix. Do you have Yunya with you?"

I pulled the mirror out of my sleeve, flashed it at him, and slid it back into the sleeve pocket.

"Good." He sighed and brushed his knuckles against my cheek. "Together, they should be able to keep you out of harm's way, but do not hesitate to call me next time if you need aid."

The ugly leers of the men scrolled across my mind and I shuddered. "I will."

He stepped back and bowed. "I shall return to the palace. My thanks for your forbearance, *Shimu.*"

"Your Imperial Highness." My grandmother curtsied in turn.

He nodded again and disappeared.

I looked at Aedrian. "Have you had breakfast yet?"

"Yes, Your Grace."

My grandmother opened her mouth, paused, sighed, and shut it again without saying anything.

"Let's go then." I huffed out a breath and turned to my grandmother, "Wish me luck?"

My grandmother arched an arrogant brow. "You are my granddaughter. You do not need anything so fickle as luck. You are all you need to be."

That was warm and fuzzy and all, but to be honest, I really just wanted a simple good luck. If only she knew how my intestines had cat-cradled themselves into painful knots.

Aedrian handed me up into the carriage. He

settled in opposite me, sword loosened in its sheath and laid across his lap.

I swallowed. "Do you think that's really necessary?"

He raised his gaze to mine. "Yes, Your Grace."

"Do people get attacked often in the city?"

"Not frequently, no. However, you are precious to many and that coupled with your status does make you a target. Better to be prepared than not."

I blinked. There was an odd edge to his voice when he said precious.

"Are you going to call me Your Grace from now on with every sentence? Could you not?"

His brows arched. "It wouldn't be proper, Your Grace."

Too tired to quibble, I shook my head.

CHAPTER TWENTY-TWO

S ethalor cocked his head, his eyes intent on Helena Hauville as she walked into the audience chamber.

Gorgeous in silver and gold silk, her hair had been bound up in intricate braids knotted with strands of pearl. She glided across the floor, the epitome of aristocratic perfection.

I looked back at Sethalor and my heart stuttered at the lethal consideration in his eyes. That wasn't the look of a man admiring a beautiful woman; that was a warrior assessing danger and risk and contemplating cutting it out at the root.

Sethalor noticed my attention and gave me a barely there shake of his head.

Don't alert the quarry. Right.

The warm scent of summer woods and leather drifted to me just before I turned my head, coming face to face with Riordan. Managing to suppress my gasp and the urge to leap sideways only by virtue of having survived childhood with a sneaky older brother, I gave him a sweet smile. "Good morning to you too."

He answered with a warm smile full of both approval and good humor. "With your company, a very good morning indeed."

Seth slanted us a look rife with suspicion.

Riordan leaned in closer, his scent drifting over me, and I fought the urge to shrink back. Any closer and he'd be centimeters away from kissing me and that was the last thing I wanted, but I didn't want to give the impression I was afraid of him either.

Somewhere in the palace a gong chimed and he leaned back, returning Seth's stare with a flirtatious smile.

Breathing out with the additional distance, I took a closer look at his face, then Helena's.

Was it my imagination, or did the marks on their faces look slightly more faded than they did before?

My hand rose to brush the lotus on my forehead, almost against my will, and I dropped my hand before I called attention to myself.

It was crimson before, but when I looked in the mirror this morning it looked darker, the red of dried blood rather than fresh.

The outer doors swung open, pushed apart and held in place by two guards. After the lords filed in, the guards closed the doors behind them.

"Anything to report?"

One of the lords stepped forward and bowed. Angular and gaunt in figure, with sharp features, but weariness lined brackets around his mouth and eyes.

"Lord Lin."

"Imperial Highness, the Fong Jiang dries further and the magistrates along the Fong Jiang valley have sent scrolls detailing the situation. They fear famine and rebellion in the western provinces if it does not rain soon. As the situation worsens, they fear the imperial city may soon be impacted as well."

Sethalor motioned in our direction. "Candidates?"

Helena answered first, voice smooth and measured. "Waiving their taxes for this year would aid in alleviating tensions and the plight of the people. If the drought continues as it has or worsens, the waiver should extend to next year's taxes as well."

A slow nod of approval from Hauville in the front row, his eyes narrowed in thought.

Interesting. So it appeared that the lord wasn't a complete waste of air.

Riordan tapped his fingers on the armrest. "Have there been subsidies made to the people? If not, open the granaries to them."

Handouts would help, but it would be a bandage over a gaping wound if the drought continued. Taxes being waived were all well and good, but it wasn't going to save people dying of thirst. With the drought going on for as long as it had, there were few options left.

"What about underground water? Do wells still have water in that region?" I asked.

"Your Grace, the people there do not have wells. They live on the banks of the largest river in

Tavaneth."Lord Lin's voice held barely veiled impatience and a trace of contempt.

"And much good that's doing them. Send the troops in and dig some wells."

A low murmur spread through the ranks.

Lord Lin opened and closed his mouth several times. "The troops?"

"Our army should be well fed and rested, are they not? As we are not at war, we might as well put the men to work for the people. They should be at least marginally more efficient and will give the people a sign that their government is willing to put action to words. Having the army there will also discourage any worries of rebellion."

"Your Imperial Highness?" He turned to Sethalor,

"The candidates have been more than clear. Make it so, Lord Lin."

The murmur grew to a buzz.

Lord Lin bowed and stepped back into line, a narrow crease appearing between his brows, his eyes thoughtful.

"Any other reports?"

Sethalor turned to me when court was over and Helena had departed the audience chamber. "Riordan will escort you to the library while Aedrian makes his report and I meet with your grandparents. He will join you later and accompany you back home."

"What about my grandparents?"

His expression chilled, his eyes turning to shards of green ice.

I frowned. "You're not going to tell me what they're doing, are you? Can I remind you that I'm not a child to be shielded from unpleasant truths?"

Lines drew tight around his mouth and he sucked in a slow breath before replying through gritted teeth. "I am not trying to spare you anything. My goal was to not enter a judgment predisposed to killing all who were involved in the incident yesterday."

Cold curled in my stomach. *The incident.* His choice of words didn't bother me. In fact, I preferred how bloodless and tidy they were compared to what I had gone through. But that *he* chose to use them...

Rage flickered in his eyes, gold burning away the green. "I do not wish to speak of this before I must, else I might give in to the urge to paint the halls with their blood. Instead, I must be regent and just."

I swallowed hard as I realized he didn't intend to diminish what happened yesterday but to distance himself from his emotions.

Be fair, Estyria.

I had to remember that Seth's heart was as easily bruised as mine, perhaps more.

"All right. I will wait with Riordan." I hesitated, then, "I'm sorry."

His eyes closed for a moment and he shook his head sharply. "No. You should never have been attacked. No woman should have to fear for their life and virtue."

"Seth...."

"No. I cannot speak of this now. Especially not to you."

He gave me a curt nod before striding from the room.

I slumped back against the chair and stared at the door, my heart trembling. Perhaps my grandparents would be willing to talk about it. My grandmother's cold expression from this morning flashed across my mind and I swallowed against the knot in my throat. Maybe not.

Riordan studied me. "You seem surprised, Princess."

He shook his head at my quizzical look. "That he is skating the killing edge."

"He said that he wants to paint the halls with their blood. I didn't get the impression that was hyperbole."

"It wasn't. You must understand there is more untrammeled danger and savagery in the men here than in your world, be they ally or foe. Unlike in your world, his reaction would be seen as just and to be expected. Sethalor is a warrior, born, bred and blooded. Never mistake him for anything less."

I made a face. "Not going to be hard if he keeps being so open about his bloodthirsty urges."

His scrutiny intensified before a slow smile unfurled across his face. "Let's go, Princess."

Wending our way through arcades and hallways, I lost track of the turns and twists and settled for just following him. We were walking down a corridor of trees in the gardens when I realized what he was doing and stopped short.

"Riordan. I don't know why you're taking the long way around, but I did notice just now that we walked around half the garden to get to this point when we could have just taken that path back there. What are you trying to do?"

He shook his head and kept moving. "We're almost there. Hush now, you don't want to distract them."

Huffing out a breath in frustration, I had no choice but to follow. The tree lined path opened out onto a dirt clearing surrounded by a wall of shrubs.

Two men stood in the center, naked blades gleaming in the sunshine.

Aedrian circled Sethalor, twin blades in hand, eyes molten with fury, lips bared in a snarl.

Seth pivoted in place, his eyes chips of green ice, completely expressionless except for a slow tic at his jaw.

Aedrian darted forward, his swords a silver blur, moving almost too fast for me to track.

Seth burst into motion the same time he did, and I realized that he didn't wield long swords but two flexible blades that twisted and wove into a web of defense, blocking all of the redhead's attacks.

They appeared evenly matched, each giving as well as they got, but Aedrian seemed to have the benefit of greater strength, pressing forward centimeter by centimeter every time they clashed.

Seth's jaw hardened, his motions getting impossibly faster, finally twisting his blades together around one of Aedrian's swords, disarming him.

"Why did you bring me here, Riordan?"

"Shhh. Watch."

Now it was Aedrian's turn to retreat, his motions speeding up as he tried to keep up with Seth, but it was clearly a matter of time.

Seth pressed forward, a small, cold smile edging his lips, the green in his eyes lightening to a brilliant gold. He caught Aedrian's remaining blade between his two and wrenched it out of his grasp.

I thought Aedrian would concede defeat, but he merely grinned, gathered his muscles, and launched himself straight into the path of Seth's spinning blades.

Seth's eyes widened. Surprise and horror flashed across his face before he tossed aside his blades, just as Aedrian hurtled past their trajectory. The redhead missed decapitation by mere millimeters, crashed into him, and drove the prince to the ground. In the same instant, he grabbed Seth's hands, and crossed them over his chest so he couldn't move.

They stared at each other, blazing silver into luminous gold, panting, their faces centimeters apart.

I glanced at Riordan as pain unfurled in my chest. His return gaze held a hint of challenge. Not knowing what he was testing me for, I dragged out humor as a shield, choosing to address the situation head-on.

Plastering a smile on my face, I nudged Riordan and whispered, "This is where they kiss, right?"

Aedrian's head whipped around, eyes wide, hands loosening and his body falling back as he shifted to a position more suited for defense.

Seth took advantage of his distraction and

wedged a leg between them, dislodging him with an upward jerk of his knee, then rolling away when Aedrian flinched back.

They sprang to their feet, collecting their weaponry, matching flags of color rising in their cheeks.

Riordan looked at me. "Well, now that you've interrupted, we'll never know, will we?"

I shrugged. "Sorry. But it's for the best, really. Imagine the awkwardness if we actually caught them snogging."

"Why would it be awkward? For all you know, I might want to join in. Nothing like a good sparring session to get the blood going."

I tipped my head towards the men. "Hey, don't let me stop you."

Aedrian and Seth stopped short of us, their gazes narrowed and the set of their shoulders tense, a dark flush mantling their cheekbones.

Seth growled. "Why is she here, Riordan? I thought I made myself clear."

The blond raised his shoulders in an easy shrug, but his eyes held a cold clarity. "Your princess doesn't seem to properly appreciate what it might mean if you should lose control. I thought I'd show her a taste for it."

Emerald eyes darkened and his gaze swept my way before he slanted a glare at Riordan. "You thought to show her what a barbarian I could be? What did you think to accomplish with that?"

"Perhaps she'd be more amenable to prudence if

she believes that you really will paint the halls with blood if she came to harm."

Seth's jaw worked for a moment. "I am not in the habit of making idle threats, Phoenix." He swept a lethal look at Riordan. "As you claim to believe I mean what I say, perhaps you will escort the princess to the library posthaste?"

I looked from one man to the other, completely lost. No way Riordan went to this much trouble and ran the risk of infuriating Seth further just to prove his point about Seth's level of rage.

Riordan gave Seth a sardonic bow. "Yes, milord. At once, milord."

Seth pivoted on the spot and walked away.

Aedrian gave me an inscrutable look before following.

Riordan turned to me, the challenging glint back. "Do you understand now?"

I thought I did, but I wasn't certain, not with him having so much fun playing riddler.

I started walking back the way we came. "Riordan, if you could take us back? The direct route this time, please. I think I've had quite as much exercise as I'm willing to tolerate before breakfast."

I waited until we were in the library before pinning Riordan down with my suspicions. "Can you do that aural shield?"

"No need. This room is automatically protected

against eavesdroppers with an entire battery of spells." A faint dimple appeared, a teasing glint lighting sapphire eyes to sky blue. "Why? Did you want to avail yourself of my numerous charms?"

"You wanted me to see them together. Why? It's nothing I haven't already seen."

"What do you think I wanted to show you, Princess? As I told Seth, I wanted you to be aware of what you are dealing with."

"Do you ever tire of speaking like that? Full of half-hints and double meanings."

His smile remained cocky and easy. "Do you not like the way I speak, Princess? Pity. I've been told I'm very good at flirtation."

"Why do you keep calling me princess? I have a name and I'd prefer if you used it."

"I call you what you are to remind you that you are a princess, with the associated duties, rights and privileges."

Was it my imagination, or was there a slight emphasis on the last word?

"What sort of rights and privileges are we talking about?"

"You're aware that the emperor has traditionally possessed a harem, yes?"

My nod was hesitant. Where was he going with this? Surely not...

"As a princess who is tied to the earth, you have the right and some may even say the duty of ensuring the health of the land through any and all means necessary."

"And what does that have to do with what you showed me earlier?"

A flicker of impatience crossed his face. "Aedrian and Seth share a strong bond, one that brings balance to them both."

More than a little impatient myself, I tapped my foot and cocked my head in a deliberate show of confusion. "Riordan. I hate to admit to this, but you're going to have to be a little more explicit. I might have some inkling of where you're going but I really, truly don't want to assume."

"Anyone who wishes to have one cannot but take the other; they come as a pair. The bond between them will not allow otherwise."

"You speak as if it's simply a matter of paying more for a matched set of goblets rather than men."

"Isn't it? Remember what I told you the last time we met."

"You're assuming much, aren't you?"

"Am I?"

"I haven't said that I want one, much less two... goblets and there's been no indicator that they will even contemplate what you're so cavalierly arranging for them."

He rolled his eyes. "Someone has to because clearly it isn't going to happen in time on its own. And you should cease looking at them both like a child eyes the pudding if you want me to believe you don't want them."

"In time?"

"You will need help with feeding the land besides

the fact that an empress will not be able to remain unwed for long. Best to forestall pressure from the court on your terms and not theirs. It's not as if it would be a hardship."

I rubbed the point between my eyebrows. "What the hell makes you think they'd go along with it, that they even want it? Besides, if we're talking about the same thing, those two are so firmly in denial about each other you couldn't pay me to touch it."

A soft laugh escaped him. "Princess, I am a man. Believe me when I say that I'm more than passing familiar with the way a man looks when he has interest in a woman. As for their repudiations..." He shook his head. "I'm not suggesting that you storm the gates or lay siege to their defenses. I recommend covert warfare in the form of guerrilla tactics and infiltration. They will likely not succumb to forthright attacks but I'm certain they'd fall to softer methods."

"I can't believe I'm listening to this. You seem to be very invested in this. Why?"

A golden brow arched. "Why not? They are my comrades, brothers in all but having come from the same womb."

"So the first thing you do when you arrive is to try and marry them off?"

He studied me for a long moment. "Pay closer attention, Princess. Everything may depend upon it. From all reports, Seth has been dead flesh walking these past years and Aedrian's happiness is inextricable from his. Less than a week you've been here and already Seth looks more like a living man than he's been since his family died. Aedrian is more than capable of observing that for himself. If you leverage that correctly, coupled with Aedrian's fascination, there would be no reason for them to demur."

"No pressure at all, oh no."

"Choosing to stay was the wrong decision if you wanted to be a sheltered orchid."

"I suppose I should be grateful you're not suggesting that I whack them over the head with a club and drag them off into a cave somewhere and make it a *fait accompli*."

His brows sprang up and he blinked once. "Not a terrible idea, all things considered, but I merely ask that you remain open to possibilities and consider taking advantage of any opportunities that come your way. After all, it was your people that pointed out that only silk gauze separates courtship initiated by a woman but a mountain obstructs the pursuit of a man."

The door slid open and Aedrian walked in.

Riordan lifted my hand to his lips and brushed a light kiss over the back of my fingers. "*En garde.*"

CHAPTER TWENTY-THREE

"**W**ake up." I sat beside the girl's bed, willing her to open her eyes.

Her slight figure was motionless under the counterpane, her face lax in sleep. Only a day and her lips were already split and dry, her cheekbones sharp enough to cut glass.

Squeezing my eyes shut, I prayed to all the gods of my childhood. *"Dazizai wangfou. Namo guanshiyin pusha.* Please let her be all right. Please."

Warmth trickled down my cheek and bitter salt spread across my tongue.

A knock at the door and then Aedrian's voice came from behind me. "Princess."

Swiping at the tears, I turned to face him.

Stormy silver eyes flared before narrowing on my face. "Why do you weep?"

His eyes narrowed further when I gestured at the girl, not trusting my voice. "Surely your grandparents have told you that she merely sleeps?"

I shrugged. There was sleeping and then there was sleeping. Didn't change the fact that had I acted faster, she probably wouldn't have been hit.

His expression turned quizzical. "Don't tell me you feel responsible?"

My mouth tightened at the incredulous note in his voice and I looked away.

"Don't be ridiculous." His words were a cold slap, his tone unyielding.

I whipped back to glare at him. "What?"

"You risked your life to save her. What more are you asking of yourself?"

"If I'd acted sooner..."

"It wouldn't have changed anything. At most, you hesitated for minutes. The men would have come along and that wasn't the first time they've terrorized women at will in the streets."

"But if she didn't have that sign up anymore, then she would have been safe from them."

He shook his head. "Perhaps she would have been safe, but only because they would have fixated upon you."

"Why?"

His eyes darkened and the twist of his mouth turned rueful. "That delicate innocence of yours would have been sufficient to draw them to savagery but they wouldn't have been able to resist the defiance in your eyes. They're the sort of men who like to grind women beneath their cocks. Your fine clothing might have made them hesitate, but I know their sort. There were enough of them that they would have goaded each other into assailing you. It was only a matter of time."

My jaw dropped. *What* did he just say?

"They would have accosted you because you brought no guard. You would have said something suitably scathing. Then you would have been the one thrown to the ground. As it was, it was better that you had not drawn their attention first."

"Better? For whom?"

"Better for the men, who have narrowly escaped with their lives. Better for their fathers, who will only need to pay bloodgild instead of having Seth and your grandfather torch their ancestral homes."

I shivered at the matter-of-fact savagery in his words.

"Better for you, also, since I know you will suffer should the men around you descend into unreasoning rage. It took much to persuade him and your grandfather to settle for seconding me to your protection instead of surrounding you with an entire regiment of guards."

It took me a moment to find my tongue. "Thank you?"

His answering smile was razor-edged. "You can thank me by never trying to lose me or complaining about what I consider necessary for your safety."

"Believe me, I'm not going to go running off on my own after *that*." If anything, it was going to take a while before I could imagine going out without someone with me.

A tap came at the door before my grandfather

walked in.

Aedrian bowed. "Your Illustriousness."

Grandfather nodded at him. "Lord McKenna."

Then he turned his attention to me. "Fengxun, I have some business to attend to in town. I thought you might wish to accompany me."

Speaking of which.

Fear leaped into my throat even though I knew exactly what my grandfather was about. Here was someone to make sure I got right back on the horse, so to speak.

The box in my mind creaked, panic threatening to spill out and I kicked at it.

I exhaled slowly past the fear and gave him an I'm-onto-you look. "In what capacity? Tourist, granddaughter, or as the scion?"

He grinned, his expression so similar to my brother's in that moment that I pressed a hand to my chest to still the pang. It was one thing to be told we were family, another thing to see the evidence before me. "That is your choice, Granddaughter."

"Will Grandmother be going as well?

Grandfather winked. "Your grandmother, being the head of the household, has too much on her plate to be able to go wandering around at will. You'll have to settle for just my company."

I bit my lip, swallowing hard.

The box rattled harder.

The logical side of my brain told me going out would be a good idea. The frisson of fear creeping up my spine disagreed.

He picked up my hand where it fisted at my heart and patted it, "Lord McKenna will be with us at all times. Also," he lifted his other hand, turning it palm up, and tongues of fire blossomed between his fingers. "Your old grandfather is not entirely without teeth. I would not let any harm you."

I forced a smile. "Sure, that sounds like fun. Unless I have more lessons coming my way?"

I wasn't quite sure if I would have remained even if my grandmother had said yes to more lessons, but it was worth asking. I ached in the strangest places after her rigorous walk through of all the various curtsies and obeisances that I needed to know for court. Who would have thought etiquette lessons could give yoga and pilates lessons a run for their money?

"No. I thought you might be ready for a respite from everything for an afternoon."

I *was* ready for a bit of something not super dramatic or terribly serious. I just doubted I'd find it in town.

CHAPTER TWENTY-FOUR

I pressed my face to the glass in the carriage's window, Aedrian beside me, his solid presence a comfort. My grandfather kept his eyes on me and continued a pattering monologue about buildings and monuments as we passed them. A few turns and we moved into a different area of the city, one that was clearly the market and entertainment district.

The road teemed with people, horses, palanquins, and other carriages. *Che shui ma long*, carriages like water and horses like dragons. A common idiom in Chinese, but somehow it was different to see the sort of scene that prompted the saying. The way people and animals moved and paused in synchronized harmony was almost a living thing in of itself.

Hawkers peddled their wares along the stone paved street, from steamed meat buns, kabobs, and scallion pancakes to tiny wreaths of jasmine and white jade orchid flowers.

But it was the people who really caught my

attention. The unexpected diversity of the people walking the streets knocked me out of my daze. If diversity was what one called the glittering confusion.

I stared after the tall man striding down the street away from us, the one with hair the color of kelp and skin of a luminescent pearl. "*A-gong?*"

"Yes?"

"I'm seeing a lot of... foreigners."

A golden-haired man walked hand in arm with a woman, her skin a glimmering cream gold. A woman wearing a vibrant caftan and dreadlocks to her waist haggled with a full-bearded, turbaned merchant with sharply pointed ears.

"What of it, Fengxun?" His brow furrowed slightly.

"I... just..." I trailed off, my attention drawn to a girl at the side of the road who...glittered.

Damn. Don't tell me that there are vampires and they do glitter.

"Do you have a problem with foreigners?" Grandfather stared at me with ill-disguised concern.

I broke out laughing. "Oh gods no. Of course not. It's just that I didn't expect this many of them. It almost feels as if I'm in a modern day city in my world." If Boston were the setting for an urban fantasy. How had I missed the supernatural on my previous foray out of the residence?

He blinked, his posture relaxing, "I'd wager that the portals allowing for international travel would be the cause of that. As capital of Tavaneth, Ziyang has portals to and from almost everywhere. Even to the deep sea clans."

Right. Magic.

"So how permeable are the borders?"

"Quite. Perhaps you didn't notice, but there are also a number of foreigners in court."

"I did notice, actually. How did that happen?"

Ancient Chang'an, the capital of the Tang dynasty, was known for being cosmopolitan, with a significant foreign population, but I didn't imagine that diversity extending to the court.

"There have been some intermarriages with members of other royal courts. Lord Hauville's foremother was our own Queen Morgance, and the siren clan she belonged to lived off the coast of Faransi."

Faransi? Fair enough. Did this mean that the European royal families in this universe weren't quite as inbred?

"Um. I'm also noticing some people that don't seem quite ... human?"

"Yes. Being the capital, the people here are usually more tolerant of the supernaturals and there is an enclave of them in the city."

I frowned. "Wait. They're segregated?"

Grandfather quirked his lips in a wry smile. "That's as much for the safety of others as for theirs, Fengxun. It is not always safe to house firebreathers near those who build with straw, and a sleepwalking siren can be very dangerous to the unsuspecting."

"*Oh.*"

The carriage rolled to a stop in front of a red stone building, striking in contrast to the mostly wooden buildings around it. The sign said simply, "Xuanyuan", in golden lettering upon ebony wood. Two loosely woven cloth panels hung from the doorway, with stylized clouds embroidered in silver upon a dark blue background.

Aedrian opened the carriage door, one hand on his sword, gray eyes alert and wary.

A man stood beside the door at parade rest, dark eyes scanning the throng. Smooth skinned with no hint of stubble and pleasant features, he appeared not much older than I. His amiable expression contrasted with the way he held himself, relaxed yet coiled like a snake, ready to strike. His hunter green robe was woven of fine cotton but bore no embroidery, sashed plainly with a belt of the same color, his only ornament the bone hairpin keeping his topknot secure.

He bowed. "Lord Xuanyuan."

His eyes flickered over me, cataloging, judging. No surprise, just a calm scrutiny.

Grandfather smiled. "Lan Xin."

Lan Xin eyed Aedrian, summed him up in one glance, and turned his focus back to his employer.

"Might I assume that this maiden with you is our *shaogongzhu?*"

Shaogongzhu? That could be either little princess or lesser princess. Was that because technically my mother was the princess, even if she wasn't the heir?

My grandfather's tone was amused. "You might. I see you've kept up with news."

"It was hard to miss, Your Illustriousness."

"I'm sure."

He turned to me. "Granddaughter, this is my man of affairs. All of the people in my employ answer to him."

So kind of like his executive manager.

"Pleasure to meet you, Lan *gongzi*." I chose to use the honorific instead of calling him by his name directly the way my grandfather did.

"My honor, Your Grace." He bowed again.

Grandfather led the way in.

Aedrian entered with us, but remained at the door, turning so he wouldn't obstruct anyone coming or leaving, his sword hand still at the ready. It was surreal, the way he stayed on guard, the fact he believed his every action necessary. Then again, I knew first hand the possibility of violence.

The great room was furnished with an oval table carved from the stump of a massive tree. Four seats were set out around it, but it could easily seat six. Silk scrolls of calligraphy and watercolors of scenery hung on the walls. Bamboo blinds loosely woven to let in light but provide privacy covered the two large picture windows. The scent of sandalwood incense drifted in the air, blending with the fragrance of the jade orchid flowers in a ceramic dish on the table.

Lan Xin poured three cups of green tea. The aroma of jasmine rose with the gently curling steam.

"Shall I begin with the usual reports?"

"Yes."

"The caravans have returned from the Tea Pass and from the Silk Road. They..."

The sound of indistinct shouting came from the street.

My throat tightened and my hands shook. So much for something non-dramatic.

Stay in my seat or investigate?

Whatever helps you sleep at night, Estyria, the small voice murmured.

My gaze met Aedrian's calm one and the band around my chest loosened. If there was trouble, if someone needed help, Aedrian was here this time and there was nothing to be afraid of.

I got up and walked to the door, lifting a corner of the cloth panels so I could see out.

The noise of the street swelled in my ears and I realized the cloth must have been magicked to be at least somewhat soundproof.

A wagon piled high with carrots, cabbages, and potatoes had stopped a few feet away from the door. A man in rough blue homespun stood at the head of the ox, his bamboo hat hanging from his neck, down his back. His hair was bound back in a simple braid tied off with red string.

Three men blocked his way. The man at the forefront wore silks of red and a supercilious expression. Two men flanked him, the guards in robes of plain blue. Their hands rested on the their hilts, swords loosened.

Beady little rat eyes narrowed in condescension. "You should be grateful that someone is willing to take your wares off your hands, peasant." His voice sounded just as oily and superior as he looked.

I disliked him on sight. He looked like a bully and definitely sounded like one.

"Fifty coppers is an insult, and you know it!"

Rat-man sneered. "Those pathetic vegetables of yours are barely big enough to take note of and it's already past midday. You're unlikely to get a better price."

"Not after you have announced to the entire city that you want to buy me out with that pittance!" The farmer's voice rose to a shout.

Ratty buffed his nails on his robe front and inspected them. "It's what they're worth. Take my price or do not. If you come round later and wish to sell, it will be forty coppers."

The farmer's hands fisted at his sides as he sputtered.

I took a half-step forward before I remembered myself and stopped. My heart pounded in my ears. My hands grew cold and clammy. What did I even expect to do?

I felt another presence beside me and turned.

Grandfather stood there, his lips thinned, eyes narrowed.

Ratty took another step forward, coin in hand, and made up my mind.

I swallowed past the bitter taste of fear and looked my grandfather in the eye. If I was going to stay... If I was going to claim that I wanted to help... I was going to have to get over my fear.

"We do own restaurants, right, *A-gong*?"

Amusement lit his face. "Yes." He waggled his

brows. "Don't forget you are my scion, heir to House Xuanyuan, and a princess of the realm."

I smiled at him. If that wasn't *carte blanche*, I didn't know what was.

Aedrian grinned and tipped his head toward the drama, as if to say after you.

I stepped into the street. "What is going on here?"

Ratty flicked a glance my way and his lip curled. "None of your business, little girl. Stay clear while men conduct their business."

Little girl?

I gave him my best imperious look, the one I used on too-forward drunk men and turned to the farmer. "What is your name?"

The farmer gave me a quick once over, then his eyes dropped and he bowed his head. "Zhang Dawei, my lady."

"I hear that this man is offering you fifty coppers for your entire wagon."

"Forty now, for his insolence." Clearly Ratty just didn't know when to stop.

Zhang Dawei clenched his jaw. "Fifty coppers for a month's work of backbreaking labor hauling water from the wells, raising cover so the crops don't burn in the drought, weeding, and chasing away pests?"

"More than you deserve, peasant. Will you sell or not?"

"If I did, my children would go cold this winter."

"How much were you looking for, Zhang Dawei?"

He turned back to me. "My lady..."

Ratty sneered. "Cease your petty interference,

woman. I was here first."

"It's a free market, isn't it? He also clearly doesn't want to sell to you at that price."

"I was hoping for a silver." His words were hesitant, the look on his face showing surprise at his own daring. A silver was a hundred coppers. Twice what Ratty was offering. If that was what he considered a fair price, no wonder he was pissed.

Ratty pressed a hand to his chest, an overblown look of shock on his face. "That's tantamount to highway robbery. You see what happens when you women let your soft hearts overpower sense?"

Seriously?

I half-turned, and motioned to Lan Xin. "Lan *gongzi*, if you please."

Lan Xin moved to my side. "Yes, Your Grace."

I ignored how Ratty's jaw dropped.

Aedrian caught the farmer by the elbow before he could kneel and I slanted him a quick smile.

"Can you estimate roughly how much revenue this wagon of vegetables would fetch?"

"Yes, Your Grace." Wariness slipped through Lan Xin's eyes.

I bit back a sigh. No, I wasn't quite that naive as to ask him to broadcast it to the street. I just needed him to play along.

"Would the profit be significantly more than a silver?"

"Rather much so, Your Grace." Understanding curved his lips into a faint smile. "In fact, the numbers assure me that you could safely pay the man fifty coppers more than the silver he desires and we would still turn a profit."

"Ah. In that case." I held out my palm and waggled my fingers at Lan Xin.

Zhang Dawei stared at me, mouth slack.

The man of affairs pulled out a silver coin from his sleeve, then a string of copper coins and handed them to the farmer. "Take this to the Drunken Fragrance and unload there."

He grasped the money in his hand, disbelieving, his eyes shimmering with emotion. "Thank you, Your Grace. Thank you."

Ratty sniffed and turned on his heel. "Fools, the lot of you."

I waited until he was three steps away before raising my voice, "Zhang Dawei, have you and your brethren considered boycotting the merchants unless they paid you a fair price?"

Rat-face stopped mid-stride and spun around.

The street noise went from a low hum to an excited buzz.

"The merchants would just threaten to close their doors and let our food rot. There's always those who will sell for lower than they ought."

"If you all band together and unionize, the merchants will have to come to heel eventually." I lifted my chin and stared Ratty straight in the face as I said, "I'll provide you incentive: House Xuanyuan will buy any surplus that you do not sell at the end of the day if you promise to cooperate in this."

"What? You're crazy." Rat-face came storming

back.

Zhang Dawei's eyes were wide, searching mine as if he also thought I had a screw loose.

I shrugged. "Zhang Dawei, organize all the farmers you know. Tell them to insist on a fair price and not to sell for anything less than what will keep their families fed and clothed. Any surplus that remains will be bought by House Xuanyuan."

"That is insanity. You can't do this." Ratty's face turned bright red, a vein ticking at his temple.

Oh yeah? Watch me.

"No. What is insanity is maltreating the people who feed you and who keep our armies marching." I looked around. "This is the capitol, is it not? I don't believe you'd all rather lose the profit of shutting down for even a day or two than pay these people a fair wage. And if you do, believe me, I can and will outwait you."

"What will you even do with all that produce? Where will you store it?"

"That's hardly your concern, is it? But if you must know, I was thinking that I could organize some free food for the poor. I'm sure there are many who would be happy for a hot meal."

He growled under his breath, threw up his arms, and stomped off.

I looked at Zhang Dawei, who was standing there, a dazed expression on his face. "So, will you do it?"

CHAPTER TWENTY-FIVE

My grandfather and I were seated on the balcony that wrapped around the second level of the restaurant. Bamboo blinds gave the illusion of being separate from the rest of the dining room. The city bustled underneath, the smell and chatter drifting up on the wind.

After my fifth glance behind my shoulder and about the tenth time I shifted in my seat to see if the waitress was bringing the food yet, my grandfather put down his chopsticks. "Lord McKenna, please have a seat and join us for lunch."

"Your Illustriousness, that would be inappropriate."

He snorted. "Allowing your charge to have indigestion because of your pride would be inappropriate. I believe you are an astute enough man to notice her distress at your waiting upon us to eat."

Grandfather ignored my frantic kick at him under the table. He shifted his legs and continued, implacable. "Aside from my granddaughter's tender heart and my desire to keep her happy, we both know that your station is our equal if not better. Unless it is your consequence that would be hurt by joining us?"

A soft huff of air from behind me. "My prince charged her care to my honor, Your Illustriousness."

My grandfather tipped his head, an edged smile curving his mouth. "You do realize that I am a votary of the Vermillion Bird? Believe me when I assure you that anything short of an army is unlikely to harm her under my watch."

His tone hardened. "Do not make me order you. Unlike my granddaughter, I have no qualms about doing so. The only obstacle currently in my path is that I do not think that would lessen her dismay."

"As it pleases my princess." Aedrian moved out from behind me, taking a seat at the table with elegant poise.

"Thank you."

Silver eyes met mine, surprise in their depths. "I should thank you for your courtesy, Your Grace."

My grandfather poured a cup of tea and pushed it in his direction. "Hmph. You should both thank me for my tolerance of your youthful antics."

I rolled my eyes. "Thanks, *A-gong*. I guess."

A platter of stir-fried noodles went by, wafting steam fragrant with the scent of garlic, shitake mushrooms, and beef. I turned my head to track it, wondering at how removed we all were from the events of earlier.

To see it, you wouldn't think there was a drought

or shortage of food. Two tables away, a customer placed an order for a suckling pig and called for another four flagons of wine. Where he thought it would go I didn't know since the table was already groaning under the weight of the plates that covered it. Another table called for another round of swallow's nests and lotus seed soup.

"*A-gong?*"

He looked up from the dish of fried peanuts. "Yes?"

"About the farmers. I'm just surprised that no one has thought of unionizing before. Shouldn't there be guilds or something to protect their interests?"

He shook his head. "The artisans have guilds, but those are more in line with apprenticeships than to protect the interests of the members. The lower crafts and farmers do not have guilds at all."

"Why not?"

Grandfather spread his hands. "In part because farmers are at the very lowest rung of society and the more intelligent amongst them pin their hopes upon the imperial exams to raise them out of that echelon. Little to no thought is given to how to better their lives within that framework as most people simply want to get out. Those who remain farmers are usually illiterate and spend all of their time and energy trying to subsist."

I frowned. "What about school?"

He shook his head. "Sometimes families will hire a scholar to teach their children writing and reading in exchange for room and board and a small stipend.

However, that requires an ample harvest. One that brings in enough for the families to feed themselves, pay taxes, and have enough to keep a scholar. Of course, the drought has not been kind to the people."

Yeah, that would have been why life in dynastic China sucked. However...

"I would have thought that having magic would help."

His brows arched. "How so? The majority of the populace have no magic ability and weather working is both forbidden and beyond the abilities of the strongest mages we currently have."

I drummed my fingertips on the table. In a way it sounded like tech in my world: magical as it could be, it didn't necessarily mean a better life for those caught in the poverty trap. Especially if they were illiterate.

"Why forbidden?" Of course, being impossible made it moot anyway.

"It is the province of the dragon princes. To interlope is to go against the will of the gods. "

"Right. Weather work is forbidden. Got it." If I had my mythology correct, the dragon princes were the ones who danced in lightning and brought the rain. Not really good people to get on the bad side of, not unless you liked being served up extra crispy frizzy.

I chewed on my lower lip and ran my finger around and around the rim of the plate. "The farmers need their kids for work, so it's going to be difficult to try and encourage mandatory schooling which then makes raising overall education unlikely. Little to no upward mobility means bad things for social change."

I glared at the dish of peanuts. "When's the industrial revolution when you need it?"

"Industrial revolution?" Grandfather frowned.

I tapped my finger against my plate. "*A-gong*, do you know of any peoples who have started using self-moving machinery to supplant labor?"

His brow furrowed in perplexed thought before he shook his head. "Not that I recall, no."

Not particularly surprised, I still let out a groan. "That's right. Anything mechanical would have been more of a curiosity than anything else." Why go to the bother of inventing and perfecting machinery when you had no shortage of people to throw at problems?

Knuckling my forehead, I tried to organize my thoughts. Part of the problem was I really didn't have a good bead on what time I was in and there was no telling how closely the history here would mirror that of Earth. Having magic around, even if it wasn't widespread, probably also skewed the progression of technology.

"What are you thinking, Fengxun?"

"I'm thinking of how to set up mandatory schooling for children and how to shove this country into the industrial revolution."

The waitress set down a tureen of eggdrop chicken soup in the center of the table and ladled out three bowls, sprinkling minced scallion on the surface of each bowl before serving us.

Arching a brow, my grandfather pushed a bowl closer to me. "On your own and immediately, of course, all before lunch."

He laughed at the wounded look I shot him. "It would be easy enough to establish schools, if that's what you wish. However, you are correct in that most families would balk at sending their children to school when they need them at home. Oftentimes it is a simple matter of needing to eat."

"You could consider abolishing taxes for those families who send their children to school, with additional rewards should the children perform well," Aedrian interjected.

I set down my bowl. "Would that be sufficient?"

"It should be sufficient for your needs. The current taxation is three bushels of grain for every ten, in addition to corvée labor of two months a year for every man and woman of majority and one month a year for all citizens of age ten and above. Relief from the same should be adequate incentive." Corvée labor, or taxes taken in the form of labor, was a large part of what kept feudal societies going. It was probably also a large part of why it was so hard to get ahead.

"And whatever corvée labor lost to the lords would be compensated labor gained for the commoners."

He inclined his head. "Precisely."

"Would that be possible?"

My grandfather frowned. "I am more than happy to advance your social experiments, however, the other lords may not be as sanguine about this idea. You should realize, there are distinct castes in society, and it is one thing when the odd gentleman farmer whose genteel family has fallen on hard times succeeds at the imperial exams but quite another should you start advocating for educating the masses."

Grandfather raised a hand when I opened my mouth. "I'm not trying to dissuade you from this. It is a laudable goal and I can see the long-term benefits. However, you should be aware that all actions have consequences. This will not endear you to the other lords."

"I'm not going to let that stop me. I can't." Something occurred to me, however. "Will this adversely affect our family? To lose this income?"

A teasing glint lit his eyes. "Oh indubitably. However, we can more than afford it. You and your grandmother will simply have to content yourself with silk instead of brocade and I might need to decrease your dowry from the original hundred wagons to a paltry fifty, that's all."

"Thanks, *A-gong*." I wrinkled my nose at him. "I'm sure I'll cope with a mere fifty."

His face sobered. "Granddaughter, you must know that this is only feasible because of who you are right now. You are a candidate for the throne and you carry the mandate of a goddess. Otherwise, you must never forget that *gong gao zhen zhu*. Should you not be chosen, then you will have to be more careful about what you espouse and who you offend. Xuanyuan House can weather more than most, as evidenced by what happened with your mother, but you must not test that too much."

Gong gao zhen zhu. Glory so high it shook the throne.

I nodded. I'd read my history and watched my share of historical dramas. I knew precisely what happened to those who were so popular as to threaten the rule of the emperor.

The waitress appeared with a platter of fried rice, a clay pot of three cup chicken, and a bowl of stir-fried greens. The heady aroma of basil, garlic, and sesame oil filled the air.

"Now that we have a plan, perhaps your appetite can be tempted by something more substantial than worry?"

I nodded again, hearing the imperative couched as suggestion.

CHAPTER TWENTY-SIX

A nother day. Another session at court. Frighteningly, it was already starting to be just another thing. My stomach still roiled, but the carnivorous butterflies in my stomach had started to die off, and part of the terror was that I couldn't be sure if I was rolling with things or if I was in a protracted state of shock that would eventually wear off. And then, hysteria. Precisely what I couldn't afford, what none of us could afford.

I would have preferred to think that it was superior powers of adaptation at play, but the chained boxes in the back of my mind laughed at me.

Hauville moved forward, a predatory gleam in his eyes, and I brought my focus back to what was happening rather than what could happen.

"Imperial Highness, in light of the dire situation and the imperative needs of our people, I would like to suggest reviving the use of the Great Rites. The benefits are two-fold as it would alleviate the drought and serve as a method of further proving the candidates."

Helena leaned forward slightly, her gaze narrowing on Hauville.

Sethalor's expression froze, his body gone stone still, an aura of palpable violence radiating outward.

"Which Great Rite are you thinking of, Weiyuan-*wang*? All but one have been discontinued due to the inherent danger. The remaining one is for fertility and therefore hardly appropriate to the situation."

Hauville's lips curled, his expression avid. "The Great Rite in which the candidates make an offering to the land in blood and magic to call forth rain. According to historical texts, he who brings the most rainfall is the rightful claimant to the throne. Your Imperial Highness."

There was just a beat too long between the end of his sentence and the honorific due Seth. Was Hauville one of those who resented him for not taking the throne?

"Weiyuan-*wang*, if we are referring to the same historical texts, may I remind you that seven times out of ten the candidates were drained by the rite unto death? These have been banned for generations for very good reason." Sethalor's voice was controlled, his words even, but his rage was a living thing in the room.

"Most of those rites were conducted without the auspices of healers present. Of course, in current times we would hardly be so barbaric and unfeeling. With healers standing ready, the danger should be minimal. It is my opinion that healing the land and revealing the true candidate is well worth the risk."

Lord Lai bowed and stepped forward. "Imperial Highness, Weiyuan-*wang*'s plan has merit. I believe the rite will be successful under the watchful eyes of our healers. There can be no good reason not to pursue this solution, especially as the drought worsens."

Hauville took another step forward. "Imperial Highness, this is my daughter's welfare we are discussing. Do you believe that I would willingly cast her in harm's way?"

Judging from the cold gleam in his eyes, I wouldn't precisely put it past him.

I glanced at my fellow candidate. Helena's lips curved in a sardonic smile, her eyes glittering.

Riordan sat back in his chair, tapping his steepled fingertips together, his gaze moving from Sethalor to Helena to Hauville and back again.

"Imperial Highness. Desperate times call for desperate measures. If you are unwilling to entertain this plan when our people are starving and the land is dying of thirst, I must say I understand why the gods did not deem you worthy of the throne."

A low murmur of shock and appalled titillation spread through the room. Several lords looked askance at Hauville while others more nodded in approval.

Sethalor's hand fisted. "Enough. Do not think that you are above the charges of contempt simply because of your position as a king and contemporary of my father, Weiyuan-*wang*. I will perform the rite. Given how difficult it has been to find appropriate candidates, I will not condone placing them at any risk."

"Imperial Highness. As one refused by the gods, how valuable is your sacrifice compared to those who have been touched by celestial favor? It pains me to be so blunt, but I'm sure you'll forgive the offense when you consider the needs of our people."

Sethalor inhaled sharply, his eyes flaring molten gold. "As an imperial prince of the House currently bonded to the land and former blood heir, I warrant that my blood and magic will be more than enough to grant the land a reprieve until the rightful heir takes the throne. This is not a matter for debate. It is my will as regent and you will not gainsay me."

Hauville bowed, "As you will, Imperial Highness."

He backed into place, his smirk clearly saying, *lord it over us all you want now, but you're going down sooner or later*.

"Any other reports?"

Silence.

"Court is adjourned."

Helena stood, smoothing her skirts out, her face expressionless.

She hesitated, then turned to Sethalor. "If you need aid, Imperial Highness, you have my direction."

Sethalor bowed his head. "My thanks, Princess Helena, but I do not think it necessary. As I said to your father, it is a great risk and I will not place your health at jeopardy."

A faint smile touched her lips. She swept Riordan and I a glance, curtsied, and left.

The aural shield went up as soon as the door shut behind her.

Riordan crossed his ankle over his knee. "That was not good."

Sethalor closed his eyes and tipped his head back. "It was, in fact, a disaster."

I looked between them. "Placing all his potshots at you aside for later, is it because Riordan isn't actually god-touched?"

Riordan slanted me a mocking smile, sapphire eyes glinting. "Actually, I'm the safest one to do the rite. As the only one who isn't connected to the land by the gods, I am the least likely to be drained of all life and magic. You are the one Seth is protecting. Between the magic expended when you arrived to heal your injuries and the magic you threw out recently, you have none to spare."

He reached out a finger and brushed the tip across the mark on my forehead. "This shows you to be a favorite of the gods. It also probably means that you have a deeper connection than most to the land. Once you start giving, it will be very difficult to stop."

He flung Sethalor a cynical look. "On the other hand, if she is beloved of the gods, then they are unlikely to let her die. After all, there was that rather handy shower of rain the other day."

Sethalor opened his eyes, his pupils dilated to dark pools in glittering gold. "No. I will not risk her."

"So you're going to do the rite." His tone was

acerbic. "Might I remind you that your power levels are nowhere near replenished yourself?"

Seth tipped his head back again, a sharp laugh escaping. "Haven't you heard? I'm the most expendable. Unloved by the gods and unwanted by the land. Why not me? Might as well do something useful for once. Perhaps it'll redeem me."

I slapped my palm on his chest. "Stop that."

He flinched, his eyes opening and focusing on me.

"Riordan. How is the rite performed and how dangerous is this for him?"

"Blood and magic." He shrugged, the movement casual, but his eyes were intent on my face. "It usually involved opening a vein or two, calling power, and hoping the gods don't take your offering as an invitation to kill you."

"If I'm parsing what Lord Evil was saying correctly, others can join in, right?"

Sethalor sat up. "No. I forbid it."

I put my hand over his mouth. "So, what do your energy levels look like? What about Aedrian? Does he have power? Can I get my grandparents to help?"

He pulled my hand off his mouth. "I absolutely forbid it. Were you not paying attention when I said that there is a good likelihood of death?"

"Shut up. You don't get to always play the martyr."

His eyes widened in shocked affront, and I slapped my hand back over his open mouth. "Stop interrupting my conversation with Riordan, or I swear I'll go out, find a patch of earth, and slit my wrists to see what happens."

He yanked my hand away. "Aedrian wouldn't let you."

I narrowed my eyes at him and smacked my palm back across his mouth. "I told you, stop interrupting me. Also, how much do you wanna bet that Aedrian would be perfectly happy to let me do it if it meant keeping you safe? Don't think I've forgotten what he said about you being his first priority."

His mouth snapped shut, his lips firming under my palm as his eyes promised retribution.

Riordan tilted his head, his eyes considering. "Aedrian is not a mage, but he has power and he is bonded to Seth. I could supplement, but it will not be as potent." He slid a look at Sethalor, who looked ready to spit nails. "However, I agree with Seth that you should stay out of it. I can tell you're dangerously drained already and it would be folly to place you in a more vulnerable situation."

Sethalor relaxed under my hand.

"If you and Aedrian help, however, he won't be in any danger?"

"It shouldn't be a problem. Seth is one of the strongest mages I know and he doesn't use power lightly. He'll probably have to sacrifice his hair though."

"Really?" I couldn't keep the note of disappointment out of my voice.

Riordan shrugged. "It's why most mages keep their hair long. It's a way to store power. Hair, blood, flesh, and so forth. Hair is the most painless option."

Oh. In that case.

"How much power can I raise if I cut my hair?"

They gave me identical looks of shock and horror. "No."

Sethalor caught my wrists in an unbreakable grip and held them captive between us. "I forb..."

That line was seriously getting irritating.

I narrowed my eyes at Sethalor. "If you finish that sentence, I'll cut my hair to my chin first chance I get."

His pupils flared, his mouth firming in an angry slash. "It is unnecessary. Between Aedrian, Riordan and I, we should have more than enough power."

Riordan touched his finger to a lock of my hair, his eyes narrowing. "Frankly, considering you've never used magic before, your hair should have quite a bit of power stored in it. How much were you thinking about cutting?"

"As much as necessary. I don't think it's a good idea for any of you to be drained."

Riordan looked at Sethalor, who was giving him a death glare of betrayed affront. "I understand your feelings on this, but if she has not used her magic before coming here, her hair should hold more than enough power. Even six inches would be helpful."

Sethalor stood, his face set in lines of implacable fury, and disappeared.

"I really hate when he does that."

Riordan sighed. "Much as I appreciate your pragmatism, you are not making this easy for him."

"Huh?"

"He considers you his to protect and cherish. First you arrive half-dead. Then it turns out that you have amnesia due to nearly dying of an illness. Then the incident of yesterday. Now you are threatening to disfigure yourself as a result of him not being strong enough to keep you safe."

"Disfigure? Seriously?"

He shrugged. "A woman's hair is sacrosanct. They do not usually cut it except in times of great mourning."

"Um. He's been to my world. There are women who shave their heads there."

His eyes were serious. "Yes, but clearly you care for your hair, or you would not have left it so long. Therefore it is an affront to him that you should need to cut it on his behalf."

"I like it, but it's really not that big a deal, not compared to his safety. And it's necessary, isn't it?"

"Yes. It would be suspicious if either Aedrian or I showed signs of having aided in the rite after Seth clearly said it wouldn't be allowed."

"Do you think he's coming back?"

Riordan shrugged.

"I'm going home to breakfast then. Don't let him do anything stupid, all right?"

He huffed out a surprised laugh.

"I'm serious."

He stood and bowed, his right hand over his heart. "Yes, Princess."

I stood up and headed for the door, hoping that court wasn't always going to be that exciting. Having a boatload of drama unloaded every day before the sun was even up was really too much to ask of anyone.

And to think that I worried about it being just another Thing.

CHAPTER TWENTY-SEVEN

I sat on my bed and tried to focus on the knots in my hair instead of obsessing over what Sethalor was doing at that moment. No use. I'd stayed in the shower until my fingertips pruned and it didn't help. Ridiculous man. Ridiculous, macho, prick ass man. He acted like asking for help would kill him when it was his pride that would get him killed. My chest ached at the thought of him dead and drained. I rubbed my fist over my breastbone and took a deep breath.

"Hubristic fucker." I said the words out loud. Somehow, that made the ache easier to bear. Was hubristic even a word? Did it matter?

"Prick ass prideful fucker who should have learned better about machismo in high school or whatever the equivalent is here."

"Your concern quite warms my heart, darling."

I spun towards the door.

Sethalor stood, half in half out of the doorway.

His hair was loose around his shoulders and he wore a simple white robe instead of his usual black. His eyes gleamed gold with magic and irritation.

I shifted so my hair fell over my face and continued pulling the comb through the knots.

"I don't really care what you think so long as you don't care what I think, Seth."

The temperature in the room dropped a few degrees.

Whatever. I wasn't going to give in if he wasn't going to.

He snarled. "It won't grow as fast here. You'll have to live with it for longer than you expected."

"What won't? The hair? Why not?"

I pulled my hair over my shoulder. Wet, it was a significant weight and I coiled it up, hefting it in my hands. To be honest, I was more than happy to have an excuse to cut at least part of it off.

"You will be using your magic, therefore there will be much less power to store."

"All right." I shrugged. I liked my hair, sure, but I wasn't so terribly attached to it that I'd prefer him to suffer instead.

He stepped closer, hooked a finger around a lock of my hair, and stretched it between his hands, his gaze pensive. "I don't want you to do this."

I sighed and pulled my hair back. "Seth. It's just *hair*. Furthermore, it's my hair. It'll grow back. That's for one. For two, do you know how irritating it can be to wash and dry hair this long? It takes forever and a day just to untangle it after a shower."

His lips tightened. "Then why did you keep it so long?"

I shrugged again. "After I got sick, my mother suddenly got a bee in her bonnet about me and haircuts. She would trim my hair, but she would get really upset if I talked about chopping it off. It might be some superstition about longevity and the length of hair, but I'm not sure. She wouldn't explain."

He looked away, but not before I saw the pain and rage in his eyes.

I reached out to him. "Hey. It's all right. I'm fine now. Just missing a few pieces and maybe with some cracks, but who doesn't?"

My attempt didn't work. His muscles were rock hard under my palm, almost vibrating with tension. "And you didn't find it odd?"

"I nearly died." I kept my voice soft, willing him to understand. "I was in a coma with an unexplainable fever for two weeks and when I woke, my mother looked like she'd gone to Death's door with me. I could never forget the way she looked when she realized I was conscious and aware. If not cutting my hair would keep her happy, it was a small enough thing and I wasn't going to question her about it."

I patted his cheek, where a muscle tic was starting up. "Why? You seem to think there's something important about her request."

He shook his head. "Nothing."

Liar. He didn't look like he was in any mood to let me try and tease out the answers though.

I tried to shrug it off. "Fine. Don't tell me. So are

we good with the cutting of the hair then?"

He pulled a hank of hair over my shoulder, stroking it through his fingers. "Are you sure?"

I rolled my eyes. "Yes. It's *just hair*. I showered so it's clean and everything. Do I need to do anything else?"

A slow shake of his head, his eyes losing focus and going distant.

"Do I just cut it then?"

"No. I'll do it." He sounded distracted and abstract, his voice taking on a detached quality.

"Stand with your back to me and pass me the comb."

I passed him the comb and turned my back.

Sethalor stroked the comb through my hair, from the crown of my head to the tips, over and over, never once tugging on my scalp. His movements were slow and sure, his hands infinitely gentle on me, but his dark mood stretched the silence between us, and I found myself uncertain of more than just his thoughts. Words crowded in my mind, but not one seemed appropriate. He combed my hair until it was dry and fell in a sleek curtain.

A faint tugging sensation, then the weight pulling at my scalp diminished. Released from his hold, my hair swung forward, still longer than waist length. A hint of burnt hair's acrid smell hung in the air. Power shimmered between us, stretched like a rubber band and then dissipated with a snap that I felt down to my core.

"It is done."

I turned to face him. "That wasn't so bad, was it?"

He averted his face. "Thank you."

The words weren't so much grudging as sulky.

I bit back a laugh. "If you really want to thank me, tell me what was going on today."

His entire body tensed. His brows lowered, his mouth already halfway to forming the *nothing*.

"Don't tell me nothing. Lord Hauville clearly has some kind of vendetta against you. What's going on there?"

A tic started up in his jaw. "What is there to say? I've mentioned his ambition before."

I stood on my tiptoes and cupped his cheek. "It seems much more personal than that."

He lifted his hand to cover mine, his eyes closing. "He has ambition. Always had more than his share of it and I think his lack of success has turned him bitter. My father was born very late to my grandparents and there was a chance he could be next in line for the throne if they had no issue. From what I've heard, he was just old enough to appreciate being the heir apparent and to hate having it taken away from him. Then my father had the extreme bad taste to have his heir and two spares."

A bitter laugh escaped him. "He must have been thrilled when they were so accommodating as to get killed by assassins. When I returned after hearing the news," His voice turned jagged. "I think he was very disappointed. He must have been hoping I'd managed to get myself killed in my travels."

Tugging my hand from his grasp, I slipped my

arms around his waist and pressed my face to his chest. "I'm sorry."

Another harsh sound, but his arms wrapped around me with a tenderness at odds with the rough tone of his voice. "Of course, he was furious when it turned out the throne was still out of reach, even after it was clear I would be regent, not emperor. Yet another reason he hates me: he knows, somehow, that I threw away what he desires most in this world as if it were so much trash."

I tightened my grip, my heart shredding at the pain in his voice.

"It killed my parents, Estyria. My parents and both of my brothers, lost, all because someone didn't want them on the throne. And it cost me you. How could I love it after all it'd taken from me?"

"How could anyone blame you for not wanting it?"

"Even if no one else did, I would blame myself, now that you have been dragged into this muck because I unmanned myself with cowardice and faithlessness."

His arms dropped and he stepped back and away, fury roiling in his eyes. "I never wanted you to be touched by darkness, yet I have brought you nothing but peril and saddled you with a burden that was mine to bear. And now," he laughed, the sound wild, "you must give yet more of yourself to supplement my inabilities. Gods, what a disgrace you must find me." His mouth twisted and he disappeared.

I stared at the space he'd vacated, the jagged edges

of sorrow slicing through my chest with each breath. There were times when my very presence here felt like walking through a minefield, made worse that every step was a gamble on his pain rather than my own. Guilt, regret and the heartbreak of being the cause of his despair made carrying through my plans almost unbearable, but I couldn't walk away from this, from him, even if I knew that it was what he wanted.

CHAPTER TWENTY-EIGHT

I sank yet another arrow into the target, growling when it went wide of the bull's eye.

"It is dangerous to continue if you cannot focus, for the sake of others if not yourself," Aedrian said.

Only ingrained respect for a weapon kept me from tossing the bow aside in frustration. He tugged on the bow and I let him have it, throwing myself to the ground instead.

"How long does it usually take?"

Aedrian glanced at the sky. "As long as it takes."

I let my head fall back with a thunk, almost welcoming the jolt of pain. "I suck at waiting. I hate waiting. I don't *want* to wait."

He knelt beside me, his expression contemplative. "I've heard it said that it is harder to wait for a warrior to return than it is to be the warrior. There is some truth in that."

I fixed him with a flat look. "Better pray that a war requiring the personal attentions of those I care about doesn't happen then."

Horror slid into his eyes along with dawning realization. "You wouldn't... it wouldn't be allowed..."

"Because I've shown myself to be so very adept at doing what is expected of me?"

"The head of the country does not personally enter the battlefield."

Enjoying the debate now, I sat up. We were putting together assumptions out of broadcloth, but it wasn't like I had anything more productive to do. "Out of choice, usually, not by law. Isn't there that saying of how a true general rides with the vanguard?"

A muscle leaped at his jaw. I kept my expression bland and my gaze flat. Giving Aedrian hell instead of Seth wasn't quite sporting on top of being just a bit cruel. But I figured if I made him miserable enough, it might tip him over into working harder at stopping Seth from being stupid.

"Sethalor and your grandfather would never stand for it."

I arched a brow at him, mimicking Seth's arrogance. "If push came to shove, what makes you think I would care? Also, the only way in which they would go to war is if they were under my command. What makes you think I need to have their agreement to lead my own armies?"

Molten silver eyes narrowed. "You're deliberately taunting me. Why? What do you want of me?"

"I'm not yanking your chain." I totally was.

I nearly lost the straight face at the look of disbelief he shot me.

"Let me rephrase. What would appease you right now?"

Stung at his tone, I pouted. "You're making me sound like a trial. Careful. You might hurt my feelings."

"Oddly enough, I have significantly less fear of that than I usually would."

Now that did bruise my feelings, even if I knew I deserved it for rattling his cage. It was almost a relief, however. If he didn't care if I cried, then there was no need for me to restrain myself on his account. I just didn't want to saddle him with a weeping woman on top of his worry for Seth.

The stranglehold I had on my frustration and fear crumbled.

Tears stung my eyes and overflowed, a sob rising in my throat. What if Seth were lying somewhere, bleeding out, eyes dulled by the proximity of death? What if an assassin found him in his weakened state and took advantage? What if he was too weak to return and *that* was what ended up killing him?

Aedrian flinched. "Hells. No need for that. Didn't I already ask you what would make you happy?"

"I want to know he's safe. You know where he is, don't you?"

His eyes darkened. "He left explicit orders that I wasn't to let you interfere. And I *don't* know where he went. He did take Riordan with him and I trust Riordan to keep him alive."

Not safe. Alive.

I blinked again, more tears welling up. What if he

needed help and wanted us, but had no way of letting us know? Yunya didn't know the last time I checked and she said he wasn't responding to his mirror.

"Oh hells." He swiped a hand over his face. "I'm going to *kill* him if he tries to string me up for this. I'll take you to his residence and we'll wait for him there. Just. Stop crying."

I looked at the incense clock for the umpteenth time. The stick of incense was perhaps one millimeter shorter than when I last checked. Giving into the itchiness, I started swinging my feet under the table, the only way of fidgeting I had that wouldn't alert Aedrian.

He stood at the window, white-knuckled fists at his side, the set of his shoulders getting progressively stonier as time dragged on.

I'd stopped teasing him shortly after he brought me to the palace, when I realized the banter was doing nothing to alleviate the tension for either of us and was in fact likely to start something that would end poorly for everyone concerned.

There was the faint pop of air being displaced before Riordan and Sethalor appeared, the regent's arm slung over the blond's shoulders, his body limp in his grasp.

I jumped up, my heart stuttering.

"Seth!" Aedrian made an aborted move forward, as if to grab him.

Riordan dumped him on the bed with a faint sound of disgust and swept me a weary look. "There you go, Princess. I've brought him back, alive." He snorted. "Barely and no thanks to him."

The Aierlan lord pulled back Seth's sleeves, revealing his forearms, wrapped in blood-stained bandages. More red blossomed with each breath he took. "He refused to have a healer present. I did what I could, but I'm a killer by nature and fixing things isn't exactly my forte."

"Hells," Aedrian breathed out.

Two lines of crimson ran down his arms. My blood chilled at the sight. "Gods. Down the street and not across the road. Goddammit, Seth, you could have bled out."

I ignored the looks of startled confusion the other two men gave me. "So what now? We just wait for it to magically stop bleeding on its own? Shouldn't we find a healer?"

Inky lashes fluttered at that last. "No. No healer." The breathy words were barely out of his mouth before his eyes closed again.

"What? *Why*, you bastard?"

No response. I fought the urge to slap him until he woke up and made sense.

"You're a water mage, Princess. That means you can heal, theoretically."

My head snapped up and around. "How?"

Riordan shrugged. "Blood is liquid, is it not?"

Good point.

Reaching out, I curled my fingers around Seth's

hands, suppressing the jolt of fear at how cold he was. More than half a human's body was water. I could work with that.

I unspooled power from my core, wincing a bit at the pang of reminder that I'd overdone it and sent it into his body. Ignoring the twinges, I grabbed strands of the blood seeping through the bandages and wove them into a net, knitting the edges of his wounds together. It was slow, painstaking work made more difficult that I had to keep my metaphysical hand on the net as I went to keep it intact and in place.

Blood red stars danced behind my eyelids, another warning I'd be laid out like him if I wasn't careful.

"Stop."

I opened my eyes, startled by the inhuman growl running under the command.

Aedrian reached out and untangled my hands from Seth's before he lifted me up and away from the bed.

"Let it go." He shook me lightly. "Your body cannot endure this much abuse."

Blinking away the dizziness, I managed a slight shake of my head. "No. I'm not done yet."

"You cannot continue or you will burn out."

Magical burnout would leave me weakened and without magic, but...

Hooking the chair with his foot, he dragged it further from the bed and set me on it. "You can continue if you can walk to him," he snarled.

Challenge accepted. I braced my feet against the

ground and stood. Or tried to. The ground rushed up at me and all I could manage was to thrust out my hands to break my fall. Aedrian caught me before I face planted and put me back on the chair.

Riordan snorted. "No wonder you're bonded to each other. All three of you, one more suicidal than the last and only God's grace and your bondeds' efforts keeping you alive. The gods knew what they were doing when they tied you together. You'd never survive elsewise."

Aedrian snarled at him, a low wordless sound of rage.

The blond narrowed his eyes at him. "Don't think I don't know that you nearly killed yourself to bring Seth back the last time and now she's trying the same. If you don't want an early death for one or all of you, you might want to make it clear to our dear Seth over there that he won't be able to kill himself unless he kills you both first. And if he's not trying to kill himself, then you should remind him that weakening the two of you to save his ass only means that all three of you are placed in more danger."

He pivoted on his heel and stalked toward the door. "I'm going to go wash this blood off. I'll see you tomorrow at court. You all, *try* to be sensible and get some rest."

CHAPTER TWENTY-NINE

ilence suffocated the room after Riordan left.
Aedrian stalked the perimeter of the room, silent as a wraith, fury building until it was a living presence swirling around him.

I sat in my chair, holding the cup of sweetened lemon water he'd shoved in my hand and fought the urge to curl up in a fetal position and rock until the sick feeling in my stomach went away.

Was Riordan's guess right? Did Seth have a death wish?

"Phoenix. What are you doing here?"

Sethalor.

I turned to face him. His face was ashen and his lips bloodless. Worry clutched at my chest at how clear his veins showed against the paleness, the way his bones pressed stark against his skin. Anger rose along with the worry, simmering slowly in my veins.

I shoved my cup of tea at him. It was more than half honey and nauseating. It was also probably the best option we had at the moment since the ubiquitous post-blood-donation orange juice wasn't available.

He stared blankly at the cup in his hands.

"Drink that. Now. I'm going to get you something and you're going to eat it. Then we're going to talk."

Wariness slid across his face before he smiled, soft and devastating, the lazy look in his dazed green eyes adding the perfect note of sensual vulnerability. "It's lovely to see you as well, darling."

I narrowed my eyes. "I'm glad that's the case, since apparently you've been doing your best to be unable to see anyone else again."

Something dark slipped across his eyes, but his smile didn't falter. "I would never, my heart. How could I bear to leave you?"

"Drink, Seth, or I'll have Aedrian pour it down your throat."

He drained the cup and handed it back to me. "You sound angry, dearling."

"That would be because I *am* angry, *darling*." I slammed the cup down on the table, refilled it and thrust it at him. "What were you thinking, pushing yourself like that, refusing a healer and then teleporting yourself around as if you weren't already drained?"

"I don't trust the healers in the palace, Estyria. I judged the risk to outweigh the potential benefits."

I didn't flinch at the coldness of his tone. Rage filled my veins, more than a match for whatever he could throw at me.

"Don't your healers have some sort of code that says harm not? Also, why the hell do you retain healers who you don't trust?"

"No code speaks quite as volubly as lucre, pet."

"You could have called for Morgan," Aedrian interjected in a cutting tone.

Seth arched a brow. "I should think that Morgan has better things to do than be dragged halfway across the world into my mess. Besides, there was no earthly way he could have made it here before the rite."

"You were perfectly willing to pull Riordan into it," Aedrian's voice grew lower and colder.

"Yes, because he is the best at what he does. He sees patterns and clues where we do not. We could not keep her safe without his help," Seth snapped back.

"Wait." I raised my hand. "Do you mean to say that there's actually someone else Seth trusts who also happens to be a healer?"

"Where we do not? We haven't been *looking*. Why not be truthful, Seth and admit you haven't kept your house clean, not because of lack of ability, but because you didn't care before she appeared." Aedrian sounded like he was on the verge of violence.

Seth's mouth tightened.

I looked between the men, at the truth in Seth's silence and Aedrian's rage and my own anger cooled to a searing chill.

"Seth." Grief for them weighed so heavily upon my chest I had to force breath in and the words out.

He looked at me, his mouth impatient.

"If you have no healers that you can trust, have

you ever considered what that means?"

"What does it mean, darling?" he asked, his voice silky.

I looked down at my hands and slowly closed them into fists against the pain spreading through me. "I think you don't care if you're hurt, but do you also value Aedrian's life so little? And Riordan's? And you say you care for me, but clearly not enough if you're willing to hurt me like this."

"I think you should explain yourself," he clipped out the words, his voice icy.

Meeting his gaze squarely, I swallowed hard. "Today, what if assassins tried to kill you while you were weakened? You were clearly in no position to help Riordan. If he came halfway across the world to help you when you called, I can't see him just letting them kill you and I can't see them letting him go. Isn't it possible that he could have died trying to defend you?"

His eyes flared wide before his lashes dropped, hiding his emotions from me.

I pushed on, forcing my words into the charged silence. "If you don't have a healer you trust, what happens when Aedrian gets sick or hurt? Who do you trust with *his* life?"

Aedrian made a low sound, as if to stop me from continuing. I shook my head at him.

"Riordan said today that Aedrian nearly killed himself trying to save you last time. Clearly he loves you a great deal, perhaps more than his own life. What do you think would happen if you died?"

Sethalor's jaw clenched and he looked away, his hands slowly fisting in his lap.

"And me. Don't you think it would hurt me if you died? Especially if you died because you were trying to save me from pain?"

I stood up and walked toward the door, blinking away the tears. The man was driving me crazy. I couldn't bear to look at him, to see how he'd pushed himself so close to death, to see how he was going to insist on pushing, even if it might mean his life.

CHAPTER THIRTY

Twining my fingers together, I bit down on my tongue and kept my eyes forward. It took effort not to jump up and demand that Seth end court and return immediately to bed. It got harder and harder to remember why that would be a bad idea as his pallor went from ashen to translucent and his words came slower and softer throughout the morning.

"Report."

A lord stood forward, beady eyes feverish, mustache quivering. "The peasants are uprising, Imperial Highness. You must send your men to quell them and teach them not to try and rise above their betters."

Sethalor tapped his fingers against his knee. "What is this uprising of which you speak?"

"The farmers! They are refusing to sell to us, saying that they would rather the food rot. It's unconscionable!"

I blinked and sat up straighter, focusing on

something other than Seth's complexion for the first time that morning.

Wait, were they talking about what I'd started with Zhang Dawei?

"Unconscionable?"

Clearly taking Sethalor's tone as encouragement, his voice rose. "They are peasants. They should be grateful that we don't just take our just rights from them in exchange for what we do for them. How dare they try to raise their profits at our expense?"

"What we do for them," Sethalor paused, "and what exactly do we do for them, Lord Guo, that they should be grateful for?"

"Imperial Highness!" Lord Guo's eyes widened in consternation, his mouth flapping soundlessly for a few moments before he rallied. "We protect them from the barbarians without and from brigands within. We build bridges and pave roads for their use, without which they couldn't even bring their paltry offerings to market. We allow them the use of our land on more than generous terms. Everything that they have is due to our benevolence. What *don't* they owe to us?"

"You said uprising, Lord Guo. What, aside from raising the prices on their wares are the peasants doing to warrant this accusation?"

"What is it if not treasonous for peasants to raise arms towards us? They have piled all their produce into the center of the market square and have men surrounding it with pitchforks. In the capitol, no less! None may approach but their own men and then they dole out their vegetables as if they were the Queen Mother's own faery peaches. If anyone tries to get near, they brandish their sticks and hoes and enact violence upon their betters."

"If anyone tries to get near? What have you attempted, Lord Guo?"

"Nothing at all. I just had one of my men escort my housekeeper to the market to confront them about their unsavory market practices. Who knew they would resort to violence when all my man did was try to persuade them that they should make an exception for the nobles out of loyalty to the ruling class?"

Persuade? I chewed over the word in my mind. Lovely euphemism, that. I wondered if they called stealing re-appropriation?

"Imperial Highness, you simply must put an end to this before they get a taste of power and decide that they can get more if they put their minds to it."

"And what would you suggest, Lord Guo?"

"Send in the army to put them down once and for all, of course. There can be no other alternative."

"Is that so? Candidates, what are your thoughts on this matter?"

"Imperial Highness! This matter hardly necessitates the consideration of our august candidates. It is but a simple matter. One of brute force to be sure, but simple in execution."

"If that is true, then this should be a simple matter of getting their agreement before proceeding."

Lord Guo opened his mouth, closed it, and

subsided with a scowl.

"I agree with Lord Guo that troops should be sent out. The people should be protected from the coercion of their betters." Riordan spat the last word, derision clear in his tone.

Lord Guo initially perked up at the first part of his sentence, then the words sank in and his cheeks went ruddy.

Sethalor turned his gaze upon me, a mocking smile tipping his mouth. "And you?"

I tilted my head, "I would suggest that restitution be made if Lord Guo's men has harmed anyone."

"What?" Lord Guo's eyes bugged out and he looked about ready to keel over with apoplectic rage.

"If your men has harmed any of them, then they might have effectively ruined their ability to work. Depending on what kind of crops they have and if they have someone else who can take over their work for them, this could be disastrous for them. Restitution should be made in that case."

Lord Guo lost what was left of his composure. "Nothing would have happened if they hadn't gotten this thrice bedamned notion in their head that they could hold their wares hostage. They deserved whatever they got and more. You and that foreign lord may be sentimental fools, but surely Weiyuan-wang's get will know better than to let the common masses climb atop our heads."

There was a curious glint in Helena Hauville's eyes as she shook her head slowly. "I have nothing to add."

Take that, you worm.

Lord Guo's mouth dropped open, his look of betrayed horror almost comical.

Hauville moved, a squaring of the shoulders, a barely perceptible shake of the head. Striking green eyes identical to that of Helena's stared at her with undisguised disapproval, his mouth turned down in distaste.

"I'm afraid that I'll have to turn down your request, Lord Gao. As you can see, your methods have not found favor here."

"You can't just let them run amok like this!"

Sethalor shifted lazily, a sardonic edge to his words. "I can't?"

Only just now realizing that he might have made a misstep, Lord Guo shook his head frantically. "I meant, we can't just let them carry on like this without doing something, Imperial Highness."

"Oh, in that we are in accord. The will of the candidates will be carried out. I trust that should be sufficient action. Or do you wish to challenge their will?"

"Not at all." Lord Guo bowed deep and stepped back in line, but not before turning a venomous look on us.

Hauville stepped forward. "Imperial Highness. Is it truly wise to allow the commoners to display their contempt thus and ride upon our heads? Mercy is one thing, but to encourage thoughts of insurgence would only make the court and throne appear weak. I understand that you feel your guilt heavily, but you must not succumb to intemperance as a result."

I stared at him. Would it kill him to let *one* court session pass without bringing that up?

Sethalor moved his shoulders. "Candidates, what say you to this assertion?"

Helena stared straight at her father. "The wares of the people are theirs to do as they will or not. I do not see how allowing them their freemen rights would constitute encouraging them to revolt."

I shrugged. "It appears to me, in fact, that permitting them to do as they can to feed their families will keep them from outright mutiny. A man who cannot protect his family and loved ones is a desperate man. I would rather not face such a man across a blade."

"The princesses have said it well. It is our right and our privilege to protect those under our care. Those in power who do not remember that are liable to end under the blade via revolution," Riordan added.

Hauville's face paled, spots of color rising in his cheeks. He jerked his head once, his expression stony, and stepped back into formation.

"Is there anything else to report?"

The lords looked at each other, then a ripple of head shaking went through the ranks.

CHAPTER THIRTY-ONE

I stopped outside my grandmother's study and stared out over the gardens for a long moment. A light rain fell, slow and steady, wreathing the grounds in mist. Perhaps the gentle drizzle was a blessing as a downpour would create more problems than it solved. Perhaps it was because Seth's sacrifice wasn't enough. With the gods, who knew?

The wet air irritated the back of my nose and throat and I sneezed.

"If you want to stare out at the wet, might I remind you that the study has very lovely windows?" Aedrian said dryly.

Making a face at him, I knocked on the door of my grandmother's study. "*A-mah*, it's me."

"Come in." There was a note of surprise in my grandmother's voice, but no irritation.

I walked in and shut the door. This was one conversation I didn't want Aedrian to be present for.

Grandmother sat behind her desk, mirror in one

hand, red-inked brush in the other and piles of scrolls scattered in front of her.

"Are you busy?"

She chuckled. "Not with anything more important than you. There is always more work."

I settled into the papasan chair opposite her desk, pulling my legs up and wrapping my arms around my knees.

Her expression froze before a wry smile touched her mouth. "Your mother used to sit there, in that exact same position." Sorrow flickered across her eyes. "And that was the same expression she had when she spoke to me of leaving."

I blinked, resisting the urge to pull out my mirror. "Um."

"So tell me" -- she folded her hands and gave me a knowing look -- "did you come to talk about the prince, the guard, or both?"

"Neither, actually. Why does everyone want to talk to me about the guys?"

Her eyebrows arched. "Ah, not what you wanted to talk about? That's somewhat surprising. I would have thought them quicker on their feet and I thought you were more curious than that."

"It isn't as if I haven't had other things to think about. More important, politics-type stuff."

Also hello, trying not to fail the Bechdel test here.

She cocked her head. "More important than who you've chosen to bind yourself to? You have odd priorities, granddaughter. Important as the throne, the politics of court and your ideas of reform are, do not forget what they say. Correct the mind and heart, cultivate the self, order the home, rule the state, bring peace to the land. There's a reason for that order, after all. How can you truly bring about harmony to the country when your mind is uneasy and your house in disarray?"

I ducked her piercing gaze, settling my focus on my fingers.

She sighed. "If you didn't come to talk about that, what's on your mind?"

"I wanted to know what would happen to Sethalor after someone new takes the throne." Drat. We were still talking about a guy. So much for the Bechdel test.

"In what way?"

"What sort of position, if any, he'd hold with the court. Does he have any estates elsewhere. Stuff like that."

She folded her hands, her eyes pensive. "House Qiandai probably does have some ancestral estates that are not entailed to the throne. However, why do you ask? I assumed that no matter the result, the imperial prince would remain with you."

A short laugh escaped. "Quite the opposite. No matter what happens, I do not think Seth will remain in the picture."

"Is that by your choice or his?"

"With how much he hates the throne, I don't think he'd want to stick around. But, given my druthers, I don't want him anywhere near this mess. I don't trust him not to play the martyr and break hearts in the process."

"Tch." She shook her head, pinning me with a sharp look. "Speaking of the imperial prince, you're starting to sound far too much like him. Don't make decisions for anyone other than yourself. Rather than planning his exit strategy for him, why not ask him what he has in mind?"

Ah yes, that would be the reasonable, *rational* thing to do, wouldn't it?

"Ah, Fengxun," she sighed. "I was hoping you would face your fears and take the lead in moving beyond the past to see the possibilities of what could be. You may have been deeply disappointed by someone you loved, but that doesn't mean you should stop loving."

"Have I disappointed you?" I asked softly.

"No, granddaughter. I do not believe you are capable of disappointing us. Any of us. I simply wish things were different."

"I doubt it," I let out a bitter laugh. "I think I disappoint one of the guys at least once a day. I'm glad that you don't think so though."

"Fengxun. I have not pried, because it is your choice to confide in us or not. However, I will remind you that it is unfair to color your perceptions of those who care for you based on previous betrayals from others."

I bit my lip. "What do you mean? Did they say something?"

"I am a mind mage, child. Even if the imperial prince hadn't mentioned something, which he hasn't, it is more than obvious to me. I wouldn't have said anything, except it is clear you are deliberately being obtuse in an effort not to see. And I would not gainsay you if you made a conscious decision to deny them, but I don't wish you to miss this chance at happiness because of something so base as fear."

Frustration flared. "What shape and form does this happiness you see take? Do you also subscribe to Riordan's ridiculous claims that I can simply open my hand and men will fall into it like ripe fruit? Besides, we're not talking about petty backstabbing or malicious gossip. We're talking about people I knew for years, who I loved and who I thought loved me, not only dumping me, but dragging me and my reputation through the mud."

Instead of taking offense at my snippy tone, she laughed. "Oh, nothing quite so simple as that, I'm afraid. Falling into your hand like ripe fruit? I think not. As for your former friends... Fengxun, don't destroy your life when they failed to."

"Then what *do* you see?"

She shook her head. "I see a man who is willing to lay down his life to further your dreams and another man whose soul is drawn to and warmed by the fire of your spirit. As a woman, it would be an extravagant misuse to give that up simply because you didn't want to put forth the effort of taming their love to your hand. As a ruler, it shows a distinct lack of skills in husbandry. I cannot condone the waste either way."

Lack of skills in husbandry. I almost laughed. Brilliant word choice there.

"How do you save someone who doesn't want to

be saved? How do you protect someone from himself?"

The glance she slanted me was filled with wry humor. "You mean like yourself? I've never seen a child quite so adept at attracting trouble."

"You know that's not what I mean and it's not the same at all."

All humor disappeared from her face. "Maybe not in degree, little phoenix. But it is the same in principle. What binds you to care for yourself? So far as I've observed, it isn't fear of personal pain but your distaste for the worry of others that concerns you. Ultimately, his emotions are an easy enough tether. I don't believe that he will engage in further self-destructive behavior if you make it clear that any pain visited upon him wounds you."

I looked away.

"I suppose, first he needs to persuade you that his heart is true. I cannot imagine what other proof you need, but that is between you and him."

"Can I truly trust the gift of a life unvalued by its owner? Death is simple enough, but it takes far more courage to live for someone, to carry the weight of their dreams and the burden of their disappointments."

She stared at me a moment before responding, her tone gentle but unyielding. "It seems somewhat cruel to castigate a man who feels that the world is better served by his death than anything else he might do rather than persuading him otherwise."

My breath solidified in my chest and hardened

into a painful lump.

"What can I do that Aedrian hasn't already? It seems the height of arrogance to assume that I can change anything when all of his devotion clearly hasn't made a dent."

"How do you know it hasn't made a dent?" -- she paused -- "and Fengxun, something you need to remember is that you are an individual unlike any other. Lord McKenna's status in Seth's life doesn't preclude yours."

"Not you too. Bad enough that Riordan is talking about it, but surely you're not also telling me that it's a good idea to get involved in that snarl of drama."

Her shoulders lifted and fell in an elegant shrug, somehow managing to convey both resignation and humor. "Why are you so opposed to the idea?"

"It's ..." I threw my hands up. "It's just not done."

Her brows arched, amusement dancing in her eyes. "Careful, child, you're starting to sound like something hidebound and on the verge of ossifying. It may not be done where you grew up, but I can assure that it very much is done here."

"*You* don't have a harem."

"Ah, yes, and of course you structure all your major life decisions according to what others have done. That is the granddaughter I have come to know."

"Sarcasm isn't helpful, Grandmama."

"Neither is denial, Granddaughter." Her tone was similarly acerbic. "You didn't come here just so I could pat you on your head and tell you that you were making the right decision by hiding, did you?"

My mouth tightened. "No."

"And who are you truly asking these questions for?"

Blood drained so fast from my face the tip of my nose went numb.

"But we don't need to talk about that right now if you don't want to. Think on it, however. As for your men, it would be unfortunate if you had an insurmountable attachment to the concept of monogamy, especially in the path you have chosen. If you take the throne, which is well within the realm of possibility, then you will likely be pressured to take more than one consort. Peace treaties are commonly sealed with marriage and you would be the most likely candidate as there would be no one else of the ruling house available."

"You mean I can't import my siblings and draft them into service?" When all else fails, take refuge in sarcasm.

"Assuming your siblings were willing to live here, you'd know the answer to that better than I would. I suppose you could adopt some more relatives, however. Other rulers have done so in the past."

"It wouldn't go well, no. I know that." My siblings would kill me first if I even dared mentioning marrying them off for political gain. Then they'd get around to strangling me for even contemplating the idea of marrying without love. That's if they didn't laugh themselves silly at the idea of me and a harem.

"Setting politics aside, you've seen how the Great

Rite affected the imperial prince. House Xuanyuan might have sufficient reserves to carry the country through this drought, but should you drain that cache, you or later generations will have that much less to fall back upon in the future. As far as I'm concerned, there are many reasons to accept them and none not to."

I looked heavenward. "There's something very wrong with my life if my grandmother is telling me that she can't see anything wrong in my engaging in a threesome and is in fact encouraging it."

"Think about it, Fengxun. Really think about it. Don't just react to the past and your fear or you would be doing yourself and them a disservice."

A knock came at the door.

"Your Illustriousness, a missive has arrived from Princess Helena for Her Grace."

I rose from my seat with alacrity, ignoring the sardonic look my grandmother sent me.

"Think about it." Her voice followed me out the door.

CHAPTER THIRTY-TWO

Helena Hauville and I sat in a stone gazebo set amid a thicket of roses on Lord Hauville's estate. Unlike my grandparent's home, the grounds here reflected a more European aesthetic. A stone manor stood in the center of the grounds, surrounded by verdant lawns and groves of fruit trees placed so as to evoke a bucolic paradise.

Helena inclined her head. "Thank you for coming, Phoenix Princess. I didn't think you would."

She poured a cup of tea redolent with bergamot and passed it to me, every movement elegant and graceful as if scripted. Perhaps they had been. My mother had tried to enroll us in tea ceremony classes, but I'd retained very little of it.

"Why not?" I took a sip of the Earl Grey.

Emerald eyes gleamed with humor. She flicked a glance behind me where Aedrian stood guard and the curve of her mouth deepened. "I didn't think any who cared for you would have been in support of the idea."

"They weren't."

"I suspected as much, judging from the murderous look Lord McKenna wears" -- she paused, a glint crossing her eyes -- "and I expect the imperial prince would have some strongly worded opinions about this as well."

She chuckled at the quick flare of my eyes I couldn't quite tamp down in time. "All know that Lord McKenna is the imperial prince's right hand and bows his proud head to no other. That he should guard you speaks volumes of the prince's regard for you. I can't imagine he'd take kindly to you braving the tiger's den. Why did you come, Princess? We are rivals, after all."

The gathering edge of Aedrian's anger and distrust rose behind me, lifting the fine hairs on my nape.

"Odd question from the person who extended the invitation. I came because I was curious and because we may be rivals, but we don't need to be enemies. From what I've seen in court, we share similar ideals and that's a fairly good basis for friendship, not enmity."

A barely suppressed sigh of disgust came from behind me.

Helena looked past me and laughed, presumably at Aedrian's disgruntled look.

I tilted my head. Her laughter sounded very different from her speaking voice. It was deeper, more resonant, almost a warm baritone in timbre.

"Be at ease, warrior. I mean your princess no harm. I'll swear it upon my mother's life if that will help."

The sense of menace eased and I took a breath of relief.

Helena searched my face, her gaze intent. Long moments later, her mouth set briefly in lines of determination before she put on her smile again. "The invitation may have been sent in my name, but it is my father who issued it. I decided to waylay you when I heard you actually accepted the invitation and were standing at our front door."

Well, shit. Maybe this was a bad idea. Accepting an invitation to tea with Helena was one thing. Walking into a trap Hauville set up was quite another.

Aedrian snarled and the air thickened with the intensity of a predator waiting to strike.

My overset stomach clenched at his tacit agreement that things were going tits up fast.

"Pay attention, Princess. We have maybe five minutes before they arrive and what you do next might mean the difference between life and death to many people, not the least of whom are yourself and Lord McKenna. You cannot leave now without giving offense or tipping our hand. Nod if you understand."

I nodded.

"There is an orb that holds a choice portal floating about. I don't know anything else except that someone in my father's employ has it and will not hesitate to use it on you if they get a chance. If you see a shimmering rend in the air, run in the opposite direction if you do not wish to have your heart's choice tested. If you enter it, it will send you to the place dearest to your heart. Unfortunately, the place dearest to your heart may not be where you need or want to be.

"One other tactic that my father likes to employ is the art of seduction and aphrodisiacs. Be aware and alert. I would ask that you not refuse food or drink that he offers you lest my duplicity be revealed, but try to consume as little as possible. It is good that you have Lord McKenna with you, as your chances of escaping unscathed are much better with him present as he is known to be loyal and incorruptible."

She reached out and covered my trembling hand with hers. "Smile, Princess. You cannot let them know that you suspect anything. As for you, Lord McKenna, leash yourself before you betray your princess with your lack of control."

I forced my mouth to curve, grateful of the shock that had kept my expression frozen. The waves of rage emanating from behind me subsided and I sucked in air.

"He may have hired assassins. If I find out any more, I will send notice of some sort."

"How do you know so much yet so little?" Aedrian growled.

"For one, he doesn't trust me, especially not after my little rebellions at court. For two, even if he did trust me, he cannot let me know of any wrongdoing or I would be honor bound to report him. If I do not, I will lose the gods' approval, thus subverting all he is working for. Right now all I have are snippets I've overheard, insufficient to try and judge him."

"What made you decide to tell us this? You clearly

fear what he might do if you opposed him openly," I asked.

Her smile took on a vicious edge. "I had to make sure you were worth saving, first. He had my mother imprisoned and held hostage against my good behavior. I hope you'll understand if I temporarily placed my mother's safety at a higher priority than yours."

"Held hostage? Can we do anything? Can Seth do anything?"

Aedrian let loose a low growl of frustration.

Helena's eyes warmed and she squeezed my hand. "Thank you for asking, but there's nothing you can do. I don't know where he's keeping her and I only know she's alive because he allows her to mirror me every night. The regent can do nothing, as a man has the right to keep his wife by him. Unless I can expose him for the traitor he is, there is no case to be made against him."

"But..."

She squeezed my hand again, harder. "Hush. Smile. They come. Remember what I said about eating and drinking. This pot of tea is safe, but anything else is suspect."

Helena's gaze flickered to a point behind me and back again before she poured me another cup of tea. She gave the cup a deliberate nudge when I didn't pick it up immediately, a warning light in her eyes.

Why...

Realization dawned and I chugged it down with more haste than grace. If she was right and he planned to dose me with something, then having more liquid in my system would only help. Especially if I needed to try and throw up later.

"Phoenix Princess. What auspicious day is this that you have graced my home with your presence?"

Hauville's smooth tones came from behind me a moment before he stepped into sight, a blue-robed man shadowing him. Despite the exquisite embroidery on their clothing and the luster of the silk, it was plain they were both trying to appear approachable, as if this was a casual day at home and they just happened across us in their wanderings.

Helena rose and made a courtesy. "Father. My lord."

I followed suit, bending my neck just so, careful not to give him more of an obeisance than I needed to. "Your Illustriousness, pray do not say so. It was my pleasure to accept the invitation. You have a lovely home."

Either Hauville had put some effort into finding someone he thought I could be attracted to, or it was simply good luck. Dark brows slashed over long tilted black eyes, combining with his high cheekbones, thin lips and strong jaw for a face that was reminiscent of a raptor. In a good way, mind, but it was hardly the time to be admiring the results of his family's good breeding.

Hauville tilted his head at the other man. "Allow me to introduce Lord Hu, Your Grace. He is the son of an old family friend and hails from the Western Lands."

The other lord bowed deeply, his waist-length black braid slipping over his shoulder. "It is my inestimable honor and pleasure to meet such beauty and grace." Tall and muscular, he moved with economical grace, much the way Hauville did. It wouldn't surprise me if they were also well versed in martial arts, which put a damper on the wild idea of making a break for it.

"Do you mind if we join you, Daughter?"

Despite the smooth question, Hauville didn't wait for Helena's response before seating himself and gesturing for the other lord to do the same.

Helena's father clapped his hands. "Lord Hu has brought some wine from the Western Lands that is prized for its rarity and quality. I cannot imagine a better time to open the bottle than now, for when else will I have the pleasure of drinking with such esteemed guests?"

A servant stepped out of the shadows, bearing a glass decanter filled with a clear liquor and eggshell porcelain cups. He filled the cups, set the decanter in the center of the table and ghosted away again. The fragrance rose around us from the simple disturbance of pouring, rich and haunting, with a tempting sweetness.

Hauville raised his cup, a small smile playing around his mouth. "To old allies and new friends."

"*Ganbei.*" I lifted my cup in return salute.

Hauville drained his cup and set it down on the table with a hint of challenge.

I held my breath and followed suit. The liquor

went down smooth and sweet, with delicate notes of jasmine and pear, but heat spread through my veins almost immediately. Even if it weren't drugged, it would take little to drink myself silly on it.

Lord Hu arched his brows, a considering gleam sliding through his eyes as he nudged his empty cup forward to be refilled. "I see that you are as valiant as you are beautiful, my lady. Even in my country, some find the fire of Moonlit Spring to be overwhelming."

I could only smile. Truth be told, I'd had much worse. Most college students couldn't afford much more than paint thinner masquerading as rotgut. "Moonlit Spring? That's a lovely name."

Hauville refilled our cups and pushed them back. "I would not underestimate the lady if I were you. Her mother, Xuanyuan Yalian, was known for her oceanic capacity for drink. The previous emperor himself couldn't compete." Bitterness threaded his tone and a shade of something darker underlaid his words.

"You knew my mother?"

He tossed his drink back before replying. "Who in the court didn't? Xuanyuan Yalian, the only woman Qiandai Jin could see and the imperial family's only choice for their daughter-in-law."

Resentment simmered in his eyes, his mouth twisting. Then he blinked, the faint sneer melting away and he forced a smile. "To Xuanyuan Yalian, chosen daughter of the gods."

The second cup joined the first and embers in my blood flared to life. Heat pooled in my cheeks and the world took on a pleasant blurriness.

"But yes, your mother and I were childhood companions of Qiandai Jin. The emperor and empress thought it ill befit an imperial prince to be without peer in theory if not in practice."

"If the lady's mother was half as beautiful as she is, I'm surprised that she was lost to Tavaneth. I cannot imagine the emperor or Your Illustriousness sparing any effort to court her," Lord Hu said.

Hauville shrugged, his smile taking on a sharp edge. "I do not question the gods' choice as so many in our court do, but I have to admit that I have my own reservations regarding the suitability of women as rulers. Xuanyuan Yalian's intelligence and political acumen couldn't be denied, yet she chose exile and her professed true love over loyalty to her childhood friend and emperor."

Lord Hu shifted closer as he poured more wine into my cup. The scent of leather and steel and musk drifted around me, raising a shiver of awareness down my spine and between my legs. He remained close, his thigh and arm almost touching mine, even after he'd returned the decanter to its place.

"Then again, that particular quirk of a woman is easily remedied, is it not?" the lord asked, his smile warming to one of sensual invite.

"Indeed," Hauville murmured with a searching look at me. "*Shi zhinû*, your House and mine have known each other for generations. If your mother had stayed and married Qiandai Jin, you would be my niece in reality and not just by wishful naming. As such, I hope you'll forgive my bluntness."

Shi zhinû. Niece by virtue of generational alliances. And niece in reality? House Hauville wasn't that closely related to House Qiandai...that I knew of. Seth had said something about Hauville and the throne, but I hadn't gotten the impression that Hauville was anything so close as his uncle.

A wave of faintness washed over me and desire flared to life in my core. I gritted my teeth and tensed, remaining upright with an effort.

"Ah, well, they do say that loyal and well-meaning words prick the ear, do they not? Your treatment of Seth at court is the best example, is it not? You must truly care for him that you would so clearly state your views, regardless of how they must sound. As such, I could hardly be offended at suggestions made with my best interests at heart." I managed to finish my thought before another wave of dizziness swept through me, my tongue almost tripping over itself.

Hauville's eyes hooded and his mouth tightened. "Seth, is it? I wonder that you name the imperial prince so intimately. Beware, *shi zhinû*, that you do not fall prey to the same weakness your mother did."

"Weakness?" Who was the old goat calling weak? Anger pushed away some of the dizziness and I straightened my back. A finger of ice trailed down my spine and banished more of the heat as I realized I'd almost leaned onto the foreign lord's arm.

Arousal licked at my nerve endings, melting the ice and cooking my brain. I didn't have much time left before I'd start doing something irreparable.

"Your grandparents did your mother no favors by

allowing her contact with such an eminently unsuitable man. I have taken pains to allow my Helena no contact with any that do not pass muster so she cannot be betrayed by her heart and heat into something foolish. When she marries, it will be to someone who will benefit her and the country rather than for something so transient and foolish as love."

There was an old pain there, barely covered by the sneer. I bit down on my tongue before I made some unfortunate comment about how his being unlucky in love didn't mean it didn't work for the rest of the world.

Hauville poured me another drink. "To Tavaneth, *shi zhinû*, long may she prosper."

No option but to drink to that. Giving the pot of tea a longing look, I regretted not chugging more cups of tea when I had the chance as the liquor hit my veins and filled them with liquid fire. Good thing the decanter only held about two more rounds. On the other hand, whatever they were filling me with seemed to have an exponential effect with each additional cup.

Even Hauville was starting to look attractive, if you liked your men coldly bitter and supercilious.

Hot damn. Bad news if I had really thought, even for a moment, of licking his mouth to see if he was so cold my tongue would stick or if he would melt given the right incentive.

Gross. Eww. I was clearly losing my mind.

"The regent is fire, is he not? I thought I heard rumors the lady is a water mage. Aren't the two historically incompatible? Something about being potentially lethal for one another," Lord Hu asked.

Water. I could kill for some water. My cheeks felt sunburned, the top of my head about ready to fly off.

The foreign lord smiled at me and it took all my willpower not to lean forward and nip his mouth, just to see if I could break that look of easy amusement in his eyes.

"Tish. Don't tell her that; it'll just make him seem the more attractive," Hauville scoffed.

"But it's true, isn't it?" Helena interjected, "Fire tends to burn away water or water douses fire. Rarely can the two co-exist, since the two are lethal in their own ways. Fire can consume the flesh, but water can boil the very blood in your veins. Historically, fire mages and water mages do not mate as the results can often result in death. Even if not, the union tends to be infertile."

Everyone's attention focused on her, with varying degrees of nonplussed speechlessness.

Water. Boiling.

Her gaze caught mine, begging me to understand as her mouth curved up in a smile. "Ah, sorry. That was perhaps tactless of me. Magic holds a fascination for me and I don't always remember others do not necessarily share my preoccupation for the details."

Water. What was it about water?

Lord Hu took a sip of wine, his tongue slipping out to catch a stray drop from the corner of his mouth. I stared at the shimmer on his lips, wanting to lick it away and replace it with my scent, my mark.

"On a more promising note, isn't there that legend about how the gods-promised lovers can marry fire and water? How did the poem go? The meeting on the eve of golden wind and jade dew, their union prized above the usual matings of mortals," Helena murmured, her gaze pleading.

I blinked. That...wasn't one of the interpretations of that poem I'd learned in elementary.

Helena's mouth tightened when I didn't respond, despair flitting across her eyes and I knew that would be last of the hints I'd get from her. Any more and she'd risk discovery. Hauville was already looking at her with a very strange expression and Lord Hu looked torn between amusement and bewilderment. Damn this cloak and dagger speaking in code bullshit anyway. I'd never been particularly enamored of playing James Bond.

"Ah. The promised lovers," Hauville snorted, dark red mantling his cheekbones. "Don't speak to me of that ridiculous prophecy. It was one of the reasons that Qiandai Jin was so very reluctant to part with Xuanyuan Yalian, the promise that the successful union of a fire and water mage would usher in a prosperity the likes of which have not been seen since Queen Morgance was first brought to Tavaneth as the emperor's bride. Whoever came up with that saying should be damned to the deepest bowels of the eighteenth hell."

His rage... Water... What was I missing?

In desperation, I called up everything I could remember about water. Water. Steam, liquid, solid.

Relentless and strong enough to carve rock. Cradle of life. Can be distilled to its purest form. Carries nutrients in the body. Human body more than half water.

And it clicked.

I envisioned strands of water in my blood forming nets to catch anything undesirable, wrapping the bad stuff in water and pushing it out. My palms dampened and the dizziness receded. Unreeling a thin thread of magic to keep the process going, I smoothed my hands over my skirts and gave Hauville my sweetest smile. If the rules of guesting meant I couldn't think about leaving until the wine was gone, then we might as well get on with it.

Reaching for the decanter, I refilled everyone's cup. "To patriotism, duty and honor."

Hauville's expression flickered with wry amusement before he upended the cup and poured another round. "To Tavaneth."

"Indeed." I tipped my cup to him in salute.

A man in imperial livery approached, coming to a stop just outside the pavilion.

Hauville's eyes narrowed in scrutiny on my face, a look of bewildered dissatisfaction crossing his eyes before he snapped his fingers at the man.

"My lord, His Imperial Highness has sent a summons for the princess and an imperial carriage awaits at the doors."

Aggravation lined his mouth. "Ah, the heavy-handedness of youth and privilege," he murmured. Raising his voice, he asked, "Did His Imperial

Highness reveal the reason for his haste?"

"No, my lord, His Imperial Highness simply asked for Her Grace's presence as soon as is convenient for her."

"As His Imperial Highness demands," Hauville responded smoothly.

"It was my pleasure, my lady. I look forward to seeing you again," Lord Hu murmured.

I smiled at the foreign lord. "It was mine as well. I must thank you for sharing the wine with me."

A considering look slid through Hauville's eyes. "I will make sure it is on hand for your next visit, *shi zhinû*."

Next time? There wasn't gonna be a next time. I'd be grounded for life once my grandparents found out. As for Seth, I had no illusions regarding his knowing. There could be only one reason he was summoning me in flagrant disregard for his preference to keep my association with him on the down low.

Rising to my feet, I locked my knees until I was certain I wasn't going to waver straight into Lord Hu's arms. The foreign lord poured the last of the wine into his glass and saluted me with it, a knowing gleam in his eyes. Hauville glared at the decanter, his hand white-knuckling around his cup before he bent his head in tight acknowledgment of my courtesy.

CHAPTER THIRTY-THREE

I let my head fall back against the seat, closing my eyes against the waves of dizziness and heat. It was getting worse faster than it was getting better and the more magic I expended on trying to push the drug out of my system, the hotter my blood burned.

"You're radiating heat." Aedrian's voice came from far away. A cool hand cupped my cheek before coming to rest on my forehead. I caught hold of his wrist, holding fast when he tried to pull away.

"You're cool."

Another wave of coolness spread through me when he pressed his other palm to the side of my neck. "That's because you're burning up. The footwarmer filled with red hot coals doesn't put forth half as much heat as you're throwing off now. What possessed you to drink as much of the wine as you did, knowing that it would be drugged?"

I wrapped my hands around his wrists, soaking in the relief of his touch. "You know I had no choice according to the rules of hospitality. To refuse to drink with your host is tantamount to slapping him in public."

A menacing growl tore from his throat and made the tension in my core coil tighter, arousal burning brighter than before. Letting my head fall back to expose my neck, I tugged the hand covering my forehead down and nuzzled into his palm, drinking in his scent.

"Gods be damned. Was it in the air too?"

His voice was husky, the sentences coming in a slow drawl unlike his usual clipped words. Curses blistered the air, but his hands remained gentle on me.

"What's wrong?" I forced my eyes open.

Aedrian knelt on the floor of the carriage, eyes dilated to pools of black rimmed in silver, a faint pink tinging his cheekbones. That sensual mouth was compressed in rage, his jaw tight with restraint. I leaned forward and nipped his lower lip before I could stop myself.

Heat flared in his eyes, his mouth softening into a curve filled with devastating promise before he pushed me back with a grimace. "No. It is the aphrodisiac speaking. You were strong enough to fight it before. You must fight it now."

That's right. Not mine. No touching.

I moved away from him, grateful for the silken robes that kept friction to a minimum and curled up in the opposite corner of the carriage, hiding my face in my knees. Every breath I exhaled carried the fragrance of the wine, every inhale intoxicating me further, but I had no choice. I wanted to rub against him, nuzzle against his throat and nip his ear to see if I could break that icy exterior. If I didn't keep to my corner, I might find myself tearing his clothes off to see if he didn't have any passion to spare for someone else.

Another string of low curses turned the air blue. I allowed myself a grim smile, more than tempted to join in. If I were alone, I might have been able to find some comfort somehow, but I wasn't quite so far gone I'd slip my fingers under my skirts with Aedrian present.

Actually...

I lifted my head. "Aedrian. Would you mind giving me some privacy?"

Silver eyes narrowed at me.

Gods, I was in trouble when the way he stared at me heightened my arousal instead of dampening it. The overweening testosterone that would usually rub me the wrong way was instead stroking me in different ways. Not that those ways were giving me any comfort either.

"Look, if you want to keep my dignity and your virtue intact, you should go somewhere else for a while. Otherwise, I can't promise what I might or might not do. Got it? If it helps, I think it'd be easier to guard against incoming whatevers if you take up guard outside."

He blinked, the flush on his cheekbones darkening. "Ah, as to that, some aphrodisiacs are such that the... sensations they engender cannot be relieved without the help of a partner. If you're talking about trying to find some relief, it is entirely likely that you will only make it worse."

I stared at him, my brain about to implode from both heat and embarrassment. "Duly noted. My previous statement still stands. You should go elsewhere if you want us to be able to look each other in the eye when this is done."

Another long moment passed before he nodded and knocked on the roof of the carriage, signaling for a stop.

Throwing my arm over my eyes, I started thinking of the most libido-killing things I could. Sethalor better have a good way to deal with this when I saw him, or he'd be the next person I'd have to worry about pawing.

CHAPTER THIRTY-FOUR

I was in one of the eighteen hells. The one where they stuffed you into a steamer. Or maybe the one where they tossed you into cauldrons of boiling oil. Heat sealed my eyelids shut and parched my throat. My skin threatened to split from the pressure of my steaming blood.

"...not fair..." Those hells were reserved for highwaymen and pirates and killers of women and children. So far as I knew, I hadn't done anything to deserve this.

Someone picked me up, the sudden movement making my head spin harder in protest. Low murmurs wove in and out of my torment, the baritone and bass tones getting progressively more urgent and the words sharper.

"Drink this, Estyria." Something cold was held to my lips. I tried to open my eyes to see what it was, but couldn't. Tried to move my hands to take the cup and again couldn't, the lethargy from the heat too consuming.

"Now," Sethalor snapped.

Cool liquid touched my mouth, the moisture unsealing my lips and I drank. The water flowed down my throat, revitalizing, but at the same time desperately insufficient to quench the inferno, like raindrops evaporating the minute they hit sun-baked ground. I drank and drank and drank until the cup was tugged away.

"Don't you dare growl at me. You'll make yourself sick if you drink too much now. You can have more, later."

A wet cloth smoothed over my face and I forced my eyes open. I was sitting in Aedrian's embrace, my back resting against his chest and his hands manacling my wrists. Sethalor crouched in front of us, disheveled, eyes wild and with red marks down one cheek.

"Cat fighting, Seth? I never would have expected it of you," I forced the tease out, suppressing the panic and terror under determined humor. I must have done it, or Aedrian wouldn't be holding me down, but I had no memory of fighting with Seth.

Relief rushed from him in a long exhale and lightened his eyes. "You're aware again. Thank the gods."

Aedrian relaxed behind me, his fingers slipping away from my wrists, confirming my fears.

"What did I do, Seth?"

"You took some exception to my attempts to stop you from stripping, nothing else."

I looked down. My robes looked neat as ever. Then again, they'd already demonstrated their proficiency in putting a woman to rights from the skin out.

"I'm sorry."

That gorgeous mouth tightened. "You have nothing to apologize for, except perhaps agreeing to that invitation. No information is worth what might have happened to you."

I opened my mouth to respond when another wave of fire sped through me. Throwing my head back, I arched against Aedrian as a streak of lightning shot down my spine. I couldn't hold back the whimper as already sensitized skin became responsive to the very air, every breath they took stirring the flames higher. The ache between my legs intensified with each beat of my heart and my stomach hollowed in want.

"Godsdammit, Seth. Is there nothing you can do?" Aedrian snarled.

"Not without knowing what trice-cursed concoction she allowed them to pour down her throat. You know that the antidote can be worse than the aphrodisiac if the wrong one is taken," Seth growled back.

Despite his steady words, his hands shook as he brushed my hair back from my face. "Estyria."

Panting, I met his gaze, curling my hands into fists so I wouldn't reach for him. "I tried to flush it out with magic and it seemed to work for a while, but not anymore."

"That explains why you were dangerously dehydrated when you arrived and why your robes were soaked," he mused, wry amusement threading his voice, "and it explains Aedrian's reaction."

A low snarl rumbled from Aedrian's chest, the sound vibrating through my body and settling between my legs.

Dehydrated?

Another burst of heat flared in my core, the trickle of sweat down my temple an unbearably sensual touch. I dug my nails into my palms, using the pain to focus.

"More water, please."

Seth shook his head. "No. It hasn't been that long since you've had that drink. Your body hasn't had time to assimilate it. Besides, using your magic further could prove lethal in your current state."

Fire roared in my veins. Aedrian banded one arm around my waist and another around my chest as I convulsed against him.

"For the love of the gods, man, if she could try to wash it out, can't you burn it out?" Aedrian snapped.

"It's not that simple, Aedrian. You can't simply set fire to someone and hope for the best. You've seen what happens to fire mages when they lose control and their fire consumes them from the inside out. I cannot risk that happening to her."

"She's your bondmate, Seth. And you're no fledgling fire mage. If you're in control, your fire will not, and in fact, *cannot* burn her."

The prince cursed, low and fluid. Leaning

forward, he entwined our fingers so our palms met. "This might be... somewhat uncomfortable. Whatever you do, don't fight it. I don't know what will happen if your power rises to meet mine."

I gritted my teeth against the desire, fanned to new heights by his touch. "Can't be that much worse than this. Just do it."

Breathing out, I closed my eyes and relaxed in Aedrian's hold, tipping my head back to rest against his shoulder.

Breathe. Let the pain move through and over...

Pleasure hit like a tsunami, cutting off my thought and my mind blanked. Relief crested in its wake and I shuddered as the aftershocks swept through me. When the last of the tremors passed, I sagged against Aedrian, barely able to keep my eyes open.

"I feel like I should ask for a cigarette or something," I muttered and fell into sleep.

CHAPTER THIRTY-FIVE

I slunk into the dining room, aching all over. It simply wasn't fair. I felt like I'd had rough, no-holds-barred, wall-banging sex, but with none of the accompanying endorphins to go with it. Even worse, I had some inkling that this was the equivalent of the walk of shame since I had no delusions that my grandparents hadn't been informed of my adventures. Not that I'd actually experienced either, but I'd seen my share of movies. The saving grace to the day was that I didn't need to go to court.

"Couldn't you have said something about it being a vacation day earlier? Before I nearly had a crisis over being late?" I grumbled, grumpiness finally outweighing the awkwardness that'd been simmering between Aedrian and I. The other saving grace, of course, being that my grandparents weren't there to see me slinking around.

Aedrian glanced at me. "You should have trusted that we wouldn't have let you sleep in otherwise.

Besides, the calendar should have indicated that, if you'd only checked." He folded his arms instead of standing at ease the way he usually did, his jaw tightening. "Then again, your inability to trust has been well documented at this point."

My jaw dropped. "My what? Since when..."

He didn't wait for me to finish. "If you had trusted us, you would not have ventured into a tiger's den for mere information. If you had trusted us even a little, you would have informed us of your plans and discussed them and a viable exit strategy in case anything went wrong. If you had trusted us at all, you would have sent notice to Seth and Riordan before doing something so foolhardy. You didn't even tell me where we were going until we were en route to the Hauville residence. What am I to take from this except that you do not trust us?" Aedrian finished, the softness of his tone somehow only serving to underscore his lethal rage.

I stared at him, speechless in the face of his fury, incapable of an easy response to the pain I could hear beneath the rage. Was it true? Was it a matter of trust rather than independence?

Swallowing hard, I chafed my arms at the sudden chill snaking through my body, blindly walking away from him to the table and sinking down on the chair.

What my former friends did, that hurt, yes, but I hadn't thought I'd change the way I interacted with others as a result. I thought I was just being more careful, less naive and taking more responsibility for my own welfare instead of trusting...

I closed my eyes as the thought finished and kicked me in the chest. Instead of trusting others with myself. Bitter tears trailed down my cheeks and seeped into my mouth.

"Estyria? What's going on?" Seth asked.

Opening my eyes, I shook my head, not daring to open my mouth lest the wail hovering at the tip of my tongue exploded out. Burying my face in my hands, I allowed myself a silent scream into the fabric of my sleeves, tears dripping into my palms.

"Aedrian? What happened?"

Silence, punctuated by a long sigh.

"Aedrian?" he repeated, his tone sharpening.

I lifted my head, scrubbing at my face with my sleeves. "I'm just upset."

"Why?" His tone softened, but was no less commanding for that.

I tried to smile, but it crumpled under his stern look. "You mean I have to list them? That's going to take a while. I just... I just need a hug right now."

He stared at me, then opened his arms to me, the look in his eyes a bit lost.

Unable to stop myself, I dove into his embrace and keened out my grief and anger at being broken and not knowing it until I nearly broke someone else as well.

CHAPTER THIRTY-SIX

The low question woke me from a fitful doze. "Is the princess asleep?"

"She is exhausted from weeping and the after effects of the drug. I am surprised she even woke at all this morning."

I remained still, knowing Sethalor was knowingly lying about my being asleep but not why.

"Morgan has sent word that he will be arriving soon. Perhaps it would be best if I were reassigned when that happens," Aedrian murmured.

I froze at his words, a ridiculous sense of betrayal encasing my heart in ice tendrils that dug in with every breath I took. I'd thought that he was coming around, that maybe we could be friends.

Seth crooned low in his throat and cradled my head against his shoulder, gentle fingers stroking through my hair. "Best for whom, Aedrian?"

"I cannot keep the princess safe if she does not trust me, my prince. It may be that she will deal better with Morgan. Women seem to." There was no anger in his flat tone, just bone deep hurt and an unspoken accusation.

A low sigh brushed over the top of my head. "Just as Estyria too often forgets where she is now, you seem to neglect to take into account where she comes from. Remember, just days ago, she was used to going where her whim took her, without guard or escort. Her potentially fatal underestimation of Hauville's duplicity has little to do with how much she trusts you."

"I notice that you did not dispute her lack of trust."

"That is for her to say, Aedrian, not I. However, in all fairness, I should point out that she has only your word that you will guard her with your life. We two blooded each other and I know the value of your loyalty, but she hasn't the same bond. Not to mention, the two of you did not precisely meet under the most auspicious conditions." His voice shifted, taking on a stern edge. "She doesn't yet realize that any danger she walks into is twice as dangerous for you, but she will. I only hope that I do not lose you when that day comes."

The ice tendrils sank barbed hooks into my chest, stealing my breath.

Seth's other hand shifted from its place at my abdomen to press against my sternum, long fingers massaging away the ache enough so I could breathe.

"I cannot..." Aedrian's voice cracked, "You will not allow me to guard you and it's becoming painfully clear that I cannot keep her safe. I do not know if I can watch on if she insists on attempting to break herself against the world the way you do."

The body cradling mine tensed for the first time in the conversation.

"When you were wounded, years ago, you shattered me every time you stopped breathing, every time I thought you were lost to this life forever. Then you woke and I thought you would heal, but you never did."

"Aedrian..."

"I cannot do this. Asking me to stand by while she batters herself bloody is more than I have to give."

"It seems I have much to answer for," Seth murmured, "Estyria accused me of being careless with you and it appears that she was right. Her cavalier handling of your heart can be pardoned because she does not know, but I have no such excuse, do I? For what it's worth, I am sorry. I will endeavor to be more careful in the future, knowing that my life carries the weight of two hearts."

Two? Not three? But then, did I have the right to be hurt when I couldn't know where my heart was? I didn't even realize that I had become so cynical, that trust had become so hard.

Uncomfortable with the intimate turn of the conversation now that they weren't discussing me, I made a soft sound and shifted against Seth. When I opened my eyes and lifted my head, their expressions were bland as if they'd been talking about nothing more exciting than the weather.

Seth shook his head, the low chuckle at odds with the warning glint in his eyes when I opened my mouth.

He dropped a light kiss on the top of my head. "Did you have a nice nap, darling?"

I shook my head. A nice nap wasn't exactly what I'd call it.

"You should eat. Then we will need to talk about what you learned yesterday."

CHAPTER THIRTY-SEVEN

"Are they very upset?"

Seth led the way to the training grounds, nothing in his serene demeanor to suggest the same man who'd confessed so painfully to the weight of emotion earlier. His ability to seemingly turn his emotions on and off at will was really starting to worry me. And irritate me, if I were to be honest.

He glanced down at me, a quicksilver gleam of humor swimming through his eyes. "You mean to ask if your grandparents are angry with you."

I made a moue. "Yes. I can't imagine why else they would be at the training grounds with express orders for no one other than us to disturb them. On pain of immediate dismissal, no less." It simply wasn't like them to be so autocratic.

"Not that you don't deserve every moment of worry for the anxiety you've caused us, but no, I doubt they're so angry at you that they're taking it out on the staff."

"You didn't exactly assuage my concern there."

An elegant brow arched at me. "That's good, because I didn't intend to."

I supposed I deserved that. "If not that, then what?"

"It is extremely dangerous for anyone to disturb two fire mages when they're tossing around handfuls of fire on any given day. I have no question that an accident today is likely to be far more lethal than usual."

"Ah. Great." Always good to know that your actions caused your weapons-of-mass-destruction grandparents to lose it.

We turned a corner, past a wisteria-laden arch and into Hell. One corner of the training ground held a ring of packed earth with countless wooden stakes of varying heights driven deep into the ground, intended for balance training.

Jets of fire streamed through the air, interweaving into a beautiful and deadly net, with balls of flame flying like miniature comets through the gaps. The air shimmered from the heat, adding a surreal rainbow glimmer to everything. My grandparents moved from stake to stake, balancing on surfaces no more than three finger-lengths in width, their robes fluttering in the scorching breeze raised by their magic, barely missing each other by millimeters.

My grandmother threw her head back and curled her fingers at my grandfather in an unmistakable taunt.

In response, he lifted his hand and drew forth a

whip of flame from the air.

She leapt into the air to avoid the blow he snapped at her and pulled forth a bow of fire.

Bending over backwards as a flurry of flame arrows flew at him, he allowed them to pass over him before he flipped onto another stake. Just in time to miss the next volley.

I swallowed, hard. "It'd be nice to have that reminder right now that they're not super pissed at me."

"You're not going to get it, darling." Seth's voice carried an unmistakable edge. "Don't try to be glib about this. You need to be perfectly aware that this is what might be unleashed if you aren't more careful in the future. Your grandparents probably didn't tell you that they nearly ashed the men who attacked you, disregarding decades of circumspect behavior in their rage. Now, they are working out their fury in the only way open to them at the moment as a courtesy to you and me, seeing as it would be extremely impolitic if they went after Hauville and exacted their pound of flesh from him."

Emerald eyes narrowed to cool shards of ice as he studied me. "For that matter, it was a very near thing for me as well. Do not mistake my restraint for nonchalance. If you had been touched by another man in any way against your wishes, Hauville's residence would still be burning even now as a warning to whoever might think to attempt the same."

I blinked, fear inching along my spine. "Right. Duly noted."

"Do not only note it, Estyria. If I must take heed of what lives are seconded to mine, then you must do the same as well."

I swallowed again, all the fine hairs rising on my neck. "Got it."

He turned back to my grandparents and thrust out a hand.

Banners of flame flowed into being between his fingers and streamed toward them, twining into a dragon that spat out more fire.

My grandfather flicked his fingers at it. A lance of fire pierced through the dragon's mouth and dispelled it. Then he and my grandmother turned their attention to us and I nearly flinched back. An inferno blazed in their eyes, an almost invisible blaze rising off their skin, the look on their faces near wildness.

I fidgeted with my tea cup, fighting the urge to squirm. I was already tapping my toes within my slippers, but that wasn't quite cutting it.

My grandmother had tossed out something terse about needing to make herself presentable before grabbing my grandfather and walking off with him earlier. I'd been unable to dismiss the thought that maybe they were mad enough at me to wash their hands of me even as I knew it was insecurity talking.

The apology that had been circling my mind spilled out as soon as my grandparents joined us in the pavilion in the corner of the training grounds, the words tumbling over one another as I stared at my knotted hands, unable to meeting their gaze. "I'm really, really sorry that happened and I promise never to go off like that again without taking more backup and having an extraction strategy. Please don't be mad at me." The last sentence came out in a choked whisper.

My grandmother made a soft sound of censure and I flinched. Another snort of displeasure and she cupped my chin in her hand and tipped my face up. "Don't be ridiculous, child. Any anger I have is directed at its rightful owner, that cockroach Hauville."

A wry smile crossed her face as she brushed my bangs back from my face, her gaze lingering on the point between my brows for a moment before meeting my eyes. "It was just the battle rage, Fengxun. It is hard to cast it aside at a moment's notice. I promise you, your grandfather and I are not upset with you. We knew you were going and allowed it, thinking that he had more honor than that. We did not expect him to falsify the invitation or to intrude upon your meeting with Helena. It is as much our misjudgment as anyone's."

My eyes prickled, relief unwinding the tangle in my stomach. "All right. I'm glad you're not upset with me."

She laid a kiss on my forehead, soft and reverent, like a benediction. "One of these days, Fengxun, you will come to trust that true love does not punish and does not cease to be without more of a fight. But today, we will speak of Hauville's intent instead."

Just as I breathed out a sigh of relief, she flicked my earlobe hard enough to sting. "Do not be complacent, Grandchild. There is too much hinging upon you for you to hide much longer."

My grandfather bent to press a light kiss to the top of my head as my grandmother moved away, one large hand cupping my cheek in a tender caress. "You are our treasure, Phoenix, the pearl held safe in our hands. Never doubt that."

I blinked hard against the tears and nodded.

He seated himself next to my grandmother and pinned Sethalor with a flat look. "What do you plan to do about this, Imperial Highness?"

My blink was one of confusion. "Why is the onus to do something on *him*?"

"Because it is only at his behest that I have not called Hauville out for an affront to our House. Unless His Imperial Highness has a better notion of how our House can be made whole, we cannot let this insult stand. One does not simply allow their kinswomen to be so treated by another, especially not when you were under the protection of guesthood. His actions were tantamount to a declaration of war."

"According to Helena Hauville, we have a choice portal, possible assassins and a princess held hostage to contend with. Once we have decided how to counteract those problems, you have my permission and blessing to blast him to the deepest bowels of the eighteenth hell for what he's done," Seth murmured, his icy tone a reminder that he wasn't as calm as he appeared to be.

Grandmother shook her head. "We can do little regarding the first two options except to be more careful. Our previous concerns regarding Fengxun's guards still stand. We trust our men implicitly as they have all been with us for generations. It would be more of a security breach than help to hire more men. I have sent messages to my old friends in the greenwood milieu, but I doubt they will be able to find the assassin within our time constraints. However, they should be able to let us know where and how the princess is kept within the day."

"The question is, of course," my grandfather said, "whether we take what Helena Hauville said in good faith and liberate the princess now, trusting that there will be no ambush, or if we wait for a more auspicious time."

"A more auspicious time?" Seth's echo was soft and wry. "Aedrian, what do you think?"

"Things will, by necessity, come to a head soon. Hauville has overplayed his hand and he knows it. Attempting to drug the princess was not a terrible idea, but now that it has failed, he has limited ways to salvage the situation. Being on the defensive, it would be best if we rescued Helena's mother now, when it can serve as a distraction and potentially gain us an ally. We cannot wait on the rescue. The longer we wait, the more dangerous it is to leave our princess without our full attention as it gives Hauville more time to reclaim lost ground."

"Especially as there will likely be significant

backlash tomorrow when I publicly mention and approve your suggested reforms in court," Seth said.

"The reforms?"

"The reduction in taxes and building of schools," my grandfather said.

Oh. That. Was that only the other day?

"What? How is what our House does on our own demesne under the Crown's jurisdiction? And why would you say anything when we already know that it would be taken badly?"

"To tug upon a hair is to move the entire body, Estyria. For example, to abolish taxes for the people who live on your estate and lands seems a simple enough thing in concept, and one that is technically restricted to your demesnes, but the ramifications are far reaching. For one, what will you do with the influx of people once they hear that there is labor to be had on your lands with no taxation? How shall you deal with the other lords when they hear of this and claim you're destabilizing the country? For another, it is unlikely you will abolish taxes forever. What will you do then when your land hosts more people than it can support? As such, you must receive permission before you may do aught that will affect the stability of the country."

I bit my lip. "I see that, but why must it be publicly spoken of?"

His eyes darkened and his mouth flattened. "I am the regent, but I do not hold the Crown and thus do not have the authority to quietly grant permission for changes of this magnitude. You must make your case before the court and defend your position. Only after you have done so successfully can I give you that allowance."

"Brilliant. What else do I need to know?"

"The crown can command a higher tithe at will in certain situations, such as war or famine. This tithe can be taken in grain or labor. It is to the crown's benefit, therefore, to be sure a House can support such an act as abolishing taxes. Then there's the question of the corvée labor. A House is required to upkeep the roads and bridges in its demesnes, and that is most often accomplished via corvée labor. You will need to address those concerns as well."

"Of course, House Xuanyuan is more than capable of meeting our obligations, even should the Crown demand thrice our usual tithe," my grandmother said smugly.

"So where would the backlash come from?" I asked.

"They would likely object to your idea of educating the people, especially if you reveal that you are going to educate the girls as well."

"What? Seriously? It's not like I'm asking them to do it or taking money from them."

"They will see it as frivolous, at best and at worst, they will claim that it will foment rebellious thoughts that will weaken the country."

"Viva la revolución," I muttered.

My grandmother not-quite-successfully smothered a laugh. "I'd prefer if you didn't start fomenting *outright* rebellion, Fengxun. These old bones would much rather not fight off hordes of nobles intent on my head."

"All right. Fine. So I get to defend my position and get more people pissed at me. What else is new?" I sighed.

"If it makes you feel better, Phoenix, you can think of dismissing them from your court should you take the throne."

I slanted Seth a look. "Oh, are we planning on that now? What's that they say about chickens and counting?"

"It would be more foolhardy not to plan for you gaining the throne. You've seen Helena's mark and surely you've had at least a passing glance in the mirror. Unless much goes awry, the throne will be yours."

"Assassins, thrones and rebellion, oh my," I murmured, the urge to laugh hysterically an itch at the back of my throat and mind.

The entire situation was surreal to the extreme and I couldn't even begin to think of it being real lest I curl up in a dark corner and start rocking in a fetal position.

"The attendance at court is not simply for the candidates to be judged. It is also for the court to be judged by the candidates. The court functions as the limbs and senses of the monarch. As such, a court that the crown cannot trust is useless and must be formed anew. It is your prerogative to do some personnel changes when you take the throne. Within reason."

The urge to scream wasn't an itch anymore. It was

a howling inside my mind, a headless chicken running around spreading panic.

As if he could sense the impending meltdown, he laid his hand on the knotted tension at my nape and squeezed gently. "Breathe. One step at a time, Phoenix. We will not fail you."

Looking around the table, I didn't have the heart to ask, but what if I failed them?

CHAPTER THIRTY-EIGHT

A heavy weight landing across my body and the vibrations of a low snarl jolted me from sleep. The cat pressed down on my shoulder with one paw when I tried to sit up, its tail coming up to lie across my lips in a distinctive warning.

Ice slid down my spine as atavistic instincts sprang to life. *Sha qi*, or palpable killing intent, was something I'd always dismissed as hyperbole in *wuxia* novels until that moment when I experienced what it was to be hunted as prey. I strained to see through the dark, knowing someone else was in the room with us, cursing my need for utter darkness when I slept.

Or was it a good thing that they couldn't see clearly to kill me?

The faintest whisper of steel moving through air broke the silence and the cat leapt off me, launching itself at a mass of shadows.

Something crashed to the floor with a solid thump, then gave a strangled, high-pitched yelp.

I scrabbled to the corner of the bed and called a shield, relaxing only when I felt the familiar coolness of water surrounding me.

Ceramic shattered and a man cursed low and fluently. Two men then, at least.

"Lights," I managed to whisper the command, both dreading what I would find and needing to know what hid in the dark. Besides, hopefully it would destroy their night vision.

Two men in all black hung in mid-air, encased in a shimmering golden bubble. With similar builds and masks over the lower half of their faces, a scar across one brow was the only distinguishing feature between the two men.

Another man stood with his back to me, one fist upraised. Unlike the two assassins, he was dressed all in white, with hair of silvery platinum. The cat, now oddly a pale ghostly shimmer, prowled around the room, ears back and tail lashing.

Adrenaline-laced blood roared in my ears, my heart beating so fast I wanted to throw up. Assassins. Here. In my room. Dressed like the stereotypical ninjas. I pulled humor around me like another shield I could use, hysteria pounding at the edges of my self-control.

"I'm guessing since you don't share their fashion sense, that you aren't here to kill me."

The white-robed man turned around at that, brows arched over a narrowed gaze the same haunting blue of the cat's.

"So who are you?"

My door exploded inward and I flung up an arm in instinctive reaction before remembering my shield. I dropped my hand and stared.

Sethalor and Aedrian stood side by side, dressed in clothing similar to that worn by the assassins, weapons out and blooded. The redhead held his sword at the ready, a look of feral rage focused on the man in front of me. The man who now held the end of Sethalor's whip-sword in his bleeding hand.

I scrambled off the bed. "Don't! He was helping."

Dropping the whip, the stranger held up his arm, barring me from coming closer, his lips curling in a silent snarl at me.

I stopped short and the cat arrowed over, leaning its weight against my legs to herd me back to the bed.

"Put your shield back up, Estyria," Sethalor snapped.

Oh. Right. I wound safety around myself again.

"Saikhanaltai." Aedrian's low tone held nothing but loathing. "I thought you'd left."

The stranger sniffed and gestured at the two men before vanishing. With his disappearance, whatever held the two assassins up went with him and they crashed to the ground, unconscious. The cat leaned harder, its weight pushing me onto the bed.

My grandparents burst into the room, my grandfather in the lead, streamers of fire trailing behind them, also clad in all-black. They swept one look over the tableau and the flames winked out, relief spreading across their faces.

Disgruntlement narrowed my eyes. The boys

dressed for mischief was one thing, but my grandparents too? "What, is this dress-like-a-ninja day? I'm hurt that no one informed me. Now I feel all left out."

The cat huffed out what sounded like a laugh.

"Thank the gods you're safe. We feared the worst when the prince told us you were in danger," my grandmother breathed.

My grandfather literally sparked with rage, dark brown eyes now an incandescent gold. "I will have his head for this, I swear I will." Coming to the bed, he brushed a hand over my cheek. "I apologize for failing you, Granddaughter. Gods willing, I will not do again."

Grandfather pivoted and snapped his fingers at the assassins as he strode away. They floated up and toward the door, limp marionettes carried away by an unseen wind.

"I will go with him to interrogate the men. He is correct: this must end," my grandmother said, turning to follow her husband.

I turned my attention back to Sethalor and Aedrian. The prince was studying Aedrian while the redhead was intent on trying to glare daggers through the cat's pelt.

"All right. Who wants to fill me in on just what the fuck is going on tonight?"

My hands trembled and I sat on them, willing back the urge to throw up or cry or both. The cat shoved its head against me, eyes dark with concern. The tremors segued into full-out, teeth-chattering shakes, ice seeping into my marrow with every breath I took.

Seth's mouth tightened and he walked over to my bed and picked me up, cradling me in his arms. I wrapped my arms around his neck, both to stabilize myself and for the reassuring warmth. He strode toward the door, Aedrian and the cat falling into step behind him, but not before Aedrian sent a death-glare at the cat.

"Wha-- what are you doing? Where are we going?"

Seth looked down at me and nuzzled his nose against mine. "I'm taking you back to the palace with us. You need to sleep so you will be ready for the hyenas at court. Your rooms need cleansing and re-warding before you can use them again. We need rest and your grandparents will be occupied for a *shichen* at least. The palace will be safest and you will be able to sleep later in the morning."

"Are we teleporting?"

He shook his head. "No. I would not distress you further."

I bit my lip, the urge to remain with him battling with the desire to let him go to his rest earlier. "I don't think I can sleep. You should just go back without me so you can teleport."

"My own, that was not a suggestion. I don't know if you underestimate your importance to me or if you think I am a stronger man than I am, but there is no early way I can rest without knowing that you were safe and within reach. Not after tonight."

"Oh."

"As for not being able to sleep, I can help with that if you like."

"Could you?" I was still shivering, despite his warmth and nearness. Part of me didn't care that it was cowardly or escapist, I just needed to get away from it all, even for an hour or two. The pragmatic side of my brain whispered that I would also need all the resources I had to deal with court the next day.

He bent his head and brushed a kiss over my forehead. "Hush, my love and sleep."

The compulsion swept over me like a wave and I succumbed, gratefully.

CHAPTER THIRTY-NINE

"Estyria. Wake up."

I ignored the voice and clutched my pillow harder. Something bad awaited on that side of consciousness and I wanted no part of it.

"Estyria," Seth said, amused, "you can sleep in, but you should let Aedrian up."

Aedrian? What did Aedrian have to do with it?

Much to my dismay, the question and ensuing puzzlement pushed sleep away. I buried my face in the pillow and grumbled, "Stop talking to me while I'm sleeping. Questions wake me up."

The pillow wasn't as comfortable now that I was more aware, but it still smelled amazing. I rubbed my face against it and tightened my arms. Something hard pressed against my side. I reached down and tried to shove it away, but it didn't move. Making a sound of disgust, I pushed harder.

"That's not going away, lass," Aedrian's voice rumbled under my cheek, his tone wry.

Under my cheek? That woke me up.

Opening my eyes, I realized I was sprawled across Aedrian's chest, my leg thrown over his waist and the hard thing I was trying to shove aside was his hipbone.

I blinked, heat searing my cheeks. "What? How?"

Seth's voice came from behind me. "You wouldn't release him and you whimpered every time any one of us left the room." No longer filled with laughter, his words were limned with barely suppressed rage.

"I'm sorry." I tried to untangle myself, but the arms around my waist tightened.

A light brush over my head, then one of the arms shifted and the warmth behind me moved away, but Seth's voice was clear and level. "It's not your apology to make, Phoenix. Hauville is going to pay dearly for everything he's done, but especially for bringing nightmares into your eyes."

Oh. Unsure of how to respond, I dropped my gaze from Aedrian's inscrutable one and tried to roll off of him. His arm tightened before he lifted it and got off the bed, disappearing around a screen.

Something moved at my feet and I peeked under the covers. The cat blinked at me and yawned, slow and deliberate.

A pile of fabric dropped in front of me and I looked up at Seth.

"Get dressed, Estyria. You have a battle to fight."

I swallowed. He was right. No time to dwell on anything else right now.

CHAPTER FORTY

To my great disappointment, Hauville didn't betray himself by more than a further tightening of his jaw when he saw me. Then again, his face was already a study in leashed fury, so to expect anything else, like a maniacal monologue detailing all his plans might have been expecting things to be too easy.

He'd probably already assumed his ploy had failed when the assassins didn't return to report the happy news and then had sufficient time to relax about being hauled out in chains when it didn't happen sometime during the night.

Seth's voice rang out. "Report."

Lord Lin stepped out of formation and bowed. "Water has been found in some of the villages, Imperial Highness. More wells are being dug as we speak. However, the people seem to be growing more agitated rather than being comforted by the discovery of water as there is insufficient for all. The lords request that additional men be sent to the villages to maintain order."

I studied him. His tone was calm and his words level, but there was an undercurrent of tension.

"Of what water there is, I would suggest that equal portions be doled out to every person in the village, with special dispensation for children, nursing mothers, the sick and the elderly receiving a half portion more. If there is extra water, it should be taken to the surrounding villages with dry wells and portioned out there. No water is to be used for cleaning, washing or even farming until further notice. I would further propose that these measures be enforced with force," I said.

Lord Lin lifted his head and stared, his expression a study between relief and affront.

Lord Lai stepped forward. "Imperial Highness, I must object to the princess' suggestion. You cannot mean to keep the aristocracy on the same rations of water as the peasantry."

"Oh?" Seth murmured.

"I do not see why not, Lord Lai," Hauville drawled. "The only real lords remaining in the drought areas are the ministers appointed to office there. The others have all retreated to more congenial surroundings. Surely, magistrates given their mandate by the crown to serve *in loco parentis* to the people of their prefecture wouldn't begrudge their children equal shares of water."

What, did Hauville just find a spare conscience lying around?

The other lord slanted Hauville a look. When

Hauville only gazed back with a bland look, Lord Lin jerked his head in a nod before stepping back into formation.

"Anything else to report?"

Silence.

"Phoenix Princess, as scion of House Xuanyuan, has petitioned to abolish the taxes for her demesne for the next three harvests," Sethalor said.

The court erupted in a cascade of angry murmurs and hissed comments.

"Unless any wish to clearly lodge an objection, I will consider her motion approved."

Lord Lai stepped up. "To abolish the taxes for a demesne as large as that attached to House Xuanyuan is to threaten the very stability of our country. There is a threat of famine, which might lead to unrest, both situations which would require the additional tithe of grain and men from the major Houses. It could mean disaster should House Xuanyuan be incapable of meeting these tithes and it would be unfair to call upon the other Houses to make up the deficit due to carelessness of a new and untrained scion."

I sighed and laced my fingers together hard, using the pain to keep my tongue in check since biting my tongue was no longer an option. "House Xuanyuan has sufficient grain in its granaries to tithe the full amount needed three times over should famine or war occur." This due in some part to the whole situation involving buying up all the stuff that people refused to pay fair market price on.

It boggled my mind that some of the nobles were

refusing to pay for grain of all things when there was a drought going on, but there was no accounting for how the aristocracy thought.

"Aside from that, we have sufficient coin in our coffers to purchase the grain needed for the tithes elsewhere should it become necessary. As for the draft in case of unrest, it will be made clear to the men of my demesne that their services shall be conscripted and they shall be paid for their efforts and time. House Xuanyuan is also fully able to pay for mercenaries to fulfill our quota should that become imperative."

Eat on that. We have enough money to buy you all.

Lord Lai took another step forward, his face gone puce. "Imperial Highness, this cannot be allowed. House Xuanyuan is clearly undertaking policies that would undermine its stability and thus threatening the security of the country."

It took superhuman effort not to roll my eyes. "On the contrary. I'm attempting to bring my fiefdom into the modern era. Lifting the taxes temporarily will allow my tenants leeway to send their children to school. It is only to my advantage that my people be properly educated."

"That would be a criminal waste of effort and resources. Those who are intelligent enough to rise above their station do so and there is no use in trying to forcibly enlighten the masses. They are who they are because by their nature they are not suited to higher thought of philosophy and law. To educate them is only to breed resentment and dissent because they will have thoughts above their position that they cannot achieve," Hauville interjected.

I stared at him. "I disagree. It is true that there will be those more or less suited to advanced learning, but I believe that all can benefit from the rudiments of reading and writing. The people also need to know they have recourse within the law so they may have some agency when their rights are trampled upon. I believe all of this is imperative."

And just when I thought he had found a conscience and might be trying to nurture it.

A disbelieving laugh from Lord Lai. "All? Surely you don't mean all. Next you'll have us believing you intend to educate the girls as well."

Rage flared and I swallowed it back with difficulty. "In fact, yes."

If the girl who still laid unconscious had been educated, if she had been allowed more options, perhaps she would never have been placed in that situation. Better to have been a serving maid to a rich lady of a house or even the wife of an elderly shopkeeper than forced to be someone's whore.

"You jest." Lord Zhao stared bug-eyed, his mouth working.

"Enough." Sethalor's voice carried over all the mutterings, the note of finality unmistakable.

"As none have laid out sufficient cause to object to House Xuanyuan's petition, it is my will to grant their request. Unless there are any other objections, it is done."

He looked around, meeting each lord's eyes in

turn. "Anything else to report?"

No one moved to break the sullen hush.

"Court is adjourned."

CHAPTER FORTY-ONE

The cool edge of the knife pressed against my throat.

"You know, I've never really liked it when people are painfully grateful to me for something I've done, but I have to admit that this is going a bit further in the opposite direction than I'd prefer." I kept my voice level and my tone light, not wanting to antagonize the assassin further.

If there was one thing I'd expected when the maid came to tell me that the girl was awake and asking for me, this wasn't it.

The girl wrapped her hand tighter around my wrists, her fingers digging in, a thin line of pain springing up along my throat. "Believe me, this *is* gratitude, rich girl. The original plan was to have you sent to a bandit camp as a whore. This is a better way, don't you agree?"

A shimmering, spinning oval of light hung between us, a portal created when she shattered a glass orb on the floor as she leaped for me.

I blinked.

Oh gee. Death, choice portal, or being raped to death. It was an embarrassment of riches to be sure. Lucky, lucky me.

"You must know you cannot escape if you harm her. Your sentence could be commuted if you release the princess now." Aedrian stood between us and the door, his swords at his feet, hands raised in the air. Fury twisted his face and turned his eyes to molten silver. The girl had grabbed for me the moment I entered the room, Aedrian's warning for me to wait for him coming one second too late.

She laughed, the sound bitter and harsh. "I would rather not trust your word for it, my lord." Her tone made the honorific a slur.

"Name your price and we will meet it."

"What price for my life and reputation? I think not, pretty boy." She kicked my foot. "Move, rich girl. Don't try anything or you might get hurt. Badly. I can slit your throat before you can pull up one of your fancy magic tricks."

She clearly hadn't had that much experience with magic. The real problem wasn't how fast I could call up the shield, but her proximity to me. She was too close and my usual shields would wrap her in with me.

Heart thundering in my ears, I bit my lip and weighed my choices. Cardinal rule of a kidnapping situation: never go along to another location. On the other hand, killer lady had a knife to my throat and didn't appear to be shy about using it. On the other,

other hand, why hadn't she slit my throat already? The previous assassins didn't seem to have any such hesitation.

Where was Seth and his teleportation when I really needed it?

"Is that a portal? What are you going to do with me?" No need to feign the quaver, or the jelly knees. Panic hovered one wrong breath away, little pinpricks of light dancing in my field of vision.

"It's my escape is what it is. Less talking and more moving, rich girl."

I needed to stall. The longer I could delay, the more time the cavalry had to get here.

I sagged in her hold and burst into tears. "No. Please. The regent is my betrothed, he'll do anything. Please let me go. I saved you. Doesn't that count for anything?"

The girl kept hold of my wrists, dragging me up against her, the knife biting deep. Sharp pain blossomed, a trickle of warmth spreading. "Shut up."

Aedrian's face paled, his eyes snapping with pain and rage. "Stop. Harm her any further and I swear I will personally hunt you down and shred the meat from your bones." He stepped forward, placing himself between us and the portal.

Bless you, Helena, for your reminder of before.

All liquids belonged to my element. What was blood if not a liquid? I pulled power carefully, using my blood and tears to form a skintight shield under the knife that would hopefully keep her from cutting me any further. Useful if she decided to keep the knife on my throat, less than helpful if she decided to stab me in the heart. Clearly some other plan was in order.

Going limp, I continued sobbing, waiting, hoping for her to make a mistake somewhere.

The knife flashed through the air, a line of fire drawing down my arm. "Move, pretty boy, or next time I'll cut something more vital. My orders are to take her somewhere and keep her alive until you nobles figure out what to do with the throne, but they didn't specify how close to death I can take her."

Sounded like her orders came before the other assassins'.

Blood flowed down my arm in rivulets. Not spurting, thank gods. Still not enough blood to create a shield large enough to be effective. If I could use it as a weapon...

I closed my eyes and concentrated, willing my blood to flow up my arm, to seep between my skin and hers. Gritting my teeth, I imagined the blood hardening into tiny needles.

She sucked in a breath, her hand releasing my wrists, the other hand with the knife slashing down toward me.

I threw myself to the ground, diving out of the way and rolling away. Not quite fast enough. The blade stabbed into my chest and slid up, carving through my flesh. Agony exploded through me. My head spun, my thoughts blurring.

A growl split the air, a white blur carrying the girl to the floor.

I blinked and looked again. It was the cat,

crouched on the assassin, claws bared on her throat.

Aedrian dragged me to my feet, his hands banding around my wrists painfully, and shoved me at Sethalor. Sethalor who'd appeared sometime in the confusion along with the big cat, and whose face was ash pale, magic a visible aura around him.

"Heal yourself." Hard hands wrapped around my shoulders, giving me a rough shake.

"You're a water mage. Heal yourself. Now." He snarled in my face, his face centimeters from mine, his eyes a brilliant gold.

Right. Healing. I tried to remember how to heal, but my thoughts kept slipping away from me.

"Estyria!"

His face blurred in my vision and I blinked, trying to focus, but the darkness closed over me before I could open my eyes again.

"Fengxun."

The note of command was undeniable, pulling me out of the depths of sleep.

My grandmother crouched beside me, the lines in her face easing when I met her gaze. Grandfather stood by the window, facing away from us, hands white-knuckled at the small of his back.

Arms tightened around me when I tried to sit up. I was cradled in a familiar masculine embrace, wrapped in a black robe that I'd last seen on Seth.

"Don't. The healing needs to set or you'll tear the wound open again," Seth said.

I leaned back against him and turned my face into

his chest, fighting against the urge to take refuge in hysterics.

"This cannot continue," my grandfather said.

"My husband is correct. We cannot wait to act any longer. To indulge this further is to show weakness and to place Fengxun at unacceptable risk," my grandmother agreed.

Seth tensed, barely banked rage exploding outward. "Yet we have no proof," he snarled. "The assassins have admitted to nothing except that they accepted a contract on her head. We have nothing with which to charge Hauville."

"Perhaps not, but I can call down Gods' Judgment on him and see how well he fares."

"No, Qian," my grandfather said levelly. "Even for our granddaughter, I cannot agree to that."

I raised my head. "What is Gods' Judgment?"

"A sacrifice is made to advance a plea for the gods' intervention in a matter of justice."

That didn't sound promising. "What kind of sacrifice are we talking about?"

My grandfather's tone was flat. "The usual is a human life."

Great. My grandmother had gone off the deep end along with everyone else. "Right. Not an option. Moving right along."

"There's enough longevity in our line that I can afford to spare a handful of decades toward dealing with Hauville."

"No. Absolutely not."

Her indulgent smile carried an edge. "And how do

you propose to stop me, child?"

There had to be something that we could do. This world was magic, for goodness' sake. Surely there had to be something we could use. "I don't believe there's no other way of doing this. Isn't there a truth spell or something we could use on him?"

"Considering that a truth spell renders a person vulnerable magically and mentally to the mage casting the spell, it's extremely unlikely Hauville would submit to one without being compelled to. Without an accusation we can support with evidence, what could possibly make him agree to it?"

"What if Riordan abdicated his candidacy? Then, considering that the court hasn't seemed receptive to having a queen, perhaps we could claim that the truth spell was to confirm that all who served in court were okay with having a woman for a ruler?"

"That could end very poorly. There's no telling what he might do if you forced him into a corner. He's already bound to be furious once he discovers that his wife has gone missing," Aedrian said from behind us.

So that was what they'd gotten up to the other night.

"I'm not sure we have a better option" -- I looked around the room -- "and are we sure that forcing his hand isn't a good idea? Do you have divorce here? If we can slam him with a truth spell and then have his wife serve him with divorce papers, it might prompt him into doing something he normally wouldn't."

"Theoretically, his wife could petition for divorce based on *yijue* if we could persuade Helena to testify against her father, as she could argue that refusing her right to see her own daughter and using her to force Helena to conform to his wishes is against the rules of Heaven and Earth. However, I doubt that she would do so," Seth said.

Yijue. The extinction of righteousness and thus the cessation of loyalty.

"Does she need to do so or can we just imply that she has done so?"

"Careful. You don't want to perjure yourself and tarnish your honor," my grandfather said.

"So get Helena's mother to tell Helena that she's safe and put the ball in her court. No matter what you've done with her for now, we can't keep her anyway, so might as well throw it out there and see what happens."

My grandmother rubbed her forehead. "That's quite some gamble you're suggesting, Fengxun."

"That's not a no."

Seth sighed. "No, it's not a no."

"Is it a go then?"

A long pause. "I suppose it is."

CHAPTER FORTY-TWO

A low murmur traveled through the audience chamber when the doors closed and Riordan's chair remained empty.

Much as we would have preferred to keep Riordan's sword arm within reach, there was no way for him to be part of what was going to happen as an Airelan nobleman without causing more trouble than he solved.

"The mark of the gods favor has faded from Lord Bryne and his candidacy is considered to be revoked. As such, he will no longer be joining us in court," Seth said.

The murmurs intensified.

I clasped my hands together to still their trembling and pitched my voice to carry. "Imperial Highness. Before we begin, I have a request."

A muscle leaped at his jaw. "What would you ask, Lady?"

"That all in the court submit to a truth spell and

restate their intent to serve this court."

"Requesting a truth spell for the entire court is no light matter. What is your justification?"

I looked around at the court before answering. "It appears that there are some who are uncomfortable with the idea of being ruled by a queen. The point of the *tianzhe* is so that the candidates may interact with the court and develop an accord. As such, I feel that it is in everyone's best interests to ascertain who will and will not serve before we proceed further so replacements can be found if necessary."

A lord with a full beard and warrior braids stepped forward, confusion in every line of his face. "A thousand pardons, but I do not understand why that would be necessary. The queen will marry, after all."

"Lord Jin, you assume that the queen will offer her husband the crown matrimonial and make him co-sovereign. That is a faulty assumption at best," Helena said, her tone icy.

"That also assumes that the queen will marry, which is another problematic assumption," I added.

Another lord stepped forward, beady eyes wide, pencil thin mustache quivering. "It is what is expected! Do you mean to say you will not? Anathema!"

"Lord Cai, you will keep a civil tongue when speaking or you will not speak at all. Keep note of who you talk to and how," Sethalor snapped.

He bobbed an awkward bow. "My apologies, Imperial Highness. I was simply taken aback. How can a queen rule on her own without a husband to guide her hand?"

"The same way a king can rule without a queen by his side." I looked around at the lords. "This sort of reaction is precisely why we deem it necessary to employ a truth casting to determine the truth of your claims of fealty. You have two candidates for the throne, both of whom are women. This means a one hundred percent chance of your having to serve under a queen. If Lady Hauville is of like mind as I, we will not temper that fact by crowning a co-sovereign simply to assuage your fears."

"You will doom us all. A woman does not have the mental fortitude to rule; nor the ruthlessness, discipline, or tenacity," Lord Cai sputtered, his face puce, neck bulging, flecks of spittle flying forth with his vehemence.

Helena arched a brow. "I do not believe that. However, since you believe so, you may excuse yourself from being in any way involved in our country's downfall."

Lord Cai looked around for support, his eyes wild. "You are mad. Mad to believe that you can rule without a man and mad to believe that you can carry forth this crazed notion. Surely I cannot be the only one that knows that this is complete folly. What will you do when you drive away your court?"

I shrugged and sent him a sweet smile. "I believe this is what the imperial examinations are for. You are not irreplaceable, Lord Cai. Who knows, we may even fill your position with yet another woman."

He made an inarticulate sound of rage and

desperation and stormed toward the doors. "I won't stand by and watch. No, I won't. I will have no part of the demise of this court and country."

The guards opened the door and he stalked off.

"Do not close the doors." Sethalor surveyed the room. "Those who wish to depart now, may. You will be granted a half year's salary for your service when you are defrocked. Those who remain, be aware that you will be required to vow your fealty today under geis."

A lord squared his shoulders, and walked to the doors. Another followed and then another, until ten or so lords filed out of the room.

I kept my face impassive. Not including Lord Hauville and his cronies, we'd lost a fifth of the court. We'd probably only lose more before the morning was out.

"Imperial Highness," Helena said, "before we proceed further, I wish to enter a petition."

Seth narrowed his eyes. "What is your appeal, Lady?"

Helena slanted a quick look of undisguised disgust and triumph at Hauville. "Isabelle Hauville seeks termination of her marriage contract from Weiyuan-*wang* Georges Hauville on the basis of *yijue*. In connection with the breaking of the marriage contract between Georges Hauville and Isabelle Hauville, Helena Hauville seeks to disassociate from the House of Hauville on the same basis of *yijue*."

The claim to break legal ties as a consequence of broken honor and lack of righteous conduct was almost unheard of, especially when used by a wife against her husband or a child against a parent. Deadly silence filled the chamber as all eyes turned to Hauville with varying degrees of horror and shock.

CHAPTER FORTY-THREE

H auville sucked in a deep breath, his face gone bloodless. "*Yijue?*"

Helena lifted her chin and stared at him. "Yes."

The gleam of shocked fury in his eyes turned feral. "You lying, traitorous chit. I asked you where your mother was and you said you didn't know. I should have beat it out of you."

She smiled, slow and vicious and I could see when enraged in his face tipped over into homicidal.

Hauville thrust his hand sky-ward and a broadsword appeared in his hands. "*Yijue* indeed. I will cleanse my House today and strike your traitorous names from the ancestral records."

The doors of the audience chamber slammed shut, as if closed by an unseen hand. Faces contorted in shock, the guards pulled their swords and ran for us, but were blocked by an invisible wall twenty feet away.

Lord Lai let out a war-cry and charged in our direction, his hands aflame. Shouts and screams pierced the air as the lords scattered before him.

Sethalor yanked me out of the chair and shoved me at Aedrian before leaping forward into Hauville's path, sword in hand.

"Shield, Princess. That blade looks to be poisoned, so don't let your guard down until we say it's safe." Aedrian crowded me toward the door.

I nodded and pulled power. It came slowly, the effort painful; far too much energy used in too short a period of time.

Lord Zhao advanced upon us, lobbing miniature arcs of lightning at Seth. Aedrian cursed under his breath and darted forward, cutting him off.

I shrank by the side of the door, cursing my inability to do anything except cower. The pool of magic at my disposal was laughable compared to what they were throwing around and I knew it would do everyone more good if I stayed put than if I tried to cowboy it up. However, knowing it made sense didn't make inaction any easier to stomach.

Sethalor pressed forward with a rain of blows in an attempt to keep Hauville at bay.

Lord Lai shot two fireballs at Sethalor, missing by mere centimeters.

Hauville took advantage of Seth's momentary distraction to move in with a flurry of strokes as the fire mage sent a steady volley of fireballs at Sethalor, timing them to cover for Hauville's retreat.

I watched their lethal dance of sword, fire, and

poison, my palms clammy with fear, sweat trickling between my breasts, my heartbeat a rising drumbeat in my ears.

Then came the inevitable stumble when Hauville moved in with a hail of kamikaze strikes while Lord Lai shot ten small fireballs simultaneously.

Twisting in mid-air and tumbling, Sethalor managed to parry all of Hauville's attacks, but at the cost of getting hit by two of the fireballs in the shoulder and the thigh.

The fire ate through his clothing like air, burning even after it contacted skin. Seth's face went impossibly paler as Hauville pushed his advantage, the smell of burning flesh rising in the air.

Oh gods.

Ignoring the pain, I yanked on more power, summoning water to form a fog around him, pouring in magic until the layer of mist covered him and became thick enough to put out the fire still burning into him.

The fire mage growled in my direction, spun a fireball the way a child would pack a snowball between his hands, and hurled it at me.

Steam rose in a cloud around me at impact. The sphere turned dangerously thin and I had to pull hard to block the next two fireballs he threw my direction.

It held, but barely, the rich taste of iron flooding my mouth when I tried to channel more magic.

I ignored it, refusing to be a distraction when Seth and Aedrian had more than enough to occupy them.

White fur blurred through the air as the snow

leopard bounded out of nowhere and lunged for the mage's leg, claws extended.

Too intent on crafting his largest fireball thus far, the mage didn't notice the cat until it shredded the back of his leg, hamstringing him and bringing him down with a crash.

He screamed, the sound bone-chilling, and shot the fireball at the cat.

The leopard chuffed and rolled away, the fireball passing harmlessly over him. Snarling, he lunged at the mage, teeth bared, and tore his throat out.

Lord Hauville glanced over at his fallen comrade, and a savage look twisted his features. He raised a hand, made a fist, and made a yanking motion.

Helena choked, her hand fluttering to her throat, and dropped like a stone.

Shit. That was going to be a concussion. Worse, what was Hauville trying to do?

Lord Zhao sent a hail of lightning bolts at Aedrian, driving him back.

Another man shot out of the shadows, ran for the fallen lord and dropped to his knees beside him.

At first I thought he was checking to make sure he was beyond help. Then I saw how the fallen man's skin tightened over his bones and how his robes deflated.

I fought back the urge to retch, realizing that he was draining his dead comrade for power. When the other man was nothing more than a thin sheath of skin over bone, the imprint of his skull clear against his face, the mage stood and sent a wall of fire in the cat's direction.

It yowled, rolled around on the floor in an effort to put out the flames, and vanished.

Aedrian reeled back, face contorted in agony, his eyes gone luminescent.

The lightning mage laughed, a shrill sound of malicious delight, and rushed forward.

Not good. We were down two people and Aedrian and Seth didn't look like they were in great shape either. If the cavalry didn't arrive, and soon, we were likely to become martyrs to the cause.

I gritted my teeth and unspooled power from my core. If I could walk three miles in four inch heels with blistered feet, at a New York City pace, I could do this. It was just pain, after all. Nothing compared to death, right?

Grabbing power, I formed two razor sharp blades of ice and sent them at Lord Zhao. He whirled, blocking them both, a sneer on his face. "Amateur effort."

Perhaps, but it provided just enough distraction. Aedrian crossed both swords, lurched forward, and swept them in curving arcs that took off his head.

A spray of blood painted the air crimson. Nausea surged in my throat.

No. Now wasn't the time to fall to my knees and throw up. That would take energy I didn't have. That would take *time* none of us had.

The power eating mage headed for Lord Zhao.

Aedrian growled, "Oh no, you don't."

He intercepted the mage, blocking him from

cannibalizing the other mage, but his movements were slowing, dodging the other man's attacks with faltering grace.

The clang of a fallen sword drew my attention and I turned to see that Hauville had tossed aside his broadsword and was now flinging bolts of light at Sethalor.

Seth flung his swords aside, spinning shields of flame to engulf the light arrows, lobbing fireballs of his own back at Hauville.

I turned back to Aedrian, who was being inexorably pushed back by the mage.

Dragging more power forth, I sent miniature ice quarrels arrowing at the mage. He blocked them with his own bolts easily, and I tried to create more, but couldn't.

Pain exploded in my chest when I tried to pull more power, turning each breath agonizing. Going to my knees, I wheezed as I fought for breath.

"Estyria. Stop. Maintain your shield." Sethalor's voice, harsh and furious.

The imperial prince flung up his hands, a hail of fire arrows slinging toward the mage just as the power-eater caught Aedrian in the thigh with a lightning bolt.

The redhead staggered back and went to one knee, just as the shower of fire arrows blazed over his head to strike the mage in the chest.

The mage tottered back, eyes wide and incredulous, and collapsed.

Aedrian braced his hands against the ground in an

attempt to rise, but his leg crumpled under him and he crashed back to the floor.

Hauville pressed forward, still shooting bolts of light as if he were a machine gun with endless ammo.

Sethalor blocked and deflected, but his face was bone white at this point, his eyes blazing with power, too much power. A thin trickle of blood ran from his mouth, and another two from his ears.

Where the fuck was Hauville getting all his power?

Then I remembered Helena going down like a sack of rocks.

Dropping the shield, I ran to where she fell and flipped her over, grunting with the effort. For a slender woman she was surprisingly hefty. I pinched her hard on her upper lip right beneath her nose, digging my fingers in.

She spluttered, lashes rising to reveal dazed green eyes.

"If you don't take your magic back from your father, we're all going to die."

A faint nod, then she closed her eyes again.

I was about to go in for another pinch when I saw her brow furrow in concentration, white teeth gripping her lower lip.

A moment later, she opened her eyes, made a fist in the air, and jerked it down toward herself.

Hauville cursed, and I had a moment of hope that it would turn out all right.

Then Helena's eyes rolled back in her head and she collapsed again.

Fuck. Double fuck with a shit sundae and a cherry

bomb on top.

"Estyria! Shield!" Sethalor shouted.

A ball of light barreled toward me.

I tried to pull power, failed, remembered that I could still move, and rolled away. Determined to play dodgeball if I had to, I staggered back to my feet.

Seth wavered and went down on one knee. One hand shot out, arm trembling as he caught himself from face-planting. His head fell forward for a brief moment before he rallied and shoved himself upright again.

Hauville laughed and walked forward, triumph flickering across his face.

Oh no. No no no.

I shuffled to stand between them, locking my knees to keep from collapsing.

Golden brows raised and he hesitated for a moment before he continued toward us.

"Estyria. Get the hell out of the way," Seth snarled. His rage was clear, but his voice was thready.

Oh shit we're going to die.

Hauville raised his hands and fire bloomed in his palms, slow but sure.

I closed my eyes.

An explosion rocked the audience chamber.

Opening my eyes, I spun toward the sound.

There was an immense hole where the doors were, and my grandparents stood in the center of the destruction, fire lotuses blooming in their palms.

"Georges Hauville. I'll teach you to make an enemy of House Xuanyuan." My grandfather stalked forward and sent a waterfall of fire descending upon Hauville with a flick of his fingers.

My grandmother clenched her fists, extinguishing the fire in her palms. Then she reached up and pulled a longbow of fire from thin air, drew it, and sent a shower of fire arrows towards him.

Hauville cursed and disappeared just before the fire reached him.

My grandparents swore in unison, exchanged a look, and vanished.

Sethalor coughed out a mouthful of blood, took a breath, vomited up more blood, and folded to the floor.

I fell to my knees beside him and pressed one hand to his heart.

He was breathing, but only just, his breath thready and with far too much time between one inhale and the other. His heart beat sluggishly, as if on the verge of giving out.

Aedrian limped up, muttered an oath, and dropped to his knees beside me, pressing a hand to Sethalor's chest. "He's past his limit and fading fast."

"He'll be fine if we find a healer, right? Right?"

Anguish carved lines around his mouth as he shook his head. "He pushed too far and you're close to burnout yourself."

Sethalor's face was bone white, his chest barely rising with each breath, wheezing out more air on each exhale than he breathed in.

"What about you? Don't you have power?"

"Not the same kind. I'd give my last drop of blood

for him, but we've never been able to share power, bond or no bond."

I stared at Sethalor, at his slowing breaths, at the little frown between his brows every time he tried to breathe and couldn't.

Something burned in my chest. It took a moment or two of trying to breathe past the weight in my lungs before it registered as rage.

Leaning forward, crowding past Aedrian, I slapped both palms on Seth's chest and snarled into his face, "Don't you dare die on me. You do not get to just check out and leave this mess to us."

Never mind that I'd originally thought I could let him go.

But not like this. Never like this.

Spinning out what power I had left, I visualized Sethalor's heartbeat as a thread of energy, wrapped my power around his heart, and bound the two together, braiding the energy together until I could feel every beat of his heart tugging at mine.

"Princess. Estyria. You can't --"

I lifted my face to Aedrian's and said with deadly calm, "No. Either help me or go away and shut up. I'm not letting him go. He'll have to drag me kicking and screaming to the throne of Yanluo Wang with him." And even then I'd fight the Lord of the Underworld for him.

Aedrian's jaw tightened and he grabbed my hand, trying to tug it away.

I flipped my wrist, interlaced my fingers with his, and *yanked*. There was power in him, but it came sluggishly, as if through layers and layers of sediment. Didn't matter. He said he was willing and I was going to force the issue with everything left in me.

Aedrian coughed, lurching forward before he caught himself with a hand on the ground, his other hand still entangled with mine. His eyes blazed silver and his face lost what little color it had. "What are you doing?"

Ruthless in my goal, I pulled harder at him, as much to keep him from stopping me as for the power he had, pushing everything I got at Sethalor. "Live, dammit. If you think you can escape this way, you are so sadly mistaken. Live, you fucking bastard, live."

Aedrian wavered, slumping forward again before jolting upright, his lips white in a bloodless face. Worried now that I'd drawn too much, I stopped pulling from him and tried to drop his hand.

His hand closed harder around mine and power trickled through our bond. "No. We do this together or not at all."

Red spots danced in my vision, the room sliding sideways as the rest of my power spooled toward Seth.

Sethalor coughed, his lashes lifting briefly to show eyes gone black, his pupils fully dilated. "Stop." His head moved, just an inch in either direction, before his eyes closed again, his face going slack.

The bond between us slammed shut, any power I tried to feed him hitting a block.

I pushed harder, to no avail.

"Dammit." I closed my eyes, fighting back nausea, the taste of iron thick in my mouth, my ears ringing.

I could still feel his heartbeat in my chest, but it no longer drew on my power.

I opened my eyes and slapped my hands on his chest, rage and pain tearing through my heart. "Damn you, you autocratic bastard!"

"He's stabilizing, but he's so far gone it might not be enough," Aedrian murmured, his eyes dazed, a terrible pain in his voice.

I swayed forward and collapsed onto the prince, beyond drained. Emptiness gnawed at me, grief, rage and magical backlash tearing at me without mercy.

CHAPTER FORTY-FOUR

"Princess."

Helena's voice.

I looked up, shaking.

"Call for the goddess, Princess. Take the throne," she urged.

I stared blankly at her, my thoughts filtering slowly through the fatigue and shock of the day.

"Claim the throne, Princess and you will be able to pull from the land's power. If your will is strong and your heart is true, then the mantle will descend and you will be able to save Lord Qiandai."

Was it really that easy? The land had taken from Seth. Who was to say it would be willing to give up magic so he could live when it had nearly bled him dry before? According to all I'd heard, I would be lucky if I didn't get turned into a husk myself. Even if there was power to be had, what was to say that it would let me use it that way?

She shook her head when I just stared at her. "You

have nothing to lose, Princess and everything to gain. You have fought and bled for this land. Is it not time to see if it will support you in turn?"

Nothing to lose... except my life.

I swallowed and looked down.

Aedrian was slumped beside Seth, pale as death, holding Seth's bloody hand to his lips in a tender kiss. Seth's chest barely rose as he breathed, air whistling out in what sounded like a death rattle every time he exhaled.

Extending slender hands to me, she waited, her beautiful face filled with certainty.

There was really no choice at all. I reached up and let her pull me to my feet. "All right."

She waited until I'd steadied myself before she released my hands and curtsied, her skirts pooling beneath her as she bent to a full obeisance.

I stepped away and walked toward the throne, half-expecting to be struck down by lightning at any point for my less than pure motives.

Twenty steps to the foot of the dais.

I counted each step, fear and uncertainty melting away with each footfall. No longer something to be dreaded, I saw it for what it was: inevitable.

Everything that I wanted to do, everything that I wanted to change, all of it required stepping forward and seizing as much power as I could. Everything had a price, and I'd found mine.

Pressing my palms together, I bent my head, touching my fingertips to my forehead and prayed.

Goddess, I offer myself for your judgment.

Goddess of all that is holy, hear my heart, my soul, and my mind. I claim the throne of Tavaneth. I claim the crown for the people, for those that are silent, those who have been silenced, and those who are without recourse. Though I am tiny before you, my efforts minuscule, hear my will and my resolve.

A bell tolled, the sound sonorous, the reverberations resonating down my bones.

"Xuanyuan Fengxun Estyria." A woman's voice, sweetly melodic, yet forbidding.

I opened my eyes and looked up.

The goddess stood in front of the throne, hood up, her hands folded in her sleeves.

Dropping to my knees, I pressed my forehead to the floor. "Goddess."

"Raise your head."

The weight of her silent regard pressed on me, a physical pressure against my mind and my body. Long moments passed before she raised her hands, pushed back her hood, and unleashed the full force of her gaze upon me. The irises of her eyes were an endless field of stars, so deep you could lose yourself for millennia. To look into them was akin to staring into the abyss, a reminder of just how minute you were.

"You claim the throne, Xuanyuan Fengxun?"

"Yes," I managed through numb lips.

"Let the mantle and crown decide, then."

Power roared through me, my head snapping back with the force of it, my hair and robes streaming out behind me as if I stood in a gale force wind. It burned, every millimeter of my skin crawling with fire ants, acid streaming through my veins, every breath a torment as fire scorched my lungs.

I gritted my teeth, exhaling through the pain, refusing to scream. Tears of fire streamed down my cheeks, the feel of them on my skin excruciating.

A gong rang, somewhere in the distance, tinny compared to the ringing in my ears. The pain dissipated as fast as it came, leaving behind blinding relief.

"Stand, Xuanyuan Fengxun Estyria."

I stood, locking my knees to keep from falling to the ground.

The goddess raised her arms, her eyes glowing pools of night sky, her voice ringing forth like a bell. "Let it be witnessed. Xuanyuan Fengxun Estyria, scion of House Xuanyuan, is now empress of Tavaneth, holder of my mandate. Let it be known."

A small smile curved her mouth and she flicked her fingers behind me. "I have restored your consort to you, little phoenix, lest the Lord of the Underworld have to deal with you before it is his time."

A flash of golden light and she was gone.

Turning, I searched out Sethalor.

He breathed, slow and steady, and a faint pink brushed his cheekbones.

Oh. Thank the goddess. I fought the urge to sag to the ground as relief washed over me.

Helena approached, knelt, and touched her forehead to the ground. "My empress. *Wan sui wan sui wan wan sui.*"

Aedrian rose from where he knelt by Sethalor's side and walked to me. Going down to one knee, he raised my hand and brushed his lips over it. "My empress, *wan sui, wan sui, wan wan sui*." He lingered over the traditional words, his tone almost caressing.

The cluster of lords who'd been huddled in the corner dropped to their knees, pressing their foreheads against the floor. "*Wu huang wan sui wan sui wan wan sui*."

Our empress, may you live ten thousand years, ten thousand ten thousand years.

Numb and near shock, I blinked at them, my mind refusing to cope. A textured weight bore down on my shoulders, more than mere fatigue could explain, as if I were wearing a full-length mink coat. Something dragged behind me as I shifted and I peered over my shoulder.

A wall of shimmering feathers the color of flame blocked my sight. I turned, and it moved with me. All other thoughts out of my head fled as I tried to process what I saw.

Um.

I hissed in an undertone. "Aedrian. Do I have *wings*?"

Weary amusement flickered in his eyes. "Yes, and I suggest letting the lords rise and depart for the day."

Right. I squashed the urge to sit down and start hyperventilating.

"You may rise. Court is adjourned." I pitched my voice to carry, proud of how it didn't waver.

The lords rose, bowed, and filed out of the large

hole in the middle of the doors.

I reached out a hand to touch the feathers sprouting from my back the minute they were gone. "Seriously? Wings? No one told me this would happen."

Helena coughed. "You hold the goddess' mandate and you are now the will and heart of the land made manifest."

No pressure, right?

"Yes, but *wings*?"

"The king traditionally shifts into a dragon." Amusement was clear in her voice.

"Can I even fly with these? And what about clothing?"

Aedrian's mouth twitched. "If it is anything at all like shapeshifting, you should be able to recall your wings by thinking about it. Imagine them folding up and tucking inside you, under your skin."

I looked at the wings again, thought about the gaping holes in my clothing they would leave behind if I got rid of them, and shrugged. They could stay until I had a fresh set of clothing ready.

Helena curtsied. "If you will excuse me, my empress." The look in her eyes made it clear that she wasn't talking about just leaving for the day.

"Where will you go, Helena?"

A bitter smile curved her lips. "I have not decided yet."

"There will always be a place in my court for you, should you desire it."

"You honor me, my empress. Farewell." She

bowed again, and vanished.

I looked around at the empty room and sank down to the floor, light-headed and tired beyond reason.

"What now?"

CHAPTER FORTY-FIVE

I crumpled up yet another piece of paper and tossed it in the brazier. Twenty sheets of nice stationary and a merry little blaze later, I was still no closer to figuring out how to break the news to my family.

Seth looked over, still pale from his ordeal. "Still no joy?"

"I have no idea how to even start explaining everything that's happened to my parents. No idea. None." It didn't help that my grandparents still hadn't reappeared after presumably going after Hauville. I wasn't looking forward to that conversation either. "In fact, I'm not sure how I'd even explain this to my grandparents." Oh yeah, I got suckered into doing something right for the completely wrong reasons and now the country is stuck with me and I have no idea what to do.

The imperial prince set down his mirror and blinked at me. "What do you need to explain?"

Wait. Was he even the imperial prince anymore

now that I was -- choke -- technically empress?

No technically about it, Yunya snarked in my mind. *You're definitely the empress.*

Oh yeah, that was the other fun thing that happened. My magic mirror started being all proactively sassy in my mind instead of just responding when I talked to her. Cuz apparently being empress appropriately impressed her or something.

Most likely or something, but I was trying not to dig into that too much.

"Oh, the fact that I got tricked into this whole thing by Helena?"

Amusement flashed across his face before he straightened his expression into something appropriately sympathetic.

I glared at him. "Oh sure, laugh it up. You couldn't have said something before you passed out?"

"Ah, darling, I did tell you to stop."

Narrowing my eyes at him, I lobbed another failed attempt in his direction. "I thought you were just being your usual irritatingly noble self." Giving up, I put the brush in water so it wouldn't dry out and shoved the stack of paper aside.

He grinned, the expression lighter than any other I'd seen on him and my heart stuttered in wonder and quiet pain. I *remembered* that smile and the sunny boy with the clear eyes and easy laugh.

"So now I get to tell my parents that I kinda agreed to take responsibility for an entire kingdom because I forgot that I could have pulled power from our House as its scion. Does that make me sound like an empty-headed twit or what?"

Seth pulled me into his lap. "At worst, it makes you a fool for love. I find I can't argue too hard against that." His low murmur slid into my heart, warming my cheeks.

"You're fretting too hard over this, Estyria. Your parents know you. They're not going to suddenly think you're Juliet or something ridiculous like that. Don't second guess yourself or try to belittle your heart. You and I both know that you would have accepted even if my life hadn't been in the balance. You and I also both know that isn't what troubles you now."

Long fingers caught my chin and tipped my face up so I looked into his eyes when I tried to hide my face in his neck. "It is a formidable task, but you will not face it alone. This, I promise you," he murmured.

Relief warred with guilt. "But you hate it. You said you hated all of it." I remembered the loathing in his voice when he spoke of escape and hating everything the throne stood for. Much as I wanted and needed him to stay, I couldn't ask it of him. He was offering now, but...

A shadow flitted across his eyes. "I did. I do. But I can hardly walk away from you and even if I could, I would despise myself if I let you go alone into this tiger's den."

Bitterness escaped in a humorless laugh.

He'd despise himself for leaving, but I, wouldn't I despise myself for letting him stay when I knew how much it'd hurt him? It would have been different if I could have told him I loved him, if he'd ever shown any sign that my love would have made a difference, if I could believe that I brought enough to the table to justify everything he was willing to give me. But I couldn't and he couldn't. Where did that leave us?

Unable to resist, my gaze went to the door, where I could see Aedrian's silhouette against the delicately carved wood. He'd been cool and distant ever since everything went to fire and shit two days ago. I hadn't heard a single word from him in that time and when he looked at me, the blankness in his gaze was frightening.

Maybe the right thing to do was to let go. The thought sent a sharp pain arrowing through my heart, but I had to offer.

"What about Aedrian? You could leave, with him. Get a life, you know, outside of the chaos," I said lightly, trying my best for a smile as I ignored the wrench in my gut.

Dark brows snapped together, faint disbelief fanning across his face before his gaze sharpened. "You can't seriously think he'd go, even if I agreed to that bit of irrationality."

I pointed at the door. "He's been drifting around like a ghost and the way he stares past me is seriously unnerving. He clearly isn't happy and doesn't want to be here. Since you don't really want to be here either, you might take on the onus of being the one to force him to go away and be happy. With you. You know."

He exhaled, shaking his head. "Happiness doesn't

work that way, Phoenix."

Yeah, I knew it didn't, but it was worth a shot. Surely someone deserved an unequivocal happy ending.

"I just... feel like some of us should have a life they want, choices that were actually choices, et cetera."

He gave me a strange look. "Phoenix, this *is* my choice. Afford me the courtesy of assuming I know my own mind, please. Besides, what makes you think that I am the sole factor in Aedrian's happiness?"

"He loves you." Wasn't that self-explanatory?

That bemused look intensified. "Yes. And?"

I leaned back and frowned at him. "What do you mean and? What else do you need? Fireworks?"

"Estyria," he said slowly, "I suppose I might as well tell you this, since you seem determined to believe otherwise: I don't believe Aedrian loves me in the way you think he does..." -- his mouth tightened before he continued, softer than before -- "because he's never once indicated interest in that way. Ever."

I blinked. "Ever? Ever ever?"

A wry smile tipped his mouth. "We've shared tents, occasionally bedrolls and bathed in the same river countless times. Ever."

The sentence flew out before I could stop it. "What if he's impotent? Or asexual?"

I clapped my hand over my mouth as soon as the words flew out, but too late.

Seth made a strangled noise that sounded halfway between choking and death.

"Forget I said that." I waved my hand in the air,

trying to erase the words from his mind. "Just. Forget I said that."

Unholy glee lit his eyes. "Aedrian," he called.

Lunging forward, I slapped my hand over his mouth. "Don't you dare."

The door opened and Aedrian stepped in, his flat gaze turning bewildered as he look from me to Seth and back again. "Yes?"

Sethalor pulled my hand down and captured my other wrist when I tried to cover his mouth again. "Aedrian. I have a question for you."

"No!" I shouted, face alight with embarrassment and dread, not caring that I probably sounded completely ridiculous. "Go awa...mmph!" Seth leaned forward and sealed his lips to mine, cutting me off.

I blinked at him, forgetting to scream or what I was screaming about. What did he just do? Heat blazed up my face and singed my ears.

He eased back, flicking his tongue over my lower lip in a sensual tease before half-turning to face Aedrian. "Estyria wants to know..."

I made a noise and without looking, he laid his fingers on my lips, stilling my garbled protest.

"Estyria wants to know if you would be happier if we left and went elsewhere," he said, his tone carrying a distinct smirk. "Somewhere safer and more peaceful."

Auburn brows arched in sardonic disbelief. "Safer? More peaceful? Does she know that we were career soldiers by choice?"

Seth shrugged with a look of infuriating

amusement.

Aedrian narrowed his eyes at me. "My empress, if you don't feel safe with me guarding you, then you only need say so. I have notified the cadre of your need and they should be arriving soon enough."

I shoved Seth's hand away. "No. Why would you think that?" Thrusting my hands through my hair, I fought the urge to yank.

What was *wrong* with these two? I just wanted them to be *happy*. Why were they making it so hard? And what was with the kiss? Since when had we gone from *it's complicated and we're not sure what we're doing with each other* to *kissing?*

"You just seem so unhappy and I got the impression that you didn't like this whole court thing and since Seth is pretty much off the hook right now, I don't see why you two should be trapped here."

The redhead shifted his gaze to Seth. "Did the power rot her brain or something?"

"Hey!" I protested.

Aedrian moved forward and went down on one knee, intent silver eyes catching my gaze and holding it. "I am yours if you want me."

There was a note of challenge in his voice, as if he expected me to say no.

As if I ever would. Somehow he'd become an anchor in my life. For my life.

"Are you sure?"

He lifted my hand and brushed his lips over the back, his eyes never leaving mine. "Never more certain, my empress." Dark lashes fell to veil his gaze as he kissed my hand again. "Seth holds my love and loyalty, but I would second my soul to your hand if I could, much less only promising you my blade for as long as you desire it."

I stared at him, my heart full, not knowing what to say, what I *could* say.

I wanted to shout that I wasn't worthy, that I didn't know what I was doing, and that no one ever should be following me anywhere, but the words caught behind the knot in my throat.

You'll do, Yunya murmured. *You may not believe in our goddess, but she believes in you.*

That thought was somehow as terrifying as it was reassuring.

Mouth curving in gentle amusement, he rose in one lithe motion and set my hand back in my lap before walking out of the room. The sound of the door closing jolted me out of my surprise.

Seth stroked a hand over my hair. "You see, my own. Everything will be fine. *We* will be fine. Whatever comes, whatever happens, do not doubt that I have chosen this, that we have chosen you above all and will always do so."

He didn't say the word love, and somehow that made the rest believable and comforting. One didn't choose love, necessarily. Love simply is or wasn't or would be. But if they'd made their choice, knowingly, and in full faculty of their senses...

Turning tear-blurred eyes to Seth, I gave him a crooked smile, willing to just believe for the moment. "Promise?"

Brushing his lips against mine, he murmured, "Promise. I'll even seal that with a kiss."

His kiss was soft, but it held an unshakable vow. Looking into his eyes, I understood that he wasn't guaranteeing me a future without strife; he was assuring me that even should seas of flame and mountains of blades lie in our future, he would be there, walking beside me.

AUTHOR'S NOTE

Thank you for reading Phoenix Chosen. I hope you enjoyed it as much as I enjoyed writing it. If so, I would really appreciate if you could leave a review to help other readers find this book.

Estyria, Aedrian and Seth's journey isn't quite done yet – I'm currently working on book two and I anticipate there being at least three more books in the series. The series being named Heirs of Huaxia, I expect the rest of the Xuanyuan siblings will also have stories of their own. At the moment, Estella is tangled up with two dragon shifter princes and Kieran might be having a wee bit of trouble with a certain mermaid queen. As for Kendrick and Katherine... who knows? I think Katherine got dropped onto a battlefield somewhere, but knowing her, that's not going to be an issue.

If you're interested in knowing when the next book will be out, you can sign up for my newsletter at www.ekaterinexia.com, follow me on Twitter at www.twitter.com/katjexia, or like my Facebook page at www.facebook.com/ekaterine.xia.

I can also be found on Wattpad at www.wattpad.com/user/katjexia, where I post experiments in progress.

GLOSSARY

Gongzi or 公子 is an honorific for a man, usually used for young, unmarried men, but it's not a firm rule, more a matter of common usage. This is because usually by the time a man is married, he'll have a title that would be used instead of gongzi, such as 老闆 laoban. Any person who owns a business, even if it's something as simple as a food cart on the side of the street, can be called laoban.

Historically, gongzi was used for all children of the aristocracy, as it literally means "offspring of a noble", but then misogyny and common usage won out eventually.

Guniang or 姑娘 is an honorific for an unmarried young woman, much like *mademoiselle* in French. It is often also used in the context of "x and y House's daughter". If we ignored all the titles that Xuanyuan House holds, for example, Estyria would be either called Xuanyuan guniang or "the guniang of Xuanyuan House".

Shifu 師傅 / 師父 means "teacher". 師傅 where the second character 傅 also means "teacher" is gender neutral. Often 師父 with the second character of "father" is used for a teacher who is also a man. 師傅 is much less in use now, probably because the second character is complicated and tedious to write, so sometimes 師父 can also be gender neutral, depending on context.

Shimu 師母 means "wife of my teacher", but the characters are actually teacher+mother. This is to indicate that the wife of one's teacher should be respected as one's mother. It is never used for a teacher who is also a woman.

A *shichen* is two hours.

An incense stick's worth of time is thirty minutes. There's a lot of disagreement over whether it's five minutes, ten, or fifteen or even an hour, but in Tavaneth it's thirty minutes.

Time goes thusly:

One minute is sixty seconds.

One cup of tea's worth of time (yizhancha) is ten minutes.

One incense stick's worth of time is thirty minutes.

One hour is sixty minutes.

There are twelve shichen to a day.

HONORIFICS

I took some liberties (read: a lot) with the honorific/title system as much of it doesn't translate well. I thought about using direct transliterations, but I'm personally not fond of those. In part, I felt that throwing the Chinese pinyin in the middle of sentences would throw off the cadences. In other part, I wanted to write about princesses, darn it, not *gongzhu*, or *junzhu*, no matter if they're technically the same thing.

Estyria should technically be referred to as Your Imperial Highness throughout the entire book because she's Sethalor's betrothed and as such carries the higher title of imperial princess automatically. However, that's being kept a secret and so she's called Your Grace and Phoenix Princess, as befits her status as a princess of the second rank as House Xuanyuan's scion. Technically, she should be 少公主 , or "little/lesser" princess, as her mother is also a princess, but I simplified it for the sake of brevity, possibly with some loss of clarity.

Her grandmother is styled Ningxia-ji, with Ningxia as the title and ji meaning "queen" and referred to as Your Illustriousness/Her Illustriousness. I chose to use "ji" because I thought it'd be far too confusing for queens to be running around at the same time as everything else.

Georges Hauville is styled Weiyuan-wang, and referred to as Your Illustriousness/His Illustriousness. Wang, technically does mean "king", but the same reasoning applies.

Her grandfather is Lord Xuanyuan, consort to Ningxia-ji, and referred to as Your Illustriousness/His Illustriousness. As a consort to a queen, he technically ranks slightly lower than Georges Hauville, but most people ignore that because he's also Seth's *shifu*.

When Estyria's siblings show up, she'll be the empress and so they'll be some version of qinwang (high prince) and huangji (high princess).

OTHER STORIES

Ariagne

All she thought she ever wanted was freedom.

Ariagne sneaks aboard the new justiciar of Elysion's shuttle, intent on persuading him to accept her terraforming services in exchange for escape from her step-mother.

All he thought he had was law and the dispensation of order.

Aidoneus is used to being the rational one, the cold one. Serving as justiciar on an icy mining planet seems apropos for a man such as he.

Turns out that wasn't the full truth for either of them.

Sunshine

Sunshine doesn't know what she is. She was her mother's imaginary friend made flesh, and now she's little more than wisps of spirit without her parents' love to anchor her. Pure luck brings Raphael into her life, bringing her into the world again, but who is she without the definition of someone's want?

She is pure magic in a world that laughs at the notion. Raphael never knew he had an unanswered prayer until the day Sunshine stumbled into his world. Now he will fight anyone and anything that might take her from the world, even if it's the woman he loves.

Who is she? How can he keep her? How can she be purely herself in this world, without the definition of others to bind her? And how can he persuade her that his love is strong enough to let her fly unfettered?

Not Just Human - anthology

In Hunter and Prey, Isadora arrives at her new school and finds herself the focus of attention. But is all as it seems and can she trust affection so carelessly given? Who is the hunter and who is the prey?

In Made For Her Pleasure, Meredith and Damien run into a bit of trouble at the hands of her family's competitor. Fortunately, Damien is more human than their enemies think, and made to fulfill any need Meredith might have of him.

In Shifters' Daughter, Lisette is hiding the truth of herself and her werewolf fathers from her boyfriend. When she succumbs to Lysander's persuasion to meet her family, perhaps he will end up surprising her in turn.

Spicy; not for those who prefer sweet vanilla.

Goddess in Waiting

Amarantha, goddess of memory, is called to present Earth's case before the Elder Council.

If she fails to persuade them that Earth is on track to Ascension, the planet will be reset back to prehistoric days.

And that's the good ending.

The Devourer of Worlds looms in wait to claim Earth as his rightful salvage. Not content with the planet as a main course, he's also set his eyes on having godlings as appetizers.

Since drama comes in threes, not only does Amarantha have the Council and the D to contend with, but she must also negotiate the status of her marriage with Death himself.

Can a goddess nearly Faded into mortal flesh save the world, herself, and her marriage along with it?

Past Love's Triumph

Once upon a time. Or so it usually begins, does it not?

They say my parents started it all with a blunder, that the King and Queen of House Lan were *stupid* enough to offend one of the Fey by neglecting to invite her to the celebration of my birth. They also say the weapon of choice was a spinning wheel. The spindle, to be precise.

A spinning wheel. As if.

In a way it fits. Bless the young princess with all the boons a future queen would want or need and yet make the cause of her demise something that is almost exclusively the province of the *distaff* persuasion. Poetic almost, perhaps the original storyteller's bit of social commentary. A princess may become a queen and rule, but only if she stays far, far away from the feminine.

However, my king-father and queen-mother were not stupid and the Powerful One was not an enemy but an old and trusted friend. She did not utter a curse, but a warning.

Elianna didn't say a spindle would kill me, but a spear. A man would break me upon himself, hollow out all that I was to create a legacy for him, and kill me in the birthing of that immortality. I could be a princess and then a queen and *live*, but only if I forsook the feminine side of myself.

As I said, the stories tell the truth as they saw it.